A Home in the Hills

Ashes of Luukessia, Volume Three

Robert J. Crane
with Michael Winstone

A Home in the Hills
Ashes of Luukessia, Volume Three
Robert J. Crane
with Michael Winstone
Copyright © 2018 Ostiagard Press
All Rights Reserved.

1st Edition

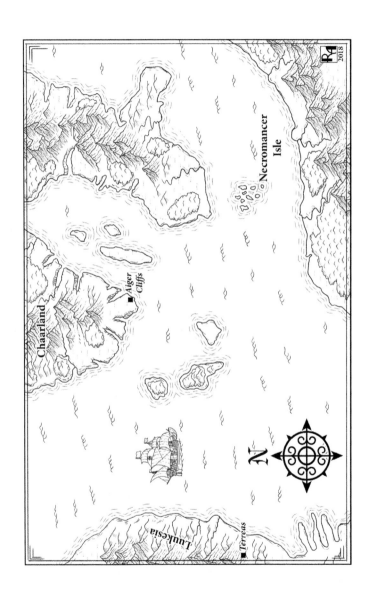

1

The *Lady Vizola* broke.

The isle of Baraghosa, a mound of dark, twisted volcanic rock, and its tower lay cocooned in fog, a misty smear of grey surrounded by the roiling sea. The sky was darker, painted in broad storm cloud strokes of grey and black. And in the building frenzy of lightning, in colors no man had ever witnessed, the waves were whipped high—

They surged over the *Lady Vizola*, pulled out from the dock, and the ship had no choice but to bow to those great blows as it was pushed inland, toward rocks—

Jasen gaped in open-mouthed horror as the boat slammed into crags that stuck up out of the water like onyx daggers.

It tilted against the surge …

And still the waters kept coming, pushing it down—under—

"*Ahn-beht!*" Kuura cried—a curse word. Already he was running, as though he could stop it, Scourgey thrown off his shoulders in a heap on the sand.

The water drew back, preparing.

The *Lady Vizola* shuddered, tilting sideways, its masts flung out in front of it, like the arms of a drowning man.

Another swell of water, pitch black and murky, overflowed the boat again.

It crashed against rocks again, and was pushed under.

The ship disappeared beneath the black, clawing waves, the sea claiming it as its own.

There was quick, muttered conversation between them: Huanatha, in her blue armor sans the shattered husk of her discarded breastplate, limping and cradling a bloodied arm, the stubby remains of her sword, Tanukke, cradled at her hip; Longwell, his lance gripped like an oversized walking cane in one enormous fist; and Alixa, who'd run

1

for Scourgey, helping the creature up even as her eyes fixed on the shattered, rising form of the *Lady Vizola* as she rose again from the waters.

Jasen hardly heard it. He hardly felt the kiss of rain on his forehead. Nor did he feel the ache in his bones, from this most recent fight, and the deeper-set ache, the one that Baraghosa had sensed in him, that which had been building for—days? Weeks? Perhaps months or longer. The poison within him, eating him from the inside.

He felt nothing but fear, beat through him in black waves by his heart thudding mercilessly in his throat. He forgot the death that Baraghosa told him awaited, for that was some far-off thing, whited out by *this* death, the one they all faced with the *Lady Vizola* crumpled, unable to save them from this no man's land.

And then the water reared back again—and where it drew backward, Jasen saw, almost dots from this distance, the *actual* arms of drowning men. They flailed, fighting desperately.

Another enormous wave rose—

Then slammed down over the heads of those men.

Then Jasen was running. He sprang down after Kuura.

"Jasen!" Alixa shouted, a high, shrill scream.

A mirthless laugh came from Longwell. "The boy has fire." He ran too, passing Jasen swiftly.

Huanatha only growled, "Faster, warrior." And she, too, overtook Jasen with powerful, leaping strides, propelled as if the wind lifted her every step.

Down the path they'd taken up here, over the smooth black rock, dodging sharp, jagged outcroppings, Jasen sprinted after Huanatha, Kuura, and Longwell, feet threatening to slip out from under him where rain and the spray of seawater had drenched the whole forsaken island.

A bolt of purest pink split the sky asunder. It boomed, a deafening roar. It connected sky and sea in one dazzling beam of electricity.

Where it touched the seawater, the water rose upward, pushed upward like a blister ...

Then came the waves.

Longwell, Kuura, and Huanatha had just reached the shoreline when the first thundered down upon the sand, pushing them back.

The spray exploded. Now Jasen did stop. A mist of salty droplets seared his eyes. The echoing boom of thunder was overshadowed by the devastating power unleashed against the isle's edge. A moment later it hit him, a weaker wave, rebounding chaotically from the island's warped circumference. He fell back, fingers grasping for purchase—

A hand on his shoulder, armored—Longwell.

"Stay back," he said, already moving back down to the shore. Jasen had not even seen him spring back up to catch him, he'd moved so quickly. "Do not endanger yourself any more than you already have."

It was not an order. And if it had been? Jasen would never have followed it. Lips tight, he pushed himself into motion again, trying to keep pace with Longwell and failing, even if his legs had to work double-time to do it.

"I want to help!" Jasen cried.

Longwell gave him a grim, over-the-shoulder look. "Then watch your step."

The noise was thunderous. Pulses of unnatural color exploded across the sky, blinding bars of illumination that kissed the surface of the ocean and churned it into new, rising blisters, slewing off tsunami-sized waves. The sea roared with all the fury of a beastly giant. The painful noise crashed down over them like a hammer forged from the foundry that had built the world. Longwell braced Jasen then, holding him firm. Jasen slammed his eyes closed so the water would not burn, and held his breath tight in his chest, trusting Longwell to hold them steady ...

Then they were running again, dragging themselves on in the respite between attacks from the sea.

The *Lady Vizola* had been pushed around the isle's edge, hull up. She'd found a field of sharp spires, risen out of the water. They braced her as the sea flowed out ... but when it crashed in again, it pushed her against the rocks, and she rolled, the top deck coming out of the water again as she righted herself.

Wood splintered, ripped apart.

The mainmast came down. How it had held for so long, Jasen could not imagine. But now it finally cracked as the ship was hammered again. They were so close now, only a hundred feet, they could hear it plain. The break was low to the deck—and it tipped, inland—

"Back!" Longwell boomed. He'd already thrust an arm around Jasen's waist, and shoved him aside—

The crow's nest crashed down upon the rock, exploding in a shower of wood.

Splinters flew. Jasen cried out, gritted his teeth. Something had winged him, he was sure of it.

Longwell's arm came away from his chest.

"You're bleeding," the dragoon said.

Jasen blinked. He was on his back, sprawled on rock.

Longwell loomed over him. Behind, the *Lady Vizola*—or what was left of her—lay against the rocks. Gouges opened dark spaces into the hull. Water flooded in. A field of debris expanded around her.

And people. Three—no, four?

Jasen blinked. A white spot clouded his vision.

Had something sunk into his actual eye?

He groped for it, frowning momentarily. His fingers found nothing—and when he blinked again, the spot vanished. Five people out there. Fighting waves—no, not all—that one, face down, was it …?

Another wave was building. They could not delay any longer.

"I'm fine," said Jasen, pushing up and ducking away from Longwell's arm. "We have to help." And he was past, running the last of the way on the slick, rocky shoreline.

Huanatha was slinging her armor aside.

Kuura had already leapt into the water.

Jasen followed, throwing himself over in an ungainly jump—

He hit the water's surface hard and hit the bottom harder; it was shallow this close, where the sea had receded in preparation for its next blow. The impact jolted up and through him, rattling his bones.

Jasen's first time swimming in the ocean had been barely a few weeks ago. It was far different from the idle swimming in the brook than wended through Terreas, the push and movement of the waves. He'd not ventured into the water since—but now he took to it as if he had been part of it his whole life. He thrust his arms out, dragging himself out as the sea fell away under him, alongside the husk of the *Lady Vizola*—oh, there were so many ragged holes …

Debris littered the water, broken boards, mostly. But there were crates too, and cages. A book floated past, perhaps one from Burund's personal collection. Maybe even one he had gifted Jasen and Alixa, before their arrival at the Aiger Cliffs. Jasen did not look closely: he was focused only on a body, face down in front of him, maybe thirty paces away. The water was dragging it back farther … and the wall kept building beyond, climbing—

Jasen kicked, pulling himself on with his arms.

Crossing the rising river with Shilara lay a lifetime behind.

How had that been so terrifying?

Twenty paces …

Fifteen …

Saltwater poured into his mouth as a pearly blast, the white of natural lightning, cleaved the air apart. It exploded on the back of the swell ahead. The flash was blinding; the boom was deafening, so close that it came in almost perfect unison with the blast.

Blinded by the flash, Jasen paddled madly.

Then the afterglow was fading, and—

A wave, easily twice the height of the *Lady Vizola*'s now-wrecked mainmast, hurtled right for him. The churning of the sea turned it into an almost black thing, an inky smear with a head of white froth riding atop it—

Jasen acted on pure instinct. He kicked himself forward, thrust all of his energy into closing that last gap between him and the dark-skinned man lying face down in the water. He swung his arms forward, sluicing through the water—

He closed his hand around the man's wrist a half second before the water hit him.

The force of it was terrifying. Buffeted, Jasen almost let the man go—almost. Instead he clung on, holding a breath in his chest, one too small, as he was swept down, pushed down against the very bedrock of the sea. He was engulfed in pitch black, the entire world swallowed.

He was ground against rock. Things were hitting him, like a rain turned solid. Stones from the seafloor? Wreckage of the *Lady Vizola*? He could not know. Nor could he gasp against the blows, or the feel of the rock digging into his back, or his spine grinding against it.

He had no choice but to endure, and to hold on.

It seemed to go on forever.

Only when he was sure he would die, a fire in his chest, his body on the verge of collapse, did the water recede. The darkness lifted, the pressure with it. He came away from the rock, freed. He kicked, not sure exactly which way was up.

He found air and sucked it in, but there was little time to relish it. A body surfaced alongside him. Those receding waters would build again.

Jasen had to get back to shore, with the unconscious sailor.

First, though, he pulled the body around. He was heavy, naturally bulky, and limp in the water—Jasen did not dare give a thought to the possibility that he was dead. Maneuvering him was not easy, and it took Jasen precious seconds to turn him so that his face was pointing upward, his airway unrestricted.

Hamisi—one of the sailors who'd wanted to throw Scourgey, and possibly by extension Jasen and Alixa, overboard that first night off the shores of Luukessia.

Well, the who of it didn't matter. Jasen slung one arm around him, hooking it under a shoulder and began an awkward paddle back to the isle's shore of blurred, onyx-dark rock. The battering wave had brought them in most of the way. But its retreat, pulling the sea back out again to build it into another swell, was dragging them backward too. And as Jasen fought, one-armed, the edge of the isle only drew farther back … His energy began to wane too, now that he carried a load at least twice his weight, prone and unhelping …

"Come on," he grunted, kicking harder.

Sweat beaded his brow, salty as the seawater.

He kicked hard, then harder—

But the sea was growing more shallow, the water rushing out beneath him, threatening to tear him from the embrace of the rocky shore. It ripped at his feet, wanting him, hungering for him. The thunderheads pelted down, great streaks of color lighting the sky, and Jasen was pulled back …

A strobing flash of purple lit the sky from behind him, casting the world in the otherworldly hue of Baraghosa's spell. It *BOOMED*, an explosive jolt of indescribable power that rattled Jasen's bones. His eardrums threatened to burst.

And the sea kept rising, kept pulling at him.

He cursed. Panic rose in his chest with the building of the water.

He was lifting too now, on the very edge of the swelling blister—

He should just let Hamisi go. Focus on steeling himself, preparing himself for the—

He had no time to think further. The suction stopped, and the first wave broke from the swell. Jasen was thrust forward on it, carried at a tremendous speed. And the shore, the mottled, twisted, blackened edge of the isle of Baraghosa, raced toward him.

He yelled—

Then he was under as it overtook him.

He saw the *Lady Vizola*'s tattered side in a blur, pocked full of ragged holes, collapsing as the water and rock ripped her apart.

Rock, jagged, flew at him—

He thrust out with his free hand, as if it would do any good—

And then blackness.

*

The next thing Jasen knew was a hammer pounding him in the chest. His ribs did not break, but the force pushed them inward, squeezed his innards.

Saltwater burst from his lungs in a cough, stringy mucus flying.

Wheezing, he

opened his eyes.

The world's contrast was wrong. All the brights were too bright, and the darks bordered on black. And the figure bowed over him was almost a shadow.

No, not a shadow—dark-skinned.

The eyes of Shipmaster Burund looked down at him. "Breathe," he said, clasping Jasen's shoulder. His deep voice was strained, his pupils dark, hidden in the whites of his eyes, which seemed entirely too wide.

Jasen obeyed, but each breath burned terribly. And though the spray of the water breaking on the rocks filled the air in a salty mist, the taste of it was stronger inside him. Each breath filling his lungs set off a cough. Something in his throat was irritated. A pool of seawater must've found a place to reside in him. He hacked and coughed, spitting murky gunk that could only have come from the deepest recesses of his lungs. Still, he couldn't ease the ache.

Someone was cursing.

Jasen squinted around, eyebrows knitting.

The *Lady Vizola* lay on her side—what was left of her, anyway. Much of it was missing, ripped away by the raking over and over of rocks. What remained appeared to be held together only by the barest framework.

A brilliant flash of pale blue split the air, accompanied by a booming explosion. Jasen flinched. For a moment he was still in the water, about to be thrown against the rocks again.

"Hamisi!" Jasen said suddenly.

"He is okay," said Burund.

"Where?"

Burund pointed, his finger coated in blood.

Hamisi lay on a rock. One of his shipmates was crouched beside him, talking. Hamisi breathed, head to the sky. His tunic had torn, revealing a strong chest with no fat upon it. It rose and fell with each haggard inhalation and exhalation.

Jasen closed his eyes, nodded. Thank the ancestors Burund had pulled them out.

But more were still in the water. There were people out there—some struggling with crates and cases, others struggling to pull their shipmates to shore. Kuura had a man slung about his shoulder. He was grunting fiercely, teeth clenched in a crazed grimace. Longwell offered the handle of his spear, from where he stood atop a gnarled crag, for Kuura to grip onto. Then he lifted Kuura almost without effort, settling him upon the rock.

Jasen forced himself upward.

Burund held out an arm to still him. "What are you doing?"

"Helping."

Burund's nostrils flared. "Do not be so reckless. You almost drowned."

"I'm fine," he lied and staggered away. "Let me help."

"JASEN!"

It was Alixa, sprinting toward him, Scourgey limping weakly behind. She tore down to the shore, slipping and staggering until she reached him.

She clutched Jasen's wrist, staring at him with desperate eyes.

"I couldn't find you! I asked Huanatha, and she said she thought—"

"I'm fine," Jasen said. He tried to wrest himself from her grip—there were people still in the water, damn it; even now, with another wave beginning its race inland, Kuura was swimming out again, the many folds of his ripped tunic billowing about him—but Alixa held firm, fingernails digging into him.

"Let me go," he said.

"You almost drowned," Burund repeated.

Alixa's eyes only grew wider. She stared in terror, gaze flicking between them.

Jasen began, "I'm fine—"

"You are not *fine,*" she said, "You ancestors-damned bloody fool. You could have died!"

Jasen almost shot back, "I *am* dying," but bit his tongue. Didn't she realize he had people to save? The *Lady Vizola* was here because of him, after all, and now she lay dying on the edge of this mist-shrouded isle.

Green lightning pulsed in strobing forks. Farther off, this one—the *BOOM* came delayed by a half-second. Nor did the explosion kiss the ocean surface.

The storm was abating.

"Please, Jasen," said Burund, squeezing his shoulder. "Let us do the work."

"You can't even swim," Alixa said. Somehow her words were harder to bear than the deafening thunder that boomed around them.

"But—" Jasen protested.

"No buts. Please. You have done more than anyone could expect. Now let us do the rest."

"But—"

"Stop." Burund gripped him hard, harder perhaps than he meant to. "You push yourself like a beast of burden against this task, but you

8

are weak. I will not permit it. Now stay." And before Jasen could protest with even a word, he broke free, strode down to the water's edge, and leapt into the water in a fluid arc, his hands out in front of him.

Jasen moved to follow—

Alixa yanked him back.

"Alixa—"

"What are you doing?" she asked.

"Helping!"

She spat a curse with such spite that Jasen flinched back from it. "You *idiot*," she growled. "The Shipmaster tells you to stop endangering yourself, and you still try to follow?"

"They're here because—"

"Sit down on the shore and let them deal with it."

They were at an impasse for a long moment. But Alixa faced him down with fierce determination, and finally, he obeyed, retreating wearily from the edge of the shore and planting his backside on a twisted, slippery rock.

Alixa lowered herself beside him. Scourgey dropped down too, sighing. Her coal-black eyes looked out sadly from above crossed paws, her head laid upon them.

Another wave hit the shore. It was weaker now though. A shower of foam rained down on Jasen and Alixa and Scourgey.

It pulled away.

"It's easing," Alixa said quietly.

Jasen said nothing.

The shattered remains of the *Lady Vizola* lay supported on the rocks that had torn her apart. She held there as the waters receded, for long seconds ... and then, with a final creaking groan, she snapped in two. The broken halves of her framework sagged into the sea, sloughing off debris into the growing mass that surrounded her.

Jasen closed his eyes, hung his head.

Alixa held onto his arm. "It's okay," she said.

Jasen shook his head. It was not—and Alixa knew it. The *Lady Vizola* was their only way off the island. It was wrecked, swept out into the ocean in pieces that could never be salvaged, much less put back together ... and in this field of accursed fog, no one was coming for them.

They were stranded—and alone.

2

Though the lightning abated, the rain did not. It carried on well into the evening, when the sun's already feeble presence began to fade. If anything, the rain grew heavier in the absence of the thunderheads.

The isle of Baraghosa did not offer much in the way of shelter. The tower itself was an option—but none of the crew appeared willing to consider it, looking upon it with fear in their weary eyes. Nor did Jasen wish to return to the place where he had faced Baraghosa again, *failed* again—and learned of his impending death. It was as though a noxious black cloud hung over it. All felt it, none wanted to chance the stay, and so alternatives were sought.

A nook was found a three-quarter-mile walk from the place where the *Lady Vizola* had finally given herself over to the sea. The rock was less smooth here, more craggy and sharp. The space was barely large enough for the full crew, let alone supplies. Yet they crowded in by necessity.

Somehow, a fire was lit. Only the one. There was little dry wood to feed it. A pile of salvaged boards from the *Lady Vizola* was spread around it in hopes that it would dry enough to burn. So far, it had not.

The ship's crew huddled around the fire. So small, not a part of their number, and with her diseased-smelling pet lolling her head upon her lap, Alixa was not permitted a space right by the fire's edge. Instead she sat a little back. An idle hand stroked the stringy, thick hairs sprouting from Scourgey's head. Girl and scourge both stared into the fire with lost eyes.

A salvage operation had been in effect for the past few hours, now that the full crew were accounted for. Though Shipmaster Burund would not allow Jasen to venture into the water for the crates and barrels that remained close enough to shore to bring back onto land—too dark, he said when Jasen questioned him, even if the waves had subsided—Jasen was allowed to help carry them back to the shelter. Once, Jasen and Hamisi were tasked with a crate with a splintered top. Jasen flashed him a weak smile as they carried it awkwardly the whole way back to the cave. Hamisi only looked sour, as ever. Once the crate was placed with the rest, building a wall up to protect further against the elements, Hamisi stalked off without waiting for Jasen to accompany him back.

Jasen sighed, watching Hamisi's back recede.

Huanatha was passing as Jasen made his way back to the shore once more. She hefted a barrel, holding it close to her belly. She nodded at Jasen and continued on her way. A minute later, having put the barrel down, she caught up to him again.

"You are a determined one," she said. "I knew I saw it in you. Your ancestors are proud."

A chill ran up Jasen's spine, nothing to do with the rain or the wind caressing his skin. They were with him now? He stumbled, missing a step.

Huanatha caught him. "Are you okay?"

"Fine," he said.

Another white spot had opened up in his vision, though. He blinked against it. It dimmed, but did not go away.

Huanatha squinted at him. She seemed unconvinced, but she released her hold of his arm. "Rest soon." And she lifted a wave before moving ahead, carried on longer legs with more energy than his.

She passed him again a few minutes later heading back with another crate in her arms. This time, she gave him only a glance and a nod.

At the wreckage, Burund was overseeing the salvage. A stack of crates had been pushed together, hauled in from the water.

When he saw Jasen, he pointed to a small one, no larger than a knapsack. "Your last one," he said. "Then you rest."

Jasen lifted an eyebrow. Had Huanatha said something?

Nevertheless, he took it, the weight pulling at his weary arms.

"I am serious, Jasen!" Burund called as he turned away. "I do not want to see you back here."

Jasen clenched his teeth. He didn't complain though, just headed back toward the cavern.

Another of those white spots was clouding his vision by the time he added his small crate to the rest. His legs were heavy too, and his arms. And that horrid salty taste in the back of his throat—that hadn't abated either. It was like a little part of the ocean must live right down at the bottom of his lungs. A little part of him wondered if he'd taste it forever.

Another part considered that forever, for him, might not be very long at all.

He sat down, more heavily than he'd intended, by Alixa's side.

Scourgey glanced at him. She pressed her nose against his skin, and breathed. The sound she made was sad.

Jasen patted her. He blinked, hard. Stupid spots. Like blank, white paint poured into clumps in the middle of his sight. A wave of dizziness ran through his head just then, and he tipped slightly before catching himself.

"What's wrong?"

He frowned at Alixa. "Hm?"

"What's wrong?" she asked again.

Jasen just shook his head. "Nothing. Tired, that's all."

A canvas sail—part of one, at any rate—had been pulled from the water. It was soaking, but had been squeezed out as much as possible by a team of shipmates who weren't able to help much with salvage—those with injuries that made walking difficult, but did not totally immobilize them. They were cloistered together, and Medleigh oversaw them, looking as though he needed a doctor too, a great wound open in his shoulder that he'd stitched and bound.

The sail was being slowly manhandled into a canopy. A new fire was lit below it as men struggled to attach the sail's corners to wooden beams. For now, the flame was low and kicking off a great deal of black smoke. Drips kept falling into it, threatening to put it out. The hope appeared to be that the smoke would dry the sail, extending their meager shelter as the night lengthened. It might be successful, though Jasen wondered if, when the sail was dry, they would have to kick the fire out to stop it from igniting the canopy.

He looked around them. He knew barely any of their names. Their faces, though, he knew those.

A frown pulled his lips downward.

Alixa touched his wrist. "Talk to me."

He sighed. "I did this."

"This was Baraghosa," Alixa said firmly.

"And we are all here because of me." Jasen gazed over the clustered bodies in this shelter, their injuries—broken arms, legs, swellings all over and innumerable wounds that oozed blood even now, soaking the improvised bandages binding them. That no one had been killed was an unbelievable stroke of luck. It did not change the fact that every one of these people were here, broken and stranded, most of their possessions lost to the ocean, because of him.

He hung his head.

"Stop it," said Alixa. "Right now." She spoke so fiercely that Jasen looked up at her. "This self-pity has gone on for long enough. Neither I nor anyone else can talk you out of whipping yourself endlessly over what has happened, so I'm not trying anymore. If you think it's your fault, fine. But now you need to start asking yourself— *what can I do to fix this?*"

What could he do?

He racked his brains, running a finger distractedly across the graze above his right eyebrow, already beginning to form a scab.

"I don't know," he said at last.

Alixa pursed her lips. "No. Me neither. But we can work on that."

What she thought they'd come up with, Jasen hadn't the first clue. The only thing he could think of was entirely unrealistic: locating another boat by which they could escape this rock. Baraghosa had fled in his and Jasen doubted the sorcerer retained a spare. And with barely any foliage on the island except for some low-growing scrubby plants, they had little in the way of materials to build a raft, let alone a sea-worthy boat.

No, he had no answers. Pondering them now likely wouldn't get anywhere either. He was tired and his head was fuzzy. He was probably hungry, although for now his stomach did not appear to know it. He'd pushed his body hard today, but now he that had stopped, he ached, all of him—his muscles, his bones, even his brain.

And those damned spots in his vision—a little one was flickering in the corner, but whenever he tried to glance at it, it darted out of sight like a bird startled from a bush.

He fingered the scab on his forehead again. Damage from the bit of wood that had winged him? Splinters in his eyes? Or had the first spot appeared before that? Now he thought about it, he couldn't quite get the timeline in order. It had happened after ... hadn't it?

He peered out of the nook of a cavern. An outcrop of boulders provided a wall against the wind. Dark as the night beyond them, Jasen could see their shape only by the flickering of flames: their curves, slick with rain ...

His heart skipped.

He stared.

Between two of the boulders, there had been another shape. A human one.

Was that ...?

"Jasen?" Alixa asked, from afar. She peered at his face, then followed his gaze. "What ...?"

He turned to her. "Did you see that?"

"See what?"

He opened his mouth—but the answer would not come. It would sound like madness. Fatigue had taken a deeper root than he'd realized.

"Nothing," he said. "Just tired." And he settled back, bunching his knees to his chest and holding them tight.

Still, he watched those boulders, and the gap between them.

She did not appear again. But then, she hadn't appeared at all. She couldn't have.

After all ... his mother was long dead.

3

Adem was angry. He was shouting, over and over, his voice was deep and frightening. Jasen cowered back from him. Adem spewed an endless slew of words Jasen didn't understand, loud like thundercracks. For some reason, Jasen associated his words with different colors of flashing lightning. And the voice … it kept *changing*.

Then Jasen's eyes were open, and he was not looking into the crossbeams of the ceiling of his home in Terreas. Instead he saw rock, dark, lit in streaks by golden firelight.

It was not his father shouting at him. Instead the raised voices came from the crew of the *Lady Vizola*.

He rolled over.

Alixa crouched beside him. Her grim expression was painted in stark colors by the fire's glow and the night's shadows. Her grip on Scourgey was white-knuckled. Unaware that Jasen had woken, she watched across the small cavern.

Jasen followed her.

Hamisi and several others were standing, crowded in the small space, their faces glowing dimly in firelight. They shouted, pointing accusatory fingers.

Shipmaster Burund stood among them, enduring their complaints. When a gap came in their rapid speech, he answered in calm.

It did not placate them. Hamisi exploded, throwing his arms skyward. He spat words in a frenzy, so quick that Jasen could scarcely recognize the sounds that made them up.

Burund responded, calm as death.

One of Hamisi's mates, a dreadlocked man with a fat stone hanging from each ear, Kosi, cut over Burund. A great barrel of a man, he got up into Burund's face, practically roaring. Burund stood stock still, placidly enduring the verbal assault.

15

"What's going on?" Jasen asked.

Alixa just said, "We should do something."

"He can take it." This was from Huanatha. She'd crept up. Clad in armor only from the waist down, a better bandage finally wrapped about her by Medleigh, she regarded the ongoing outburst with a sneer. "Besides, I do not think a fifteen-year-old girl is likely to diffuse an attack on the shipmaster. Particularly this one."

Alixa pursed her lips. "Still."

"What are they fighting about?" Jasen asked.

Huanatha stooped beside him. The glow of the fire licking the curves of her armor turned its blue to a peculiar shade of amber.

"They are unhappy with this turn of events," Huanatha said. "Their ship has been destroyed, their possessions lost, and they find themselves stranded on a cursed dot of a rock in the middle of a hostile ocean. This, they blame on the shipmaster." She paused a moment, listening as Hamisi kicked off another particularly vicious diatribe, complete with wild gesticulation and much jabbing of fingers. "This one, he accuses the shipmaster of forsaking the judgment of the crew." Another pause. Kosi, just as animated as Hamisi, was talking again. "They would never have sailed here. Not willingly." A few moments listening again. Lips tight, Huanatha finished, "Not for unpaying strangers …" Her eyes flicked sideways to Jasen and Alixa at that. He there might have been more to Kosi's speech. Whatever Kosihe'd said sounded much more venomous than Huanatha's translation.

Jasen sighed. "They have a point," he conceded wearily.

Alixa's glare softened; she apparently agreed too.

He listened for a little longer. Kuura and a few others joined in the debate to defend Burund, but he often waved them down, keeping the focus of Hamisi and his comrades firmly on himself.

After a minute or two of listening, Huanatha said, "They are questioning the possibility of a change of leadership."

Alixa looked shocked. "They're going to depose Shipmaster Burund?"

Huanatha listened intently. The conversation was rapid. Others in the shelter were weighing in too now, but it was hard to tell where they stood on it. Nor did Jasen care. He was interested only in the outcome—one in which, he hoped, Burund would keep his position—or at least that Hamisi would not replace him.

"They are not threatening it," said Huanatha at last. "Not yet, at least. Merely suggesting the possibility, albeit strongly. This has gone catastrophically, after all, they say. And no one will come to our rescue. Everyone from Firoba and Chaarland and Coricuanthi and the other lands know better than to come near here." Her lip curled. "Cowards."

Jasen watched. A wider discussion had opened. Hamisi and his group were not quite so loud now. A man who kept close to Hamisi's elbow, the tattoo of a many-legged creature imprinted across his exposed shoulder, appeared to have taken a sort of mediator role. He listened quietly, arms folded, nodding as people spoke. Then, when another pair vied for loudest, he snapped off a complaint and elected one to speak.

"Slimy creature," Huanatha growled.

Jasen glanced at her, eyebrow raised.

"That one is quieting those on the shipmaster's side. He lets only those sympathetic to Hamisi speak."

Sure enough, when the current speaker finished, and the other opened his mouth to jump in—Kosi leapt in. The 'mediator' did not intervene, initially. When the rejected speaker tried to speak more loudly, the mediator shouted at him, making a cutting motion with his hand. The rejected speaker was cowed into quiet. He seethed, eyes burning.

"Did he threaten him?" Jasen whispered.

Huanatha shook her head. "He might as well have, though. Hamisi's reputation keeps the others in check."

"Reputation?" Alixa asked.

Huanatha nodded. "All is not perfect brotherhood on the *Lady Vizola*."

Alixa asked quietly, "What sort of reputation?"

"He is a brute," said Huanatha. "Quick to use his fists."

Jasen bit his lip. What wonderful timing, learning of Hamisi's penchant for brutality now, when they were all stranded together.

He glanced at Burund. The shipmaster was not shouted down. If he was threatened by the possibility of removal from his post, whether by vote or by force, he did not show it. He appeared the same as ever, his quiet confidence intact.

Still, Jasen could not help but wonder—if Burund ceased acting as shipmaster, and someone like Hamisi took over with this stranded party, where did that leave him and Alixa? They were, after all, the "unpaying strangers." Burund had led the crew of the *Lady Vizola* into this mess—but he had done it for Jasen.

Jasen blocked out the thoughts of what might happen to him and Alixa. Too many possibilities, and all of them unpleasant.

Alixa turned to Jasen. "Who is—?"

17

"Ssh," Huanatha hissed.

Burund was talking. Huanatha listened.

Jasen alternated looks between the shipmaster and Huanatha.

"What's he saying?" Jasen finally asked.

Huanatha's face twitched with irritation. She'd probably missed something, even if Jasen whispered. Nevertheless, she said, "He is reminding them that whatever might happen in the future, he remains shipmaster. A challenge to that will be handled accordingly but not in the middle of the night. Everyone should rest for now." Her lips drew back in her familiar sneer, teeth bared. "Foolhardy man, showing his dissidents such loyalty. He ought to cast them out into the waters tonight and let it run them ragged against the rocks."

"Shipmaster Burund wouldn't do that," said Alixa. "He's a good man."

"Too good." Huanatha snorted. "This Hamisi, he will accept Burund's edict—for now. How *gracious* of him." Acid dripped from her words.

Sure enough, Hamisi appeared to have conceded, at least for the moment. He parted from Burund, the small group of instigators following him through the small cavern, between people lying or sitting on the hard ground. Hamisi's gaze passed over Jasen as he strode by. His expression was sour, his mouth twisted into almost as deep a sneer as Huanatha's. But then his eyes fell upon the warrior, poised at Jasen and Alixa's sides, and he was past them.

Huanatha cursed under her breath, a particularly unpleasant insult. It referred to one's mother as having lain with a sort of Coricuanthian dog. Perhaps even a pack of them; Jasen did not wish to ask.

Alixa's mouth fell open.

"Don't look so affronted," Huanatha said. "You know I am not wrong."

Alixa spluttered, "Well, literally I think—"

Huanatha held up her hands. Then, rising, she said, "Get some sleep. We have long, unpleasant days ahead." She, too, stalked away.

Jasen watched Burund, who remained in place and was making quiet conversation with Kuura and Medleigh. Both of them looked troubled, the former more so considering his usual wide grin.

Were they genuinely concerned that Hamisi could remove Burund from his post?

Jasen wished he knew their native tongue so that he might have caught more of the nuances to the argument that had just passed.

Then again, he would also know what Hamisi had actually said about him and Alixa and he might wish he hadn't swum out to save the wretch … But that was not a line of thought he wanted to follow at the moment. He was too weary, and he wished to save his hatred for Baraghosa.

A spark of fire kindled in Jasen's chest. Murderous sorcerer.

That was better—something worth hating. True evil, not just name-calling and a lack of gratitude.

Nevertheless, Baraghosa was not an issue at present. The growing tension within the *Lady Vizola*'s crew, however …

That was liable to explode in a way that would not be possible to escape—and perhaps very, very soon.

4

The day dawned grey.

Two nights had come and gone since the *Lady Vizola*'s cataclysmic end. Salvage was still ongoing, although the majority of what could be reclaimed had already been fished out of the water. A small team, winnowed down to just a skeleton now as their job neared its end, continued to dive into the shattered frame of the ship, or swim far out into the ocean for a barrel or crate bobbing on a crest of soft foam. Jasen volunteered his help for this, but Burund would not permit it.

"Rest," he said, every time he was asked. "Save your strength."

Anxious to be helpful, Jasen busied himself instead where he could around the camp. Although the rain had finally died off during the early hours of the morning before, they needed walls—to protect against the elements and to retain the heat from their fires.

So a wall of the salvaged crates was erected, far enough from the flames to keep them from catching should the wind howl through, but close enough to keep the heat in.

Then there was the matter of extending the canvas roof, so that the sailors were not practically lying end to end all night. New fires were lit and kept fueled at all hours. A watch was set and kept, just the same as had been on ship.

Somehow, a tattered net had been found, clinging to one of the jagged rocks that had contributed to the *Lady Vizola*'s undoing, and they flung it out into the sea.

Twice, it was dredged up empty. The third time, it snared some seaweed and a dead thing Jasen couldn't identify—much of it was missing, chewed off. Kuura cursed at it and tossed it back out into the water. Things were not yet that dire.

But they would be. The food stores were small, a fraction of what the *Lady Vizola* had carried. Two crates full of hardtack had been affected by leaks. One was much worse than the other, and the seawater had turned the bland, crunchy crackers into a slurry. The other crate was less affected. The hardtack closer to the leak had turned to mush, but once those portions were scraped away, the rest was found to be edible, if somewhat soft. It was spread out on canvas to dry in the sunlight.

There was not much sunlight, though. Grey clouds hung overhead at all hours of day and lay thick over the sorcerer's island at night, obscuring the moon and stars. As though the mood were not dark enough without the aid of their environs making it so, literally.

So the food situation was grim. And it seemed it would only get grimmer, for a party that scouted the circumference of the island found barely any foliage. The scrubby plants that did cling to life weren't fit for eating—mostly twigs, few leaves. It made Jasen wonder what exactly Baraghosa ate while here. Perhaps he didn't need to eat at all. His own heavy sense of self-satisfaction hardly seemed filling enough.

The next problem to present itself was water. A good deal of it, all in barrels, had been fished out of the sea. But it wouldn't last forever. So far, three barrels had been opened to sate the crew. The second had to be set aside as a piece of the wall only, a glorified brick, because the first taste test was overpoweringly salty. It would only dehydrate them, Kuura said.

Eight barrels of water left—eight and a half, counting the open one. Rationing wasn't in effect yet—but already, at the dawn of their second day, Jasen heard the mutterings. Huanatha relayed it to him and Alixa, in regular updates; Kuura was too busy, and Burund was overseeing operations. He might be worried, but he had a cool head about him. Had to, Jasen supposed, after Hamisi's threat of mutiny. Panicking like a chicken with its head lopped off would only seal his deposition.

That morning, when Jasen woke, the shipmaster was not to be found.

Nor was Longwell.

Hamisi, though, was griping in his own language. Sitting by one of the fires, he scowled as he ran a blade over the end of a long, thin wooden beam. It wasn't yet a sharp spike, but it would be before too long.

Alixa was already up. She sat cross-legged at Jasen's side, staring into the distance.

"Morning," she said flatly when she spied Jasen's motion had changed, from the shifting of a boy asleep to someone rousing.

He rubbed the sleep out of his eyes. No spots in them this morning, which was good. "How long have you been awake?"

Alixa shrugged. "A while."

A particularly sharp blast of wind from the ocean came, whistling through the gaps in their makeshift walls. Though Jasen had become immune to the smell of saltwater, having been surrounded by it so long—much the same as he rarely noticed Scourgey's deathly smell anymore—the blast of wind seemed to bring it back with force. His nose crinkled.

Hamisi grumbled. Kosi, at his side, added something—agreeing with him, going by the subtle incline of his head. Complaining about the weather, most likely.

"How long has he been sharpening that?" Jasen asked in a low voice. Hamisi couldn't speak his language, just the same as Jasen did not share Hamisi's, but still—it paid to be careful.

"Since before I woke," Alixa murmured. She glanced at the stave briefly, then looked away, as though staring at it too long might challenge Hamisi to test its sharpness out on her.

Jasen frowned. Hamisi wouldn't be preparing his spear for combat purposes, would he? To strike Burund down? Surely it was to fish. Kuura had said that they did that, back home in Coricuanthi, striding out into the river with poles and stabbing at fish as they passed. The most adept could catch twenty in ten minutes easily, slinging them over to women on the shore, who gutted and cleaned them.

That must be it. He was preparing to fish. Nothing more.

Still, it was disconcerting. Jasen stared, fascinated by every sliver of curled wood that Hamisi whittled away, and his apprehension grew.

Stop watching, he told himself.

He could not.

"I'm going to stretch my legs," he said, rising. "Want to come?"

Alixa shook her head distantly. "No, thank you."

"See you, then." He patted Scourgey on the head—old faithful, lying at Alixa's side with her head on Alixa's knee—and then wended his way out of the little encampment. A wide route, giving Hamisi maximum berth.

It was a cruel wind indeed that came from the sea this morning. The moment Jasen was out in it properly, he reconsidered having left the overhang and its walls and crackling fires. The wind came ceaselessly, gusting harder and harder. The mists had been dislodged by it, or at least thinned; Jasen could see much farther this morning.

He stooped around the shoreline made of mottled, blackened rock, heading for the *Lady Vizola*'s wreck. Perhaps there he'd find Burund.

He did. And Longwell, too. The shipmaster and dragoon were talking, their backs to Jasen as they looked out at sea and upon the ruined carapace of the ship Burund had once commanded.

They huddled together. At first, Jasen thought it was because the wind from the sea brought with it a chill.

As he came closer, though, their words were carried upon the wind to him.

"... situation is very dire, Longwell."

Jasen hung back, low, listened.

"I'm aware of—"

"Then you know I have more pressing matters to attend to," Burund said, cutting over the dragoon.

Longwell did not evince Jasen's shock at the shipmaster's brusqueness, at least from the back, though his helm partially obscured his face. Nor was there any surprise in his voice as he whispered, "The sorcerer is the most pressing of matters before us. You must see that—"

"The most pressing matter before me is the survival of my crew," said Burund. "We have food and water for a week, no more. Nor do we possess a vessel fit to sail off this island. Why I need to impress upon you the seriousness of this situation we find ourselves in, I do not know."

"I, too, have been wrecked at sea, Shipmaster."

"And fortunately for you, we happened upon you. We will not have the same luck. Not here, in the middle of a cursed fog, on a cursed isle."

"The fog is lifting."

"And do you see any vessel out there which might save us?"

"There is time yet."

Burund shook his head dismissively. "These are the things I have to deal with. Others, too."

Longwell stood with his spear jutting high above his head; it was easily taller than him. "You refer, I assume, to the mutiny that's brewing among your men?"

"Aye. So, as to Baraghosa—he is not on my list of priorities at this moment in time. Nor is he likely to be again, after ... this." He waved a hand at the lingering wreck of the *Lady Vizola*.

Someone called from behind, startling Jasen almost out of his skin.

Medleigh approached. He either had not seen Jasen, or did not acknowledge him; instead, he called again to Burund, and the shipmaster turned.

23

Burund's eyes flicked over Jasen.

Heat bloomed in Jasen's cheeks. Burund's face was often difficult to read—but Jasen was certain the shipmaster knew that he had been listening.

"This is my last word on the matter," Burund said to Longwell, and off he strode, to meet Medleigh and deal with whatever it was he wanted.

Longwell dawdled at the shoreline, looking pensively out to the wreck and beyond.

When Burund and Medleigh had turned to return to the camp, Jasen meandered out to join Longwell's side, pushing against the wind blowing in off the ocean. He took up position beside him, watching out to the sea just as thoughtfully as the dragoon.

Little debris was left now. Jasen spied a crate that had been eased back toward the shore by the waves. It lolled at an awkward angle, a corner pointed straight up like a mountain rendered in a miniature wooden diamond. In the distance, one of the sailors strode over to pull it out. Hopefully it would be food.

Even the scraps of wood, the boards that had splintered and come apart, were mostly gone now. Enough had washed ashore and been scavenged for firewood that the *Lady Vizola*'s crew would perish from thirst well before they perished from cold. Still, it was hardly a fraction of the material that had made up the ship and its contents. If they'd collected even ten percent of the boards, Jasen would be amazed. So it was incredible to think of how quickly the sea had dispersed the wreck's pieces and carried them away.

He felt small just thinking of it.

Eventually, Longwell sighed. "How are you keeping?" he asked.

"Fine," said Jasen. As well as could be expected, anyway.

Longwell nodded. "Of course." He ran a hand across the stubble on his chin, metal plates of his armor softly clinking. "Did you overhear …?"

If another person had been asking, Jasen would have been ashamed to admit it, but he had the feeling that Longwell would understand for some reason, so he said, "I heard some of your conversation. Not all of it."

"If you heard the end, you can surmise the start."

Longwell did not say any more. And Jasen could not bring himself to ask. So, again, it was quiet, except for the blustering of the wind, which buffeted hard all of a sudden for long seconds, then died off again in a momentary respite. The tang of salt crinkled Jasen's nose again.

There seemed to be something *off* in the air too. Very faint, it wasn't exactly the rotten, deathly smell of Scourgey ... but something unpleasant drifted on the wind. Maybe this part of the sea smelled different, part of the curse that kept boats out of these waters.

The dragoon interrupted his thoughts. "Except for Huanatha, no others among us are as determined to stop Baraghosa as we. And look at us now—stranded and stalled, the sorcerer escaped. You're thinking about it, aren't you, in spite of our circumstances? Thinking, still, on how to catch him, how to beat him. Thinking about our own defeat."

Jasen hesitated. Again, if another person were asking him this, he would surely dodge the question to hide a truth that Alixa would surely chide him for, Kuura too, perhaps even Burund, after this turn of events.

With Longwell, though, he could answer truthfully. And so, after that moment's consideration, he nodded.

Longwell nodded too. He rubbed a fist across his chin again, fingers raking stubble. "Aye. Our minds, they're more similar than you know. That desire for vengeance ... it's bred in." Turning out to the sea again, he said, "This is not the end for us, Jasen. We will find a way off this island. And the sweet satisfaction of revenge will yet be ours."

As he spoke, a fire sparked, then burned in his eyes. His jaw, which was already sharp-edged and strong, became steelier still, clenching, the muscles taut. Fiery determination flowed through his veins— Jasen could practically feel the heat of it radiating from him.

But—"How?" It was a question that had lingered in the back of his mind these past two days. He kept himself as busy as he could, but in those moments of quiet, when he got time to think, the word pulsed in his mind over and over.

How, how, how?

Longwell shook his head, lips pursing. "That I don't know yet. The *Lady Vizola* ..."

"Ignoring the boat," Jasen said, "I still don't see how. Baraghosa beat us. He threw us aside like we were dolls, mopped the floor with our bodies—and then, when it was over, he didn't even bother to kill us. We outnumbered him, we've come after him twice now, brought our best fight every time. We should be a threat—and still, *he didn't even try to kill us*. He just ... left. Like we're nothing to him."

Longwell was quiet, for perhaps ten long seconds, and the air between them was filled instead with the sound of the wind whistling around the rocks strewn about the island's edge and howling through a cranny in the *Lady Vizola*'s wreck.

Finally, Longwell pursed his lips. "That last error will be his undoing."

He elaborated no more. Now, Jasen suspected that no amount of asking would answer anything. Not with regard to their current circumstances, anyway. He and the dragoon might share a near-single-minded focus on getting their revenge, but neither of them commanded the magics that Baraghosa wielded. They could not conjure a boat to sail them from this island any more than they could sprout wings and fly from it.

Anyway—if they did, where was Baraghosa now? Looking back on it, it had been luck that Jasen and Longwell had managed to locate him in the Aiger Cliffs before the sorcerer's departure. It was chance, too, that Baraghosa had left the Aiger Cliffs to come to this accursed isle. A whole world lay open—the sorcerer might have gone anywhere, after his harvest upon the clifftops.

Now he truly *could* be anywhere.

So where to even begin?

Well, that was a silly question. The place to begin was where Jasen had stopped asking—how to leave this island.

Instead, he asked, "Do you know who he is? Baraghosa, I mean," he said after an inquisitive look from Longwell.

"That … is a long story," the dragoon said, then looked over Jasen's shoulder.

Jasen followed his gaze.

The salvage crew were approaching, or the thin skeleton that remained of them, at any rate—just three, now, and likely none of them were needed. They navigated rocks with ease, muttering amongst themselves. A gale of a wind blew, nearly dislodging the man in the lead—Chaka, if Jasen remembered correctly from Kuura's introductions. He flailed, pinwheeling his arms. He spat a double-syllabled word Jasen didn't hear for the wind. Doubtless it was a curse.

"I'll regale you with it later, if you still wish to listen," said Longwell, drawing Jasen's attention back to him. "I suspect you will. For now, here is all you need to know—I have helped defeat worse than Baraghosa." Jasen's eyes widened, but before he could ask, Longwell continued, "Yes, he defeated us. But we are not dead. And this is not the end. Keep your faith."

He clapped Jasen on the shoulder, a powerful thump, and then strode past.

"When we next speak," he called over his shoulder, "I will tell you all there is to know of him. Little of it will help you, mind—but you deserve to know." Then he pivoted and passed the salvagers with a tiny nod.

Jasen watched his receding back for a while. The wind gusted again. That *off-ness* (he could put it no other way) came with it again, but though the *Lady Vizola*'s crew were shunted by it, Longwell was barely moved.

He'd said little in their brief conversation, just exuded his typical determination, in the face of odds Jasen saw no way, as yet, of overcoming. Mostly he had promised answers, but all of them later, none of them here and now, when it mattered most—perhaps. Because, of course, if they were to never leave this island, doomed to shrivel and die and never be found—well, then Baraghosa's origins, or what he had done to garner Longwell's hatred, did not really matter.

Still, Jasen could not deny that he felt encouraged. It was only the slightest, tiniest amount, and perhaps it was more vanity at being told that he and the dragoon had something in common than anything else.

Nevertheless, there was still one matter lingering in the back of Jasen's mind.

Baraghosa had said that he had had nothing to do with the destruction of Terreas.

This, Jasen could not shake.

There was something afoot with the sorcerer. Whatever his role in the death of Terreas, he must be stopped. Like the *off-ness* that assailed his nostrils every time the wind blustered, Baraghosa too was *off*. There was no goodness about him, nothing at all, and he had to be stopped, if it was the last thing Jasen did.

Which, in light of Baraghosa's revelation … it might be.

He sidelined this thought. The questions of his mortality could wait for another day. There were too many others jostling for attention in his mind to ponder others.

He set off back toward the camp, ready for another day of—whatever the day would entail. What that might be, Jasen did not yet know. Possibly returning to the tower, to see what might be of use there. Little, that Jasen could see. If asked, he'd go, though—to help in any way he could—and, perhaps, to locate some clue that could lead him to Baraghosa once again.

He'd gone no more than fifty feet when the salvage crew began to hoot. They'd been chattering maybe ten, fifteen seconds, Jasen realized—but now they whooped, voices filling the air, words foreign but the tone undoubtedly excited.

He turned back, expecting to see them crowded around the shore over a cask of water that had been pushed inland overnight, or an unbroken crate packed with biltong and salt—

Jasen froze. His eyes bulged, wide.

Very distant, scarcely visible on the horizon—there came a ship.

5

The tasks of camp building and food foraging forgotten, the *Lady Vizola*'s crew had arranged themselves upon the mottled, rocky shoreline.

It was a boat, definitely. The last half an hour had brought it nearer. And though it was still miles out, it was certainly growing—and its peculiar shape becoming more and more apparent, though as yet, Jasen couldn't discern much beyond a boxy shape with many sails.

Jasen and Alixa stood with Huanatha, their own little cluster complete with Scourgey, who also watched the sea in silence.

"Are we being rescued?" Alixa dared to ask.

Huanatha's lips were thin. "If it does not shatter on the rocks like the *Lady Vizola* did. The wind is blowing it inland—they are not coming here willingly."

"Who are they?"

The blue-armored warrior's expression was hard. "I will not speculate."

"But you know?" Alixa asked. "Don't you?"

Huanatha was silent.

Alixa exchanged a weary, frightened look with Jasen. He could only squeeze her hand—as close to an *it'll be okay* as he felt comfortable with. Because, going by Huanatha's tight-lipped reaction, he was not convinced it would be.

The *Lady Vizola*'s crew had amassed like clots. Groups of three and four were spread out, all of their eyes glued to the boat as it pushed steadily closer to shore. Only Shipmaster Burund stood alone. Jasen glanced at him, watching his face—as though that was not a pointless activity. The shipmaster was too guarded to betray his thoughts. Still, Jasen couldn't help watching, hoping for a crack.

Kuura had run early, at Burund's orders, to Baraghosa's tower. At

29

the top, he'd be better able to assess exactly who might be coming.

Now he hurtled down the rocks again, tunic flapping behind him, shouting words Jasen couldn't understand.

The atmosphere among the crew changed immediately. Huanatha cursed under her breath.

Alixa's eyes widened in alarm. "What is it?"

"As I feared," said Huanatha. "We are approached by a Prenasian war galley."

"Who?" Jasen asked.

"Prenasians," said Huanatha. "Warmongers, from a desert land between Coricuanthi, Firoba and Amatgarosa. They besiege every land they find, spreading across it like a disease."

Guiltily, Jasen felt his gaze flick to Scourgey.

"Beastly things," said Huanatha, "with teeth for eating men. If they are to land here …"

Alixa breathed, "Men?" She exchanged a wild-eyed look with Jasen. Her grip on Scourgey's shoulder tightened.

"I must go speak with the shipmaster," Huanatha said. And she went to join the crowd that had enveloped Burund, worried people talking with lightning speed. Hamisi was among them, Kosi seemingly stitched to him at the hip.

"They eat men?" Alixa whispered to Jasen.

"I'm sure it's just exaggeration," he said lamely.

"Exaggeration? Huanatha does not exaggerate!"

Jasen wondered for a second if Alixa had met the same Huanatha as he, dramatic as she often was, but he did not ask the question aloud. Instead, he said, "It may be our only hope."

"Our only hope?" Alixa said, wheezing a high-pitched laugh. "To what? Die by being eaten alive instead of starving to death on this rock?"

Technically, Jasen thought, they would die of thirst long before starving to death—but like the last thought, he kept it to himself.

"We have to do something to get off this island," he said. "What if it's months before another boat gets blown inland, or is brave enough to scout out the mists? If this is our only chance—"

"They are warmongers, Jasen," Alixa said. "Huanatha said they *eat* people."

He closed his mouth. He couldn't argue with Alixa and had no way to make her feel better. Instead he watched the frantic conversation between the *Lady Vizola*'s crew and Burund.

At last, Burund had had enough. He hardly raised his voice, but his words cut over the crew's talking. If not for the wind, Jasen would have believed in that moment that the *Lady Vizola*'s people could be spread across the entire island and still Burund's voice would reach them.

Whatever he said was in their native tongue, so Jasen did not understand it. It was not hard to see the negative reaction it garnered, though: a full half of the crew, if not more, exploded with what sounded like objections.

Burund cut them short with a swiping motion of his hand. He spoke again, louder and clearer.

The crew parted. Some were willing—among them, Hamisi and his entourage, who hurried back toward the encampment. Others bore terrified expressions, splitting back into their groups and moving across the island, for what, Jasen was not sure.

Kuura rounded up several. He was talking at length and kept pointing up to the tower.

The eyes that followed his gesture were wary.

"What's happening?" Alixa asked.

Jasen shook his head. "I don't know."

He watched for a few seconds as the crew began to work on Burund's order. Then, when Huanatha had peeled away—

"What did he say?" Jasen asked, jogging up to meet her, Alixa and Scourgey in tow, slower because Scourgey still limped, although she was struggling less by the day.

"The fires are to be piled high to signal our presence," Huanatha said.

"Burund is alerting the Prenasians that we're here?" Alixa asked.

"And Kuura?" Jasen asked, ignoring her.

"Collecting wooden objects from the tower, I believe," said Huanatha, glancing after them. "For burning."

"Should we help?" Jasen asked.

"That, or stand and watch," said Huanatha. "I don't suppose it matters either way. They will light the fires with or without us." And then she was gone again, looking none too pleased.

"She doesn't want them to land here," said Alixa.

"No," Jasen said.

"Do you?"

He hesitated. "It's our only hope."

Alixa shook her head, her messy braid dancing on the latest burst of wind. "This is madness." Still, she fell into step with Jasen then. Realizing that he had directed them toward Baraghosa's tower, she paused. "We're not getting wood from the camp?"

"I need to see if there are any clues as to where Baraghosa is going," said Jasen, "before they end up on the pyres."

The expression on Alixa's face was so similar to Huanatha's habitual scowl that Jasen almost laughed—but he was wise enough not to. Alixa did not complain though, and instead followed along, muttering to Scourgey.

Returning to the tower was ... peculiar, Jasen thought as they entered. Something strange hung in the air, a deathly, electric sort of feeling. The hairs on his arms and the back of his neck rose. And there was a chill about it too, like the stone locked all the warmth in the world out.

The odd energy was fading, though. Like mists on the sea, it was gradually vanishing—already nowhere near as strong as the first time Jasen had climbed these steps. Perhaps, with his spellcasting complete, Baraghosa had left for good, and without the sorcerer nearby, the aura could persist no more. Maybe that was why the fog was clearing too: not from the wind, but Baraghosa's absence.

Unfortunately, there was little to salvage. Much of the tower was empty. Even clambering to the top of the tower, Jasen, Alixa, and Kuura's complement of shipmates found little more than stone brick, two writing desks with blackened, empty inkwells and scorched spots upon them, and unsalvageable sconces. The desks were brought down the steps awkwardly, but they wouldn't help the fires much.

More pressing to Jasen was the lack of clues as to Baraghosa's next whereabouts.

The Prenasian war galley was much closer by the time Jasen and Alixa returned to the shore.

A great pyre belched black smoke into the skies. Broken, salvaged furnishings from the *Lady Vizola*, empty crates, casks, shattered boards—all these things glowed a brilliant yellow-white. It reminded Jasen faintly of the blaze that had been set upon his home in Terreas, as tensions rose after his father refused to let Baraghosa take Jasen.

Pain stabbed him. He touched the pendant at his neck, from his mother.

As the ship sailed ever closer, pushed endlessly by the wind, Jasen was able to truly appreciate the ugliness of the vessel. It was an angular, dark affair. Terrifying wooden heads, ten feet tall at least, were carved on the sides. They stared out with angry expressions, their mouths open to dark holes, teeth sharp and pointed, their noses pressed flat, foreheads wide, with snakes or scorpions' tails or gripping claws instead of hair.

It was an impressive sight, and one which brooked no argument. These people on this boat came upon the shores of foreign lands for one purpose and one purpose only: bloodshed.

And there were people on it. Jasen could see their shapes, moving on the deck, saw them throwing down ladders to smaller boats clinging to the galley's side with nets and ropes. They were released, splashing down heavily, then bobbing—

And then rowers began to row inland.

Alixa clutched Jasen's wrist, fingernails pressing in hard.

"It'll be okay," Jasen said.

But he did not believe it. The tension on the shore of Baraghosa's isle was almost electric in its intensity. What little conversation there was sounded panicked, the crew's voices creeping toward crescendo as the rowboats drew closer to shore. Others clustered, looking as if they might spring up and bolt at any moment, perhaps throwing themselves into the waters on the other side of the island and just trying to swim away. Chaka sat upon the edge of a rock, tapping his leg up and down as though ants climbed it.

Another sharp gust of wind from the sea—and that off smell came again. It was sour, wrong in a way Jasen still could not exactly put his finger on ... and it most certainly came from the Prenasians.

He watched the rowboats closing in, his breath held. His heart was hammering in his chest, a double-time beat—not full speed, not like he was sprinting, but primed, ready to fuel him should he need to move.

Nearer, nearer ...

Jasen watched, confusion mounting as the seconds drew on ...

He realized it at almost the same moment as Alixa.

"They're *blue*," she gasped.

They were: a deep blue, almost the color of the ocean at night. And unlike the *Lady Vizola*'s crew, who wore tunics, these men were hardly clothed at all. Cloths were bound around their waist, and they wore bracers upon their forearms and around their shins. Otherwise, they were naked, except for maybe sandals—Jasen could not see those in the boats, and in fact could only discern this much because each rowboat was captained by a vast blue man at the front, who stood rather than rowed, staring a deathly gaze across the waters to the *Lady Vizola*'s people. Inky black tattoos adorned their chests, spiraling patterns twirling and widening as they rose up the men's torsos, like the boughs of a tree—then they snaked up the men's necks, ending just below the ears in arrowhead chevrons.

But they were not *just* blue.

Alixa's breath caught in her chest, a hitch so violent Jasen heard it.

"What are *those*?" she breathed.

At the back of each boat, behind the rowers, were something else entirely. Like a man, but not. And yellow. Almost as yellow of the middle of a daisy, maybe slightly darker or dirtier. Vast, muscled creatures, their faces were dull and miserable—like the visages upon the side of the galley. And how *enormous* they were. Even sitting, it was plain to see their sheer mammoth size, each twice as wide as a man at least, and taller—much taller.

Jasen swallowed hard against a lump in his throat. "I don't know," was all he could mutter.

He watched, slack-jawed, taking in these men and those beasts they'd brought with them. Those, he focused on more than anything. Were they what Huanatha referred to when she said spoke of "teeth for eating men"? They gnashed their jaws, like a cow chewing on cud—and Jasen had no doubt that one of those beasts could grind his bones down to dust—no doubt at all.

Four boats had been dispatched, each of them with ten men, by Jasen's count. After an age that passed by much too quickly, they reached the shore.

The captains among them dismounted.

Jasen watched. The crew of the *Lady Vizola* had lapsed into silence. Not one among them moved.

All except Burund. He moved forward, stepping past the raging signal fires, past Hamisi and Kosi and Chaka and Kuura and Huanatha and Longwell.

The first captain reached for the bracer around his shin. From it, he pulled a long, thin blade, perfectly concealed until that moment.

Jasen held his breath.

The Prenasian man took easy strides to Burund, eyes cold and calculating upon the shipmaster—and his sword held high.

6

The Prenasian man and Burund drew near, Burund still walking as though he did not face a man holding a saber skyward, a man from a race of warmongers, commanding beasts the likes of which Jasen had never seen. He approached with calm confidence, and all the while, Jasen stared in horror, his brain too muddled to even scream out inside his head to stop, to run—

At last, within a foot of the Prenasian, Burund stopped and spoke, in a language Jasen did not understand. The Prenasian stared into Burund's face with a steely, unreadable gaze. His sword gleamed dully in the faint sunlight that permeated the constant haze of cloud. He was so close, all it would take was one easy swing, and Burund's head would go toppling from his body.

How could the shipmaster just stand there?

Burund tried again, saying something else. If he could have torn his eyes away, Jasen would have searched for Kuura or Huanatha to ask them for a translation, to learn whether the anxiety that caused his heart to beat so furiously in his throat was justified.

The Prenasian cut Burund off, his voice a deep baritone, but his words, whatever they meant, hard and sharp.

Burund opened his mouth to answer, but

the Prenasian grasped him by one shoulder.

Jasen hardly had time to gasp—he was certain the blade would flash, blurring in a streak, cutting through their shipmaster—but then Burund was shoved around. A knee rose, slamming him in the back of the leg—and with a pained grunt, he went down. The Prenasian bowed with him halfway, still clasping a fold of his tunic in a tight fist, knife extended across his throat, where it hovered, yet to draw blood.

He barked orders back toward the boats. Already men were dismounting.

The mammoth yellow creatures lumbered up after them. So heavy they threatened to topple the rowboats, they were ungainly things, clad in only loincloths. Dull eyes assessed the men arrayed on the isle's shore.

Suddenly there was shouting, a cacophony running through the *Lady Vizola*'s crew. Weapons were drawn from—Jasen didn't even know where. Kuura withdrew a dagger concealed around his back. Hamisi leapt up, lifting his spear high—

Alixa gripped Jasen's arm. "What do we do?" she cried over the sudden noise.

Jasen opened his mouth to answer, "I don't know," but Huanatha spared him. Barreling across to them, Longwell in tow with his lance at the ready, she bellowed, "Get back! Behind me!" And she bundled her arms around them, thrusting them backward.

Jasen staggered and tripped. Alixa fell over him.

Scourgey whined.

"What's happening?" Alixa asked.

"Just keep back!" Huanatha said. She'd drawn the stubby remainder of Tanukke from her sheath, where she'd had to tie it to keep it from falling out now that some four-fifths of the blade had been shattered.

Jasen and Alixa watched with fearful eyes as the Prenasian crew spilled out onto the island, outnumbering the *Lady Vizola*'s people by a good margin, their superior numbers bolstered by the massive yellow beasts that lumbered behind them.

The *Lady Vizola*'s crew put up a valiant effort—for all of thirty seconds. Half were disarmed in a few moments, simply overwhelmed. Another third ran, but were quickly caught, either by Prenasians or the huge beasts they commanded. The remainder, mostly those led by Hamisi, swung with their weapons frantically, shouting curses and threats until they were swarmed, beaten down, and then their weapons wrestled from their hands.

A second captain from the rowboats, this one with long, dark hair spilling down his back, tied with string every few inches so that it bulged like a string of beads, was interrogating Burund. Leering down from where Burund knelt, his hands behind his head, he snapped off question after question.

The man with the blade to Burund's throat scoured the isle with his calm grey eyes—so damned *cold*, they were.

When they settled upon Jasen, cowering behind Huanatha and Longwell, he felt as though a bucket of freezing water had been tipped down his spine from the base of his skull.

This captain said something to his companion, something entirely too quiet. Chills came to rest in Jasen's belly.

The companion glanced over, taking in Jasen—Huanatha, actually, and Longwell. A faint light of interest sparked momentarily in his gaze; then he waved the other captain off, pointing him toward the camp, by the look of it. The captain who'd downed Burund answered with a nod, then withdrew his blade from Burund's neck and strode off, gathering men with staccato, shouted orders.

Jasen watched them recede as Burund remained on his knees, a stiff look of pain pursing his lips.

"What are they doing?" Jasen whispered.

"Looting," Longwell answered quietly. "Scoundrels. They'll take everything they can lay their hands on." He shook his head.

"Why aren't they bothering us?" Alixa asked.

"Oh, they want to," said Huanatha. "Believe me. They want to." But she said no more—and so Jasen and Alixa had little choice but to watch from behind hers and Longwell's backs as the Prenasians arrayed the *Lady Vizola*'s crew in a long line. Their weapons were tossed into a heap, where a pair of Prenasians looked through them—scouring for any of actual use, by the looks. They set aside a handful of daggers. Most were discarded. Hamisi's spear was granted hardly a look before being tossed into the fire.

The men from the *Lady Vizola* were patted down. Their pockets were emptied, possessions pulled out. Anything not of use was tossed into the fire. Items the Prenasians perceived to have value were transferred to their own pockets.

The men were then stripped down to their undergarments. A few fought this indignity, Hamisi among them. He received a nasty welt on his face, already swelling, as a result. Jasen couldn't help but admire Hamisi's resistance, foolhardy though it was.

The long-haired captain finished interrogating Burund just as the first of his crew returned from the encampment, carrying barrels of water, one apiece. He questioned them quickly—asking about the barrels' contents, Jasen presumed—and then directed his people toward the rowboats.

Then, at last, his gaze once more settled upon Huanatha and Longwell and Jasen and Alixa—and he set off for them.

"Oh no," Alixa breathed, at Jasen's side. She gripped him, so fiercely tight that her nails surely drew blood of their own.

Scourgey growled low in her throat.

"Easy, scourge," Longwell muttered. "Make this simple for us."

The captain clambered over the rocks, never once looking away from the four clustered people apart from the *Lady Vizola*'s crew.

This close, Jasen could see that the tattoos winding across his chest were jagged fractals, turning end on end over and over. Only on one side did they terminate below his ear. At the other, a single inky line swept across his cheek, reaching its end left of the bridge of his nose with a large dot.

He neared to striking distance.

The sour smell came from this man in waves, catching in the back of Jasen's throat.

He stymied a cough. Likewise, he tamped down on the urge to bolt, even as his legs were electrified, warm, black adrenaline coursing through his veins, and his heart thundering in his throat.

Unlike Hamisi and the other fighters, Jasen recognized that—at least so far—if he just went along easily with these Prenasians, the worst he would receive was a muscling about.

The Prenasian man studied them all. His gaze lingered on Longwell a moment longer than Huanatha, and on her longer than Jasen and Alixa.

Finally—"And who are you all?" he said, in heavily accented Luukessian. "To be sailing aboard a Coricuanthian merchant ship?" His expression held the a hint of a smile, but it was neither pleasant nor polite.

"I am Lord Longwell of Reikonos," announced Longwell in a commanding voice. He hefted his lance, and replanted its haft on the rock underfoot with a solid *thunk*.

"*Lord* Longwell," said the captain, very seriously, drawing out both title and name. The smile on his face disappeared, his features schooling themselves into something more plain—and, ironically, a much more polite expression than the veiled smile he had worn moments before. "You are known to us, and recognized. I accord you full honors." He bowed, slightly. "I am Rakon Brenjaack, of Farthoon, First City of Prenasia."

"Pleasant day to you, Rakon," said Longwell. There was only the slightest bit of civility in his otherwise uninflected voice. He did not extend a hand to shake, or relax his posture; he remained only in that guarded position, chest thrown out and shoulders back, the lance gripped in his fist, unmoved.

Rakon did not move to extend a hand either. Instead he turned quizzical eyes upon Huanatha. That ghost of a smile returned. This time, Jasen decided it was patronizing, almost predatory.

"And who are you, my dear?"

Huanatha bared her teeth. "I am not your dear," she spat back. "I am Huanatha, queen of Muratam."

Rakon's eyebrows rose. "Queen of the Muratam," he repeated, drawing the title out.

"Such a strong grasp of language," Huanatha replied with a sneer.

Rakon laughed, a dry boom that was over as soon as it had started. "Oh, your majesty …you are known to us." The brief humor that had crossed his place vanished. "Your title carries no weight with Prenasia. Commendations for trying, though. Nevertheless, because of your ties to Chaarland," he said, "you will be accorded with the same treatment as Lord Longwell."

Huanatha glared. "What kindness."

"This is not kindness," said Rakon. "Chaarland is a trade partner. I see no profit in antagonizing one of their protectees."

His eyes flicked over Jasen and Alixa.

"And these?" he said, directing the question over both their heads.

"My wards," said Longwell, not so quick that he would appear suspect, but before Jasen or Alixa could take it upon themselves to answer. "Jasen and Alixa—my servants." He gestured to each in turn.

Rakon granted them barely a look, before moving on to Scourgey.

His flattened nose screwed up even further still. "What is *that*?"

"Our pet," said Jasen. His quick answer drew a raised eyebrow from Rakon, but whatever Rakon thought of Jasen's response, he was sidetracked by disgust at the sight of Scourgey. He wrinkled his nose, brushing it with a wide fist, tattooed with angular drawings, in an attempt to swipe the rancid smell away. Nevertheless, he conceded, "Very well. I suppose one more … passenger … thing … will not be too much trouble."

"You're extending passage to us?" Longwell asked.

Rakon nodded. "That I am, Lord Longwell. Conditionally," he added, holding up a finger. "You will not be permitted to carry your weapon aboard *Galley 324*—neither of you," he added, directing Huanatha a short glance—her title meaningless, this conversation was for Rakon and Longwell only.

Longwell asked, "And what will become of it?"

"It will be returned to you," Rakon said, "at our next port of call."

"I see. Well, thank you, Rakon." He did not hand it over, though, and neither did Huanatha move to deprive herself of the stub of Tanukke.

Jasen couldn't help but feel uneasy. The warriors retained their weapons—for now. If they were to take passage with the Prenasians—and surely that would be soon—then heels could not be dug in any longer—and their weapons would be divested.

"I assume that you will be traveling with us," said Rakon, not quite

39

questioning. Once more, he directed this entirely at Longwell; Huanatha, Jasen and Alixa's answers were of zero importance. "Unless you are, perhaps, waiting on … other means of passage?"

Longwell did not answer this. He did say, though, "We would be most grateful to join you. Thank you."

"Excellent. Perhaps later we can discuss how the Lord Protector of Reikonos and his servant children—and a disgraced queen—" Rakon's gaze flicked over Huanatha "—came to be stranded on an island in the middle of nowhere with a bunch of lowly merchants. Many questions, I have, many questions indeed …"

Huanatha seethed, but she held her tongue—quite probably only because of Longwell's subtle touch to her wrist.

The dragoon replied instead. "I would be happy to answer them for you, at a more opportune time than this."

"I look forward to it." Rakon flashed a disingenuous smile.

Longwell answered it with a small raise of his own lips.

One of Rakon's fellow captains called to him. He turned, shouted something back, and then began marching the *Lady Vizola*'s crew, stripped and now tied together by two lengths of rope, one around each man's ankle, the other binding their wrists, toward the rowboats perched upon the shore.

Guilt shot through Jasen's chest. "What's happening to them?"

Rakon shot him a peculiar look. "There is a war on—do you not know?"

"My wards are not typically privy to global matters," said Longwell.

"Of course," Rakon nodded. Looking down at Jasen with false kindness, he said, "Amatgarosa has done much to collapse its relations with our good land. Now our wrath falls upon them, and sailors who are suspected of doing trade with the enemy—as these men are," he said, looking at the backs of the *Lady Vizola*'s crew and baring his teeth, "are subject to immediate seizure and press-ganging into the Prenasian navy. All hands are required in this time of crisis."

Jasen stared in stupefied horror. The *Lady Vizola*'s people were being forced into naval service? Made slaves?

"But don't worry," said Rakon, as Kuura, and then Burund last of all, were shoved into the last of the waiting rowboats. "You won't be a part of that. Clearly, you are not a sailor." He nodded, eyeing Jasen's hands—which were soft, not calloused, like the men of the *Lady Vizola*.

"Await us here," Rakon said to Longwell after a moment. "We will have another boat for you shortly."

"You have my word," said Longwell.

Rakon boomed that dry laugh again, and then he was off, striding for that last rowboat awaiting him.

As soon as he'd stepped aboard, the rowers began, their long oars dipping into the water over and over in perfect synchronicity. Despite the winds that had pushed the warship inland, the little craft moved swiftly through the waters, past the shattered *Lady Vizola* and the rocks she had been broken upon ... and toward the galley, on which the crew would become—

Jasen's heart thumped in his throat. Slower now, it seemed not to pulse blood through him but waves of guilty nausea.

The *Lady Vizola*'s crew were captive to the Prenasians.

And, like their wreck upon this wretched rock—it was all his fault.

7

The poetically named *Prenasian War Galley 324* was a behemoth. It had to be, to carry four additional rowboats, each capable of holding ten men plus those oversized, ugly yellow creatures—trolls, Longwell said they were called—*plus* a handful of captives. It positively teemed: the forty who'd sailed out were but a fraction of the galley's complement. Many were arrayed on the deck, ushering the *Lady Vizola*'s crewmates to work almost as soon as their bare feet touched the dark wood. More manned the sails, twisting and pulling them around, fighting the gusts.

Rakon rode the boat with Longwell, Huanatha, Jasen, Alixa and Scourgey, who sat cowering and whimpering from the time she was coaxed aboard. Rakon seemed to take some joy in this and watched Scourgey with faint interest. A ghostly smile lifted the corners of his mouth every time a shallow wave caused the rowboat to bob like a seesaw as it crested it, and Scourgey whined louder than ever.

As soon as they had boarded the war galley, Rakon barked an order to several blue-skinned sailors aboard the deck. They answered with what Jasen assumed was their language's version of *Aye!* and rushed for the rear of the ship, where a great wheel wound with chain stood, a pair of levers on each side. The chain, easily the width of Jasen's waist, descended into a hole in the deck. The men began to turn the wheel. Heavy though it must have been, their slow progress looked almost easy.

Jasen didn't have long to be impressed. Rakon swiftly diverted him, via Longwell, through a door that led into the ship.

This entrance could never accommodate trolls. They must get inside someplace else, Jasen thought. With all the activity on deck though, obscuring the smaller decks atop the galley, Jasen hadn't been able to see. And Rakon had been quick to get them inside.

"We have spare quarters," he was saying to Longwell, leading the way.

"Excellent," Longwell answered. He still had his lance, though Jasen was sure it would be taken from him soon.

The passages inside were bare. Not that the *Lady Vizola* had had a great deal of decoration, but *Prenasian War Galley 324* had none at all: just wood boards, nailed together.

Jasen had initially felt that the *Lady Vizola*, with its tight spaces and many rooms and turns, was something of a labyrinth. He'd managed to get his head around the layout quite quickly, in the end, but then it was not an over-large ship anyway, he realized, once they'd docked at the Aiger Cliffs and he'd seen some of the other vessels moored there.

The war galley really was a maze, though. With no markers whatsoever to orient by, the crew must be operating entirely on memory. A smart design choice for a war galley, Jasen supposed—if they were ever boarded by external attackers, it would be easy for the enemy to get utterly lost in here. But he could not help but realize that it also meant any attempts to escape would be severely hampered.

Jasen pushed away the thought for now. They'd barely left the isle of Baraghosa, and the next port was many days off, even if it were only half the distance from here to the Aiger Cliffs. For now, at least, they weren't going anywhere.

After numerous twists and turns, Rakon led them to a room barred by a locked door in a corner—one of many; the war galley seemed to be filled with the damned things. He retrieved a single key from somewhere in his clothing and unlocked the door. Just as quickly, the key was vanished away—though not before Jasen stole the briefest of glances at it. Nothing like any key he had ever seen, it was a very thin bar of dark metal, bent and folded into square angles. Small teeth rose from it in spindly slivers.

The door opened to a little cube of a room, with a single bed in it, bolted to the floor. It had no window.

"Your wards may stay here," said Rakon, gesturing inside. "They are happy to share, are they not?"

Jasen hesitated. "Uhm ..."

Longwell said, "Have you nowhere larger? With a light source, perhaps?"

Rakon stepped inside. He pointed at a wall.

Jasen leaned to glance around the corner.

A single shelf sat in the corner. Upon it, a half-melted candle leaned lazily inside a lantern, wax dripping down it in pale streaks that puddled on the shelf. A few drops of it had resolidified and drooped from the shelf's edge. A cup filled with long sticks of wood stuck out, which Jasen recognized as some variant of the matches Burund had acquainted him with on the *Lady Vizola*. Instant flame with but a strike.

"Your light," said Rakon. To Jasen and Alixa, he said, "Your dog will be comfortable in here with you too, will it?"

"She's not a dog," Alixa said.

Jasen cut in: "She'll be comfortable, yes. Thank you."

Rakon nodded. He stepped out, pushing past Jasen. Then he said to Longwell and Huanatha, "This way—let us find someplace to speak. I, and the other captains, await your tale with bated breath. Of course, there is the matter of your stick …"

"It is a spear," said Longwell, the first hints of irritation bleeding through his voice.

"A spear, yes, of course. Well …"

They disappeared around a corner—and Jasen and Alixa were alone—except for Scourgey, who cowered at Alixa's heel.

They dawdled awkwardly. Then: "Well …" said Jasen, and he wandered into the dim room, "I suppose this is where we're staying for … a while."

"Hmm," said Alixa. She sat down on the bed.

"I guess I'll light the candle," Jasen said.

It wasn't easy. The shelf was high enough that Jasen had to stand on tiptoe. The wick was black and lumpy where it hadn't been trimmed in a long time. The matches didn't want to light, however they were perfectly happy to snap clean in two when Jasen grew frustrated and struck them harder. In the end, he had to hold a half-match delicately between his thumb and forefinger. When eventually a flame coughed into life at its tip, he quickly touched it to the wick. It didn't light for a couple of seconds—then, just when the match had grown short enough already that Jasen was on the verge of blistering his fingers, the candle finally came alive.

Jasen blew out the match.

The room hardly seemed any lighter at all.

Funny to think of how things had changed. Weeks ago, he'd thought the *Lady Vizola* a grim place to be—too tight, somewhat damp, and everything so easily thrown about by the waves. Now he would have given anything to be back aboard it.

No … not quite anything. That bargain he reserved for Terreas. But not today's Terreas, the one of fire and ruin, ash and dust, but a Terreas of years past. One green and alive, bordered by fields and mountains, vibrant with happiness.

The Terreas he'd lived in before his mother had gotten sick and died.

Jasen touched the pendant around his neck again, murmuring a quiet thanks to his ancestors. If the Prenasians had searched him, manhandling the way they had with the *Lady Vizola*'s crew ... Jasen didn't want to think of the pendant vanishing into the pyre on the island they were leaving behind.

The last time he'd spoken to Alixa—really spoken to her—had been the first night on the island—when he'd thought, just for a moment, that he'd seen his mother, lingering out by the rocks by their makeshift camp.

Now they were alone again, and Jasen found he didn't really know what to say.

His best was a lame, "Are you all right?"

He knew his cousin well—and so he knew that he was very likely setting himself up for one sort of response: a furious, explosive rant.

Yet, surprisingly, it did not come. Alixa only sighed. Bowing her head, she closed her eyes. Her fingers pressed at the corners of them, squeezing the bridge of her nose.

She loosed another rattling sigh. "How do you think I am, Jasen? After everything that has happened to us this past—how long? Weeks? Months? I've lost track of time, honestly." She shook her head. "My parents are dead, all my brothers—and I haven't even a clue how long it has been since then." And she lifted her head again, looking at Jasen through exhausted eyes. "How do you *think* I am, Jasen?"

He hesitated, just shy of the open doorway.

"I'm sorry," he said at last.

"It's fine." Then, after a brief pat of Scourgey's shoulder—"No, it's not fine, of course it's not. Not fine at all. But it is what it is." Another sigh. It came from her like a last breath, no part of her working to hold it back, as though her lungs simply gave up the air.

"In the past two days, we have been defeated by Baraghosa a second time, stranded, and now captured by blue-skinned men who keep man-eating trolls as pets," Alixa said. "I'm trying to tell myself that things can't get any worse—but every time I tell myself that ... when the mountain exploded and destroyed the village, when we left Shilara behind and plunged into the sea, after the *Lady Vizola* rescued us, and so on, I am now sure that they can *always* get worse. And furthermore I'm certain they *will.* I just can't imagine what that might entail, at the moment."

"Things won't get any worse from here," Jasen said. He hoped he sounded at least halfway convinced of that, which would be much, much more than he felt.

Alixa regarded him with a skeptical look. "Mm."

She said no more—and so, after a long pause, Jasen finally said, "So … what now?"

"What do you mean, 'what now'?"

"What do we do? How do we get out of this?"

"Get out of this?" Alixa looked at him with the weary eyes of someone who had chased around a madman for far too long. "We're two children, without weapons, outnumbered by blue-skinned men who live for war, and their army of—of pet trolls, who Huanatha said had teeth made for eating men—probably alive, going by how these things usually work. And you want to—what, mount an escape attempt? Here?"

"No," said Jasen quickly. It hadn't been on his mind, no. But then, he hadn't had long to think about things. "I don't know what we can do. I just know we need to do *something*."

"We're always doing *something*," said Alixa. "That's what got us into this whole mess in the first place."

Jasen's eyebrows knitted. "What do you mean?"

"Following Baraghosa to the Aiger Cliffs, out to his island … even our excursion to Wayforth, that was us trying to do *something* instead of nothing."

"Our trip to Wayforth saved us," Jasen said.

"Yes, it did," said Alixa, "but look where we've ended up now. We were spared a quick death under a mountain of fire and rubble in favor of a slow, painful one sailing halfway round the world with anyone unlucky enough to happen upon us—and all in search of a crooked sorcerer who probably *didn't* split open the cratered mountain at all."

Jasen was quiet. If Baraghosa were to be believed, then he hadn't had anything to do with the mountain's destruction. What was it he'd said? That the scourge avoided entering Terreas because they'd detected the fate that would one day befall the village, the same as they could smell death upon Jasen. Baraghosa had not seen it coming—he'd missed it, he claimed.

Unwilling though he was to admit it, Jasen believed he'd spoken the truth.

That did not change things though. It was still imperative that Baraghosa be stopped. Perhaps now more than ever, with his spellcasting, whatever its intended purpose, complete.

"We should just wait things out for once," said Alixa, "rather than inviting more badness to fall on our heads."

"Badness has fallen on the heads of Shipmaster Burund and his crew," said Jasen, "because of me. They're captives because of us. Do you honestly expect me to stand by and do nothing?"

"No," said Alixa with another sigh, "but only because I know you too well."

"I have to do something."

"You're up against an entire war galley. Just wait, for once, Jasen. Please."

He pursed his lips.

Alixa was bowing out. He could feel it. She'd been reluctant from the beginning, and now that she knew that Baraghosa wasn't responsible for the loss of Terreas, she no longer wished to fight.

Jasen was alone again.

He needed to convince her otherwise. He needed her—needed all of them in the battle with Baraghosa again, and more on top of that. Whatever the number of hands needed to defeat the sorcerer, however many were required, be it dozens, hundreds, even a thousand-strong army … Jasen needed to amass them.

And it began with his cousin once again.

"Baraghosa may not be guilty of destroying Terreas," Jasen said, "but he killed Pityr. He took children from our village every year." Dying children, in some cases—but Alixa had not heard this, like she had not heard the revelation that Jasen was dying too, and he did not mention it. "He is not an innocent man. He may not have killed our families, but he is no good."

"And so we have to chase him around the world and get innocent people hurt—or worse, killed—in the process?"

Jasen opened his mouth to retort—

Alixa cut him off. "I just want to mourn my family, Jasen." She said it with a quiet, weary desperation, and the words cut through him like a blade through the chest, silencing him before he could say another word. "I want to grieve. I want to plant myself somewhere green and find a life of my own. And I can't. Not while we're doing this."

Her eyes glistened with tears. She smeared them away with the heel of her palm. Then, patting Scourgey one last time, she rolled over on the bed and faced the wall.

"Alixa—"

"I'd like to be left alone, please." There was a quiet finality in how she said it.

Jasen watched her back, watched the rise and fall of her chest. She wasn't crying, not properly; they were just breaths, in and out, in and out, her lungs filling with the scent of this strange new place they were in, all sour and woody and wrong.

Scourgey perched beside the bed. Mouth open, her tongue lolling, she looked out at everything and nothing with her black, coal-lump eyes. Whatever was going through her head—well, Jasen couldn't begin to fathom. Probably just happy to be on solid ground—and maybe, if she had the intelligence to be cognizant of it, trying to push aside the fact that she found herself once again on the water.

"I'll just … go then," Jasen said weakly.

But he had nowhere to go. And so, although he pulled the door closed, he found himself stationary. No sense, after all, in wandering and getting lost.

Instead, he lowered himself to the floor and rested his head against the door, eyes closed.

Distantly, he could feel the sway of the sea.

The war galley was moving. Taking them away from Baraghosa's isle. Onward to … wherever.

Alixa could not be right. To stand still, to just wait to see what happened … it was madness. They needed to keep moving forward, keep taking steps. Jasen was dying, damn it. If he stopped now, he might never start again.

She didn't know that though. None of them did. It was a secret—between Jasen, Baraghosa, and Scourgey. He trusted the scourge to keep it.

Himself? He was less sure.

No, he would not stop now, would not cease moving forward.

Or so he told himself. But he remained there, planted at the base of the door to his shared quarters with Alixa, and his thoughts circled and circled—and he took no steps forward at all.

8

Jasen woke the next morning, surprised. In part, he was surprised that he had slept at all: last night, slumber had seemed out of reach.

The other source of his surprise was Alixa—or rather, her absence. She'd left their quarters.

Scourgey remained.

Jasen dragged himself out from under the thin bedcovers. Evidently the night had been a troubled one for the both of them. The covers lay in a tangle around Jasen's hips and knees, knotted between them like a seeded bread from the bakery back home.

Home. A wistful pang echoed in Jasen's chest at the thought of it. It seemed present in Alixa's thoughts as well, a heavy anchor on her heart.

Need to keep moving forward, he told himself. *Can't stop moving. Not now.*

Scourgey looked particularly morose this morning. Although she'd cheered somewhat upon leaving the rowboat, that the war galley was now moving was undeniable. There was a gentle sway to its movement, not as pronounced as that of the *Lady Vizola*—this ship being much larger—but enough that Jasen was aware that the galley had left the isle of Baraghosa behind.

Where exactly they might be headed *to*—well, that was a question in need of answering, hopefully as soon as possible.

Sitting up, Jasen rubbed the sleep from his eyes. He gently rubbed Scourgey's head. She smelled particularly bad this morning, enough that Jasen noticed it even now that he was accustomed to her deathly, rotten scent. The tang of putrefaction rolled off her, almost misting in the air—a side effect of her stress, Jasen figured: she lay sadly at the foot of the cot, quivering at every soft rise and fall of the galley.

"It's okay," Jasen said. "We'll be back at port soon."

If Scourgey believed him, Jasen couldn't tell. But then, if she did not, Jasen would not blame her. He hadn't the faintest idea either. For all he knew of the Prenasians' plans, they might be seabound for months.

He hoped not. Every day at sea was another that Baraghosa grew more distant—and a day nearer to putting his plan, whatever it might be, into action.

Baraghosa's plan. What *might* it be? A sorcerer had limitless potential, and Jasen's imagination suddenly felt incredibly constrained. All he truly knew was that Baraghosa was not a good man, and that he had promised to commit sins of his own—but that was enough to propel Jasen onward.

Rising, he did the best job he could of smoothing out the creases in his clothes, and then, with a last pat on Scourgey's head, he headed out.

Navigating the mazelike interior of the war galley was something of a nightmare. Twice, Jasen got turned around—at least, he was fairly sure he'd been turned around. Everything looked so familiar, with its repetitive design, so even then he couldn't be certain that he'd managed to double back on himself. He only knew that it hadn't taken *this* long to find the stairs leading to the top deck.

The sun was low to the horizon when Jasen stepped out. The war galley was still in the fog enshrouding the isle of Baraghosa, and so the orb of yellow-white light was smeared at the edges. But the fog *was* dissipating, slow and sure. In another day or two, they might be through it altogether.

The top deck was heaving with people. Prenasians, tattooed and inky and barely clad, oversaw the *Lady Vizola*'s crew—who, chained together by metal shackles about the ankles and wrists, and hardly dressed, were arrayed in lines. They were scrubbing the deck, bowed low to it, wire-bristled brushes in each fist. Back and forth, they went, back and forth.

Another smaller task force was separate from the rest. Burund and Kuura were among them, and Hamisi too, Chaka, and one of the older shipmates from the *Lady Vizola*. Prenasians, one of the rowboat captains among them, oversaw them as they picked over a folded sail—a spare, most likely, since all the oblong ones Jasen had seen yesterday were still in position on the towering masts.

The most prominent watcher was a giant troll, skin daisy-yellow. It stood over to one side, its hulking shadow casting a long, dark bar across the galley's deck that almost blended into the wooden boards. It had a particularly miserable look upon its face.

Huanatha approached, slow and steady across the deck as Jasen watched the proceedings in horror.

"It is a dire sight," she remarked in a low voice.

"What are they doing?" Jasen asked.

"Been put to work," said Longwell from just behind him. The sound of his voice startled Jasen. The dragoon sat on the deck behind Jasen—without his lance. The stubble on his face had grown a little longer. Gazing glumly at the *Lady Vizola*'s crew, he pursed his lips and said no more.

Huanatha glared across to the captain overseeing Burund's group. "The shipmaster, repairing holes in a sail, like a common deckhand—pssh."

"He was a deckhand, once," said Longwell. "It is work he is familiar with." Still, there was a note in his voice that suggested he, too, was struggling to reconcile himself to the situation.

Jasen watched them. Huanatha was correct: Burund's group were repairing holes. Jasen he could catch their occasional glints of needles in the sun, dazzling little flashes of brilliant white light. And there was the pile of material they were using for patches, if holes were too large to simply stitch back together.

Burund was going about the job methodically with his usual stoic expression, eyes down.

Hamisi, separated from Burund by Kuura and the other shipmate whose name Jasen couldn't recall, had not adapted so easily. His jaw was clenched, a hard, solid line in the dawn sunlight. And he glared up at the Prenasians around him. Barely going a quarter of the pace Burund was, he gripped his needle tight—weighing it up as an improvised dagger?

A mad thought, if he were considering it. Too many Prenasians, only one Hamisi. And then there was that troll. Its size suggested it was not the fastest thing—but Jasen had seen them move on the isle of Baraghosa.

"Have you seen Alixa?" Jasen asked, trying to wrestle his gaze from the *Lady Vizola*'s people. A terrible guilt ate at him as he watched them, even the ones who were working on tasks that they would have upon their own ship—there, after all, they would not have been chained and forced into doing so.

"Below deck," said Longwell.

"She wasn't in our room when I woke."

"Maybe she's eating." A pause. "Or being seasick."

A cacophony of noise made Jasen jerk round to see—

The rowboat captain overseeing the sail-repairing taskforce had turned his back. Jasen could only imagine it was the briefest, slightest of twists away from the men who he stood over.

Hamisi had seen his opportunity, though—and like a snake, he had reared. Suddenly upon his feet, he leapt forward, the heavy rattle of two chains giving him away and slowing him down. He thrust out with the needle like it was a sword, brandishing it at the Prenasian's neck—

The Prenasian pivoted. His speed was lightning.

Hamisi bellowed—

The Prenasian captain dodged his strike. He swung a fist up, cracking it against the inside of Hamisi's elbow. It was a deft, fluid blur of a strike—but the *thwap!* that it made cut through the noise upon the deck like the crack of a whip. Hamisi staggered. He released the needle, and the last Jasen saw of it was a glint as it tumbled out of sight, and then the Prenasian captain slammed a fist into Hamisi's jaw. He buckled, stumbling sideways, landing on his knees—

"Ancestors," Longwell said, pushing quickly to his feet.

The *Lady Vizola*'s crew were doing the same. Brushes dropped, men pushed to their feet—

Rakon, watching the sudden action with faint interest, shouted an order to the *Lady Vizolans*.

Hamisi was on his knees. The captain stood over him, fists clenched, ready to fly again.

Burund was saying—something. Kuura too. They'd been yanked along by Hamisi's movements—the chains connecting them by wrist and ankle were short—and were scrambling to regain their balance.

Hamisi launched himself at the Prenasian's midriff.

"Idiot!" Longwell cursed—and worse, a string of expletives that came hard and fast. "He's going to get himself killed."

Huanatha bared her teeth. "Fool."

The troll lumbered over.

Hamisi and the Prenasian grappled. Hamisi was shouting—the *Lady Vizola*'s crew were too, and Jasen wished he knew their language, at the same time certain that, with so many voices all crying out at once, he'd never make head or tail of what they were saying anyway—and the Prenasian captain grunted. Hamisi had him tight. Though the Prenasian man outsized Hamisi, both in height and bulk, Hamisi had him too low and too tight for the Prenasian to do much more than flail. He landed blow after blow against Hamisi's spine—but Hamisi struck, slamming his fists knuckle-first into the captain's ribcage, using his big central knuckles to drive against bones.

But the troll was moving still. It had only been a little distance shy, barely any gap separating them at all—and it closed the last meters in two enormous steps. Gargantuan, dirty yellow fists reached down.

He pulled Hamisi and the Prenasian apart as though he were separating warring toddlers.

The Prenasian, he discarded, letting him drop onto his feet.

Hamisi, though ... Hamisi, he lifted—and Burund and Kuura and Chaka and the other crewmate yelped, dragged up by the chain too, so they dangled perilously—

The troll held Hamisi in front of his face. His fist encircled Hamisi's torso, arms swaddled to him.

Hamisi struggled.

The troll growled.

Hamisi spat—a fat glob of mucus that landed square in the troll's left eye.

Its growl deepened.

Rakon strode into the chaos.

He ordered—something—

Again, Jasen cursed himself for not knowing their language. "What's he said?"

But even as Huanatha translated, it was obvious enough. The captain who Hamisi had assaulted—Emre, Huanatha said—stepped up. He produced a glinting sliver of metal of his own. Jasen felt a stab of spiky black panic—a small blade, surely, to stab Hamisi between the ribs—but it was only a key, and he released Hamisi from the chains binding him. The dangling men dropped heavily, chains clanking round them, releasing Hamisi into the troll's grasp.

The troll stepped over the other crew, as if they were hardly an obstacle at all, and lumbered to the center of the deck, amidst the masts—and before the arrayed *Lady Vizolans*, who either stood or crouched in some state, their scrubbing forgotten, and their eyes glued to the troll.

Hamisi struggled violently in the troll's grip. He was shouting.

His eyes were wide and he snorted, readying to spit.

The troll shook him, a violent shudder that came out of nowhere—and then he slammed Hamisi's head into the mainmast—*CRACK!*

He lifted Hamisi in front of his face again.

Hamisi bled.

The troll growled, its teeth yellow—not the same as its skin, but a darker yellow-brown.

Hamisi's head rolled. The fight had gone out of him. If not for the fact his mouth hung open, and Jasen saw him dragging in great, gasping breaths, he'd think the sailor dead.

Rakon strode forward, joining the troll at its side.

He surveyed his newly assembled slaves with a grim look.

"*Discipline,*" he said in Luukessian. "It is a value above no other, in our glorious land of Prenasia—and one which, it would appear, some of our new hands aboard this galley are severely lacking."

"Why's he speaking Luukessian?" Jasen asked. "The crew don't speak it."

"He doesn't speak their language," Longwell answered. He kept his voice at a low mutter. Poised beside Jasen and Huanatha, he looked ready to spring at a moment's notice. Yet there was no lance to complete him.

"But he questioned Burund yesterday."

"In our tongue, I believe."

Rakon had not broken his monologue. "… would appear that, in your old lives, acting out of course was endured. I know these sorts well; I have encountered enough of you on these seas—ghostly hierarchies, done aside with until the moments where it matters most, in favor of a false *equality* among you.

"Do yourself away with every illusion such as this," Rakon said. "Your last captain may have blurred the lines among your crew. Here, though, you are not *family*. You are your *role*, your place upon the ladder—and at this moment, it is at the very bottom of it. Perhaps, when you show yourself to respect our system, and when I have forgiven you for trading with our enemies, you may attain higher ranks. For now, however, you are deckhands, all of you. And failure to follow orders will not be tolerated."

Hamisi was regaining some of his wits. Lolling less in the troll's grip, his eyelids were flickering now. Blood ran down his face in great rivulets.

The troll lifted him high again, right into the air, like he weighed nothing at all—

He lifted his free hand, then wrapped it around Hamisi's neck—and squeezed.

That roused Hamisi. He gasped—or rather, he *tried* to gasp. Eyes suddenly wide—no, not just wide, *bulging*—he clawed at the troll's massive fist, raking at its huge fingers—

"No!" Jasen cried, stepping forward.

Huanatha caught him. "Don't."

"But—"

"The Prenasian's speech was for all of us," said Longwell bitterly. "It's a threat."

"But Hamisi—"

"Is now an example," said Longwell. "Do not join him."

54

So Jasen could only watch, like the crew of the *Lady Vizola*, as the troll continued to squeeze Hamisi's throat, and the man tried to breathe, tried to flail and kick free, grappling with his hands in a desperate attempt to release enough pressure that he could breathe ...

Yet he could not. His dark-skinned face turned purple. His movements slowed ... until, finally, his eyes rolled back in his head, and he hung there, utterly limp.

The troll did not release him immediately. For some twenty seconds, twenty awful seconds of tense quiet, Rakon and Emre and the other Prenasians stood, alternately surveying the terrified faces of the *Lady Vizola*'s crew—and, in Rakon's case, making pointed glances at Jasen, Longwell and Huanatha—and looking at Hamisi's body as it dangled in the troll's fists.

At last, when the effect had been achieved, Rakon said something to the troll.

The troll tossed Hamisi overboard as though he were nothing. Overripe fruit, perhaps, to be got rid of with ease.

Rakon nodded to his captains. "Continue," he said to the *Lady Vizola*'s crew—and then off he went, to oversee the whole business from the front of the deck.

Jasen felt sick—sick at seeing a man so brutally, easily killed in front of him, right down to Hamisi's last twitch. Sicker still, he felt, at seeing just how swiftly the *Lady Vizola*'s crew returned to their tasks. Except for Burund and Kuura, Jasen was not aware that a single one of them could speak Luukessian, and would know what Rakon had said. But the effect was clear, no words were needed. They picked up their scrubbing brushes and returned to scrubbing the deck in a silence that was worse, somehow, than the one before.

What made him feel sickest, though, was that he knew that this was his fault. He had not liked Hamisi, that much was true ... but his was yet another death upon his conscience.

9

Longwell led Huanatha and Jasen to his own quarters—the only place, he said, where they might speak in private.

"We have much to discuss," he said quietly, guiding them back into the war galley.

"I'll see if Alixa is back," said Jasen. "She could join us."

She wasn't. Only Scourgey inhabited the room, lying on the cot in total darkness now that the candle had gone out. She raised her head when the door opened then, seeing Jasen—or more likely, Longwell—she rose and tottered weakly to her heels.

Jasen stroked the top of her head. He could smell her again now, faintly. Seeing Hamisi's death like that, so plain, so stark, seemed to have elevated all of his senses. The woody interior of the war galley was particularly pungent, but there was a sour undertone to the whole thing that Jasen couldn't get away from. What exactly it came from— the Prenasians, the trolls, perhaps from the wooden ship itself—he didn't know. But it wrinkled his nose, catching high in the back of his throat, and he was unable to rid himself of it.

How the world had changed, that Jasen found himself pleased to have Scourgey's deathly, rotted smell in his nostrils again. At least it was familiar.

Longwell, lingering at the door, cast the scourge a disgusted look. He sidestepped, putting a little extra space between them.

Scourgey watched him with her coal-lump eyes—at least, Jasen thought she was watching him. Her lack of pupils made it difficult to be certain. In turn, Huanatha watched her, a peculiar look on her face.

"Your ... beast ... thing is coming with us, then," said Longwell. He clearly wished she wasn't.

"Can she?" Jasen asked.

Longwell hesitated. "I do not think ..."

Scourgey whined, and

Huanatha's eyes widened at the sound.

She lowered to her knees, the clink of her armored greaves like a gentle chime over the creaking of the war galley. Looking very intently at Scourgey, she reached out, slowly, until her fingers were just touching Scourgey's head.

Jasen said, "Uhm …"

Longwell paled. "Huanatha, I will give you the same warning I gave the children. Those things are dangerous. They have destroyed—"

"This one is not like the others," said Huanatha.

Alixa had told Longwell as much before. He'd come to believe her, Jasen thought, at least begrudgingly. Enough that he was willing to tolerate the scourge, at any rate. But now, deprived of his spear, he seemed much less comfortable in her presence.

"You wish to be rid of her," said Huanatha slowly, still peering into Scourgey's eye. "But this one … this one is much like you."

"A scourge?" Longwell's voice was disdainful. "How do you mean?"

"She dislikes the feel of these Prenasians too," said Huanatha. "It is why she quivers and cowers, meek even now that she is in safe company."

Longwell breathed a little snort at that last part, but did not comment.

"I thought she was just seasick," Jasen said.

"She does hate the seas, yes," said Huanatha.

"All her kind do," Longwell said. "They die in water, a fact I once used to …" his voice trailed off, and Jasen barely caught what he said next. But he did catch it. "… Save a city." His voice was hollow, and Jasen wondered if perhaps he'd lost as much as he'd saved.

Huanatha ignored him. "She feels in these … these warmongers a link to the peoples like this from her own life. Despots. Conquerors. Those who would see free people put into chains." She shook her head. "She does not like it. Also, the yellow ones? The … trells, you called them?"

"Trolls," Longwell said. "That's what they're called. Or at least, the green-skinned ones on Arkaria were."

Huanatha shook her head. "These, the Prenasian version … they remind her of an old friend, long unseen." She ran a hand over Scourgey's face, scratching her behind the ears and producing a whine. "She misses him. His … sense of the absurd, I think."

Longwell stared at Scourgey, frowning. Disgust was still etched upon his face—but it had faded now, softening into a look that was almost—*almost*—the very first hints of respect. "You can tell all that about her?" he asked Huanatha. "About her life before she … became this?"

"I can." Huanatha looked up at him. "And more. For example, this one … she knew *you* in her life before."

Longwell's eyes flashed. "Impossible."

"It is true," said Huanatha. "She speaks; and I can hear her. She talks of a place where the hearth fires burned warm on every night. Where the company was loyal and true …" The queen of Muratam stared into the middle distance, hand on Scourgey's back as the grey-skinned creature let another low whine. "Where any of good heart could find a home …"

And suddenly, Jasen was aware of an almost electric energy in the air. Longwell, who moments ago had been keen to put as much of the war galley between himself and Scourgey as possible, was now looking at the beast with wide, expectant eyes, set in a rapidly paling face. He stared, unblinking, as though the scourge herself were speaking, and he was hanging on her every word, waiting for …

"Sanctuary," Huanatha breathed.

Longwell reeled back as though he had been slapped. All the color had gone from his face now. "Lies," he croaked.

Huanatha spoke, eyes closed, as if she were channelling the thoughts from Scourgey's mind.

"Sir Samwen Longwell, who came to the gates of Sanctuary from a far distant land, with a very different spear than the one you now carry." She opened her eyes, looked at Longwell. "She met you. She knew you. And you were there when her blood ran across the stones of Sanctuary."

Longwell seemed to sag, as if it were only his suit of armor holding him up. Deathly white, he stared at Scourgey. He put out a hand to clutch at the nearest wall.

"Who?" he whispered, his voice strangled. "Who was it?"

"A beautiful girl," said Huanatha. "Ageless—with pointed ears—"

"An elf." More strangled than before, as though Longwell were now in a troll's grip.

Huanatha nodded. "And long, flaming red hair …"

Longwell closed his eyes. He breathed out, a long exhalation, as if he'd held in that breath all his life—and now, only now, could he finally unburden himself from keeping it in. It left him like the entire weight of the world.

Jasen stared at Scourgey. He pictured her: an elfin woman, hair of fire streaming after her.

This was who Scourgey had been?

He'd thought her a beast. The way she loped on behind them, keeping close to heel, the way her mouth opened and her tongue lolled, the way she pressed her nose to Jasen's forehead—her dog-like behavior. But now that he looked, *really* looked, he could see there was something almost human about her—horrible and transmogrified though it was. Scourgey's body, her curved spine, those awkwardly placed legs, as though she would never be any good for running ... it was as though a person had been put in a rack and stretched, then reshaped, forced onto all fours—and then grafted with the parts of beasts, turned into an animal with pitted eyes and sharp teeth and over-large claws, wiry hairs all over her body, humanity done away with.

Yes, he could see it now—could see how Scourgey could have been human, once. And hadn't Shilara said that the scourge were people? Cursed men and women?

An elf with flaming red hair—who'd known Longwell.

And now she was this.

Huanatha looked deeply into Scourgey's eyes still, probing, perhaps reading Scourgey's mind directly.

"And she died," she whispered. The words were heavy in the air, so terribly heavy. "—with no magic to save ... to save her ..." Her eyebrows knitted. Lines crinkled about her eyes. "Her ..."

"Her arse," Longwell said finally. "To save her arse." He looked at Scourgey, his eyes filled to the brimming with a deep-seated sadness. "Niamh." The word was whisper-quiet, and came out in a low breath that Jasen had to struggle to hear. "Her name ... was Niamh."

10

He was with his parents.

He was young, so young that this distant memory—dream?—was blurry. He didn't seem to be in Terreas, so it could not be a memory, exactly … but it was so familiar.

They were walking through long grass together—a field of it. Not the hill down to the wall … no, this was someplace else in the village, or on the edge of it, or a thousand miles away.

No, he must be in Terreas. His mother was saying … what was she saying?

"One day we'll climb the mountain."

He didn't look up at her: just focused on walking. The grass was tall, so tall against his body, coming well past his little waist. It was like walking through a jungle. He'd heard of jungles, like a distant legend, only whispered about, never seen. More overgrown than this, his mother said—and Jasen knew it, knew it from a distant time that was yet to come, because he'd seen woodlands that were not close to jungles, and dimly remembered stories of somewhere called Coricuanthi, where lush vegetation abounded, and the whole place was terrifically hot and overgrown, so incredibly humid that the water beaded out of the air on the underside of leaves.

How do I know that?

Stories, from someone else. Some*when* else. Kuura—Huanatha— Burund. All and none of them, all and none.

He waded through the grass, asking—

"When?"

"Not today." His father. The voice echoed, as if it came across a cavernous room. "When you're older."

Jasen craned around to see the mountains, mottled brown and streaked with vegetation. He couldn't make out the nimble goats he'd come to watch later, moving deftly between impossible rocks and perches. He did not see the mists at the base either, condensing as the cool night air blew around the vast domes.

Nor did he see smoke rising from the cratered mountain. But then, of course he would not. This dream—or memory—it was at least a dozen years old. The mountain showed no sign of was to come.

Back to wading through the grass.

Damn it, why wouldn't he just look up at his mother?

He held her hand in his left, his father's in his right.

He longed to see her face …

But he only waded onward, deeper into the long grasses, parents at his sides.

"Swing me again," he asked.

"Very well," said his father. "You ready?"

"Yeah!"

"One … two …"

Each count, his mother and father swung their hold forward, then back … and then on three, the two of them lifted at the same time, and Jasen *flew*, arcing in their arms, legs kicking through the grass, laughing, the blue sky overhead—and there was so much *love* here, suffusing the air, he could feel it coming from them—

And then the dream ended.

He was in bed. The candle in the lamp had run right down—it would need replacing again; blasted things didn't last long at all—and it only cast a frail light into the room.

The bedcovers were a mess.

Alixa had come back at some point. Jasen's sleep didn't appear to have disturbed her. But he'd dozed off so late, he thought, probably well after sundown at the height of summer. She was probably exhausted from whatever it was she'd been doing all day.

She lay in her clothes, her back to him. A little sliver of cover remained about her, a corner that had entangled her hips and ended up coiling about her, like she was an anchor, holding it in place while Jasen tossed and turned, slowly beading with sweat and his clothes sticking to him.

So damned *hot*.

He rose, his clothes and hair plastered to him with sweat.

Better get some air.

He stepped past Scourgey—Niamh. She was sleeping too, making that throaty half-snore that indicated she'd fallen into the deepest stages of slumber. Then, easing the door open gently, he slipped out, closing it with a gentle click beside him.

He'd counted the turns leading to and from his quarters. So he reversed it in his head, moving in the direction of the deck.

He still got turned around.

Frowning, and now having lost track of where his and Alixa's room was, he tried to just follow along in the right direction. How had he got it so wrong? Probably sleepiness; he hoped the fresh air would wash away the fogginess that engulfed him.

Eventually, he found the staircase and climbed it out onto the war galley's upper deck.

The sun hadn't yet risen, but it was on its way: the thinnest sliver of orange lit the horizon to the east. With so little light available, the ship and waters almost blurred; leaning over the side, Jasen could pick out the edge of the boat but just barely.

The *Lady Vizola*'s crew were hard at work already. More deck-scrubbing was in progress. A handful of Prenasians and a single troll kept close eyes upon the crew. The troll sat upon its great backside, in its hand a cane, a long, thin one almost the full length of a human man.

Burund and Kuura had been folded back into the cleaning crew. They might be split off later, Jasen thought, when it was light enough to patch sails.

Kuura was close to Jasen. He caught the boy's eye as he stepped onto the deck. Bent double over a wire-bristled brush, he inclined his head in a tiny nod.

Jasen nodded back. He considered approaching, saying something—not that there would be a great deal he could say—"sorry" didn't exactly cut it—but that hulking troll wasn't brandishing a cane for no reason. A step out of line by any of the *Lady Vizolans*, and it would come swinging down in a blur, cutting through the pre-dawn air with a whip crack.

Rakon appeared from ahead. "Jasen?" He stuck a hand over his eyes, as though the sun were bright overhead and in need of blocking. Setting eyes upon him, he said, "What is a ward of Lord Longwell of Reikonos doing out here by himself?"

"Uhm ..." Cooling off was the answer, of course. After yesterday's speech though, apparently specifically to Jasen and the few other speakers of Luukessian, it would be a great show of impertinence for Jasen to announce that he'd excused himself from his lord's command for a brief respite.

"He—Lord Longwell," he corrected quickly, "sent me up on deck. I'm on a break." A bare-faced lie, and a bad one at that, but too late; it was out of his mouth now.

Rakon meandered over, stepping between Chaka and Medleigh as though they were not there.

"On a break, eh?" He didn't appear to believe it. Nevertheless, he relaxed his scrutinizing eye after a short up-and-down appraisal of the boy, and swept an arm out toward the front of the ship. "Well, come. Talk with me a while." And he set off again, back the way he'd come, not looking back or checking that Jasen was following. But then, he was captain of this vessel—it was unquestionable that a lowly ward would obey him.

Jasen followed.

"Tell me, young Jasen," said Rakon easily. "Where is it you come from? Not from the same lands as *these* wretches." He emphasized it by kicking the chain strung between Chaka and Medleigh as he passed, rather than stepping over it. It jolted, jerking them both sideways with small yelps.

The troll rose, fist tightening around his cane.

Rakon waved him off with a deep blue hand. The troll relaxed again. But his gaze was hungry, two mighty, pointed teeth sticking out of his bottom jaw in an underbite—waiting for any sign of insubordination from the *Lady Vizolans*.

Jasen gave Chaka and Medleigh an apologetic look as he passed. Neither looked especially appeased by it. Again, though, he couldn't say he was sorry, not without drawing ire from the Prenasians who were showing him, Alixa, Longwell and Huanatha some semblance of courtesy, masked threats aside. So he stepped past them too, making the best show he could of stepping over their chain instead of kicking it too.

"I came from Terreas," said Jasen. "A village—on Luukessia. It's no longer there."

Rakon nodded. "And Lord Longwell acquired your services … how?"

Jasen hesitated. "After I left Luukessia," he said slowly. "That's when I came to … work for Lo-Lord Longwell," he added, catching the name just in time.

Rakon inclined his head in another nod. "And how did you end up on that island? With these dogs?" With a wave he indicated the *Lady Vizolans*.

Jasen hesitated again, grateful that Rakon's back was still turned so he couldn't see the hesitation on Jasen's face.

"We were traveling with them between ports," he finally answered. "From Aiger Cliffs." Rakon nodded at that, too, and Jasen hoped this information would be enough for him. "We were wrecked two days before you came. A storm came in. It dashed the *Lady Vizola* on the rocks."

Rakon looked back over his shoulder, an eyebrow cocked. "Another royal was traveling with you?"

"Uhh—no. The *Lady Vizola*—that was the ship we were on, the name of it."

Rakon snorted. "Coricuanthians and their fancy names." Shaking his head, he continued up the steps toward the smaller deck at the fore of the war galley. Wood and metal beams crisscrossed here, forming a sort of fence around the perimeter. An angular decoration, resembling the troll-like faces on the side of the galley, rose ahead of them, pointing out to sea.

Jasen followed.

Rakon leaned against the rail, his arm thrown casually against it. Half-turned to point out to sea, he watched its smooth, inky surface. No waves still. The bar of frail sunlight, reaching up from below the horizon, was gradually widening though, and color was seeping back into the world.

"What happened to your village?" Rakon asked.

"A mountain—a volcano," Jasen said. "It erupted."

"And you got out alive."

No, Jasen thought. *I was buried under the slag, just like everyone else.*

He kept this thought to himself.

A *thwack* came from down on the deck. Rakon peered toward it. One of the *Lady Vizolans*—Jasen could not tell who, in this light—cowered forward. The troll loomed over him, swinging the cane up for a second—*thwack!* The whole rod bent, more elastic than solid wood, but it didn't snap, then came up again for a third strike.

Thwack!

Jasen flinched. He thought he heard a whimper escape the man. If a noise had got out of him, though, he stifled it just as fast.

One of the other rowboat captains, a short-haired man with bronze bars piercing his eyebrows, called Hamza, said something to the *Lady Vizolans*, a reprimand of some sort. What the caned man had done, Jasen couldn't imagine—muttered something to the men on either side of him, perhaps. There was little else he *could* do, stripped down to his underwear, wielding only a wire brush.

The troll backed off at Hamza's order.

The excitement over, Rakon turned his attentions back to Jasen. Or at least somewhat back to him. He didn't glance at the boy, just peered over the deck with the faintest sort of interest. Jasen got the feeling he was talking out of boredom.

"I heard tell of the fall of Luukessia," he said, "though I was given to understand it happened some time ago. A decade or so later, Arkaria began to topple. All rumor and secondhand knowledge, though; I've not gone so far west yet to see myself. Talk of it reaches my ears though, percolating through the Prenasian navy from those who have. A plague of grey-skinned beasts with dark souls poured over the lands, they say." He leaned toward Jasen. "Not unlike the beast your Lord Longwell has permitted you to keep—and which we have been kind enough to allow you to bring aboard." Fixing Jasen with a long, assessing look, he leaned back but did not break eye contact. "Of course, the beast of yours cannot be one of them. It is as tame as a trained falcon." His eyes flashed with a touch of amusement at that, but Jasen suspected he was probing, wondering if perhaps Scourgey *was* one of the creatures in the stories.

He schooled his expression into polite interest. If he could be half as good at keeping his emotions from leaking through as Burund, well, he might pass through this conversation without spilling anything more than the words he'd spoken.

Rakon turned his gaze back onto the war galley's top deck. No sign of any funny business from the *Lady Vizolans*; just scrubbing now, no one out of line. The man who'd been struck with the cane was back in his place. Jasen couldn't pick him out, not from here, in this light. Later, he would—by the welts on his back where he'd been struck.

"Yours might be tame," Rakon went on, "but there's no beast that isn't dangerous. Not when it's threatened. Back any creature into a corner, however intelligent ..." his gaze flicked to Jasen "... and they'll fight like animals, relying on basic instincts. This is just known."

"Of course ... all beasts can be tamed, too—man among them." He nodded toward the *Lady Vizolans*, in their shadowy line, bowed and scrubbing. "Man is different in this respect. He can rise above his animal instincts ... with the appropriate instruction, from the right source."

Jasen kept his voice carefully neutral. "Is that so?"

"Of course," said Rakon. "Sooner or later, they come to learn their place—and the fight has been disciplined out of them. It is the same with all men. They simply need discipline."

Jasen was quiet. Yes, Rakon was bored, he thought. Certainly he was not saying any of this to Jasen because he expected the boy to agree. He was just talking for the sake of talking.

"Prenasia is that order," Rakon said casually. "We will tame the world."

"Oh?" Jasen said politely.

"Not tomorrow," Rakon answered. "Our focus is in the east, for now. But the day will come when Amatgarosa is ended, their defiance comes to its natural halt in the face of our innate superiority, and Prenasia will dominate. And so—for now—we are allies with you westerners, and your disorder." He again cast Jasen a sideways look, more of a smirk than a genuine smile. Easing back once more, he leaned back on the rail: "But not these men." He looked darkly at the *Lady Vizola*'s crew.

"No?"

"Coricuanthi is too divided, you see," said Rakon. "Too many city-states, too many tribal grudges. Muratam alone is at war with three other city-states surrounding it, and bears ill will toward five others." Shaking his head, he said, "Coricuanthi lacks union. Purpose. When the appropriate moment comes, it is Prenasia's destiny to bring order to that chaos."

Jasen almost expected him to say, *But not yet. Our enemies to the east ...*

He did not. It was there, though, unspoken, lingering in the air like mist. Jasen had the measure of him, and had found it easily enough—a man who boasted, too sure of his land and its people and their superiority, and contemptuous of Prenasia's many enemies.

Rakon cast a look at the horizon. The bar of orange sunlight was widening, softening the darkness of the evaporating night.

"Your lord will be looking for you," said Rakon. "I daresay your break is not this long. And some of us have work to do."

"Yes," said Jasen, stepping away. "Thank you, Captain."

Rakon did not reply so Jasen clambered down to the main deck, past the men of the *Lady Vizola*, again taking great care to step over their chains. The Prenasians watched him, and the troll too, idly swinging the cane back and forth so it whistled as it streaked through the air, as if looking for any excuse to land it upon Jasen's back.

Huanatha had called these people warmongers. It was plain in the way Rakon spoke—and of course in the way they'd already brutalized the *Lady Vizola*'s crew. Jasen and Alixa had been lucky to escape the worst of captivity.

He needed to free them all, though. Not that there had ever been any question of that, other than the *how* of it, which he still didn't have the first answer to. But now he saw these Prenasians more clearly, and understood their belief in their innate superiority, it was more imperative than ever. He had to find a way to free the men of the *Lady Vizola* from their captors—and soon.

11

Jasen hammered on the door that he hoped was Longwell's.

A confused mumble answered him. "Who's there?"

"Jasen," he hissed, half a whisper, loud enough to penetrate the thick wood and the fog of sleep apparently clouding Longwell's mind.

"Jasen?" A yawn. "What are you …?"

Footsteps approached the door. Then it was opened—and there he stood, the dragoon, clad in cloth underclothes that must have been scavenged from the *Lady Vizola*'s stores. Striped white and blue, they looked almost comical on him in place of his usual suit of armor.

He peered at Jasen through bleary eyes, rubbing his face with his palm.

"What are you doing here?" Longwell asked. And then, suppressing another yawn: "What time is it?"

"Before dawn," said Jasen. "May I come in? I'd like to speak to you about something."

Nodding, Longwell ushered Jasen inside. Then he peeked his head out into the corridor, looking both directions. Activity had long since begun on the war galley—or, rather, it hadn't stopped: a vessel this size required working right through the night, but here Jasen and Longwell had privacy.

Longwell closed the door.

His quarters were grander than Jasen's and Alixa's. Perhaps triple the size, his room housed a larger cot with thicker blankets, currently lying in disarray at the foot of the bed, a writing desk, a chest which stood open, some meager possessions in it, all of them apparently collected from the *Lady Vizola*'s salvage, and finally, scavenged from ancestors knew where, a frame on which Longwell's armor hung. With its wooden arms, it looked like a military scarecrow, Longwell's helmet replacing a straw cap.

"I've just been on deck," Jasen began, but no sooner had he said it than there came a knock on the door.

Jasen and Longwell both froze.

Who was knocking? At this hour?

"Answer it," said Longwell.

Jasen spluttered, "Me?"

"You're my ward," Longwell whispered. "If it's Rakon or one of his captains, they'll think it odd if I answer my own door while you're present. Quickly!"

Jasen hurried to the door. He opened it, dreading the sight of Rakon greeting him once again—

But it was not Rakon. Nor was it a blue-skinned Prenasian at all—though, for a fearful half-moment as his brain caught up with reality, Jasen could've sworn it was. Huanatha stood there, faint rings under her eyes but more alert than Longwell had been. She was already clad in her blue armor—except the breastplate, of course; the Prenasians had been kind enough to donate a spare, muted and grey and very battered. Jasen couldn't help but wish he'd been there to see the moment she was given it; her sneer would've been almightily dark.

"I heard you hammering," she said to Jasen. "I did not wish to miss any discussions."

"Oh. Uhm. Come in." Jasen stepped aside.

Huanatha slipped in by him.

She nodded at Longwell, appraising. "Don't you look fetching."

Longwell huffed and lifted his helmet from the armor rack. "It's too early for your jibes."

"Who said anything about a jibe?" Huanatha countered.

A peculiar look passed between them. Jasen felt, for a moment, like an intruder, then Longwell dropped heavily onto the edge of his cot, the helmet stuck on his head and the face guard open, looking even more ridiculous than he had in just his striped underclothes. "Speak your mind, Jasen."

Jasen hesitated. "Is it safe …?" If Huanatha had been able to hear his knocking, what did that mean for their conversation?

"I did not hear with my ears," she said. "These walls are not so thin. I have other means."

Longwell made a derisive noise. "Accursed magic."

Huanatha ignored him. "I will warn if anyone should get close enough to hear our conversation. For now, we are safe. Proceed."

"All right," said Longwell. He turned to Jasen: "Speak your mind."

"We must free the men of the *Lady Vizola*," Jasen said.

"Of course we must," Longwell said. "But that is no easy task.

Perhaps not even for me ... *if* I had my spear." He screwed his face up. "Without it—without Tanukke," he added, nodding at Huanatha, "I fear it will be difficult indeed."

"Yet it must be done," she said fiercely. "The whispers of the dead fill this vessel. I hear them, lingering here ... tortured souls the Prenasians have killed, agonized in their last earthly moments, their business here unfinished and their spirits too troubled to move on." She closed her eyes, perhaps listening to them now.

Jasen wondered what it must be like—a swirl of voices, perhaps, echoing as though they came down a great long hall, or floating on the wind? How many were there? How many had these Prenasians and their trolls killed, like Hamisi upon the deck just yesterday? Was *his* voice among those Huanatha could hear?

Longwell's face paled as he watched Huanatha. Squeezing the bridge of his nose, he pursed his lips and looked away, like he'd happened upon something he should not set eyes on, and rolled his helm between his palms.

Jasen looked back to her.

Then—

A white spot opened. Directly in front of his pupil, it blotted Huanatha's shoulder from view, an eroded hole in the world to a pool of pure white underneath.

He blinked, forcing it away—

And, for just a fraction of a second—he saw them: the dead. There were so many of them, all clustered around Huanatha, vastly more than could reasonably occupy this room. They overlapped, layered one over the other. So many—and their *faces*! Sadness upon all of them ...

They were gone just as quick as they'd come.

Huanatha watched him.

Jasen's breath had caught in his chest. He let it out, slow.

She knew. Jasen didn't know how, exactly—perhaps she had shown it to him?—but Huanatha knew what he had seen.

She said nothing.

And Jasen did not ask. There was little time for questions. He'd found the measure of Rakon, and the Prenasian people by extension; and he knew that, inevitably, if they were not saved, the *Lady Vizola*'s crew would join the dead stuck upon this ship, riding it endlessly in death.

"The Prenasians will use them up," he said, "the *Lady Vizola*'s men. They'll die."

Huanatha nodded. "The Prenasian war machine grinds all men who cross it into dust."

"That may be so," said Longwell, "but there are … an awful lot of trolls," he said. "And arguably worse are the Prenasians themselves."

"They're cruel, no doubt," Jasen said, "but how can they be worse than those trolls?"

"The men from Prenasia," the dragoon said slowly, "are of a species that was wiped out on Arkaria. They built an empire ten thousand years ago, only to be rendered extinct by their own hand—by the hands of the greatest among them, specifically, cleansing their own people from the land in order to maintain their own superiority." He set his jaw. "They became the gods of Arkaria to us lesser beings, until they, too, were wiped out. All that remain of that entire race now are their offspring with humans—the dark elves." He shook his head. "Or so I thought, until I laid eyes on my first Prenasian. Their race lives on in other lands, apparently. Let us hope they do not share their Arkarian brethren's skill with magic, for the Ancients, the gods …" He let a small shiver. "They were the fiercest enemies I have ever faced."

"There is a strong magic here, I sense," said Huanatha quietly.

"Great," said Jasen. His heart sank. "Are you suggesting it's impossible, then?"

Longwell sighed. Again, he massaged the bridge of his nose. "No. But there are other difficulties to consider. If we can wrest this vessel from the Prenasians—and that is a troll-sized *if*—we have no idea where we are. Rakon has not shared our destination with me; we could be anywhere now."

"We're only a few days' travel from the isle of Baraghosa," said Jasen. "And Burund could tell. If we supplant the Prenasians, beat them and their trolls, we could give the ship over to him."

"A fine prize, for all he has been through," said Huanatha.

Longwell was quiet. Knuckling his chin, he said, "Many will die to see this done."

"Many will die if it's not," said Jasen. "Perhaps more." And Burund and his crew would remain enslaved, Jasen thought guiltily.

"Perhaps that is true. But do you know what you ask? Honestly, truly?" Longwell leaned forward, fixing Jasen with a hard look. "We will have to murder, in stealth, as many of the Prenasian crew as can we can. We will have to slit their throats in the dead of night, in perfect silence. You will have blood on your hands—like a butcher, slaughtering animals. But these will be people—your fellow men."

"These *are* animals," Huanatha growled, teeth bared in a sneer. "They are lower than that, less worthy of mercy."

"But they are men," said Longwell. "Their skin is different to ours, their beliefs, their capacity for what we perceive as evil ... but they are men all the same."

"They have decided they are better than other men," Huanatha replied. "That they are worthy above others to exercise control over the lives of free men. By seeking to crush others beneath their boot, they deserve the sword that descends on the back of their neck." She folded her arms in front of her.

Leaning back again, Longwell gave Jasen a long, cool look. "Then we are agreed. This is what must be done if we are to achieve what you propose." Longwell stooped a little lower, his eyes finding Jasen's in the shadowy cabin. "Do you realize what this will do to your soul? How it will coarsen you?"

Jasen considered. He could see it, almost, now—see himself standing behind a Prenasian captain, perhaps even Rakon, and dragging a blade across the man's neck; could almost feel the hot gush of blood as it poured out of him, flowing over his hands, and the man bucked, gurgled ...

Yes. Longwell was right. This would fracture him deeply, breaking him in ways he could not imagine.

But he could justify it. This—saving the men of the *Lady Vizola*, no matter the cost—it was right. Just as he knew it was right to stop Baraghosa, whatever his malevolent plans were.

"These Prenasians are men," Jasen said, "but so are the crew of the *Lady Vizola*. I owe Shipmaster Burund my allegiance, and more. His men—and he too—will die unless we do this. And if need be ..." He paused, and the image came back to him, Rakon's throat split open and a river of dark liquid pouring out of him, soaking his wrists. "... I will slit their throats myself."

Huanatha and Longwell traded an uncomfortable look, fraught with significance.

"You will not," said Longwell at last. Rising, he strode to his armor. Resting a hand on the breastplate, he seemed to steel himself, inclining his head in a short nod. "I will do this. I will go to the crew cabin of this ship, and I will kill these men myself."

Huanatha joined him, touching his shoulder. "And I will join you."

But Longwell shook his head. "No. Someone must be on the deck. Otherwise they might close the hatches and attempt to trap me. You must listen—and when things begin to get loud ... then you will know what to do."

Jasen expected Huanatha to argue; she was so fierce, so ready for battle, at all times. Yet she did not. She simply nodded, and exchanged a look with Jasen, silently asking if he were in on it too.

Jasen confirmed with his own resolute nod. "We will know what to do." A hesitation. "But … your spear. And Tanukke. How …?"

"Leave it to me," said Longwell. "I believe I know where they are stored. If not … there will be other weapons."

"The Prenasians carry swords," said Huanatha.

"And I am proficient with them." At her surprised look, he said, "What? You expected me to be useless with anything but my spear?"

"Yes," she said plainly. "You refuse to wield anything else. Why would I believe you capable in swordplay when you cling to the lance like it is all that tethers you to this world?"

Longwell flashed a macabre grin. "I look forward to ruining your measure of me." Looking again very serious, he looked from Huanatha to Jasen. "So it is decided then. We will do this—no matter the cost."

"Yes," said Huanatha.

Jasen nodded. "No matter the cost."

It was decided. They would do this. And if it fractured Jasen's soul, blackened it with a taint that could never be healed, for as long as he lived …

Well, he would not live much longer anyway.

12

The plan was set, and it would happen that day—almost as soon as they were done speaking, in fact, when the sun had lifted high enough to paint the deck with morning light. The shift changeover would not have long occurred, the overnight workers returned to their quarters and the day shift distracted with the tasks they had to carry out at the very beginning of the day, yet more still in the mess halls. This, Longwell said, was the best opportunity for him to reclaim his spear and slit the throats of as many Prenasians as he could.

"What should I do?" Jasen asked, rubbing his fingers against the thin, blond hairs on his arms.

"Take to the deck," said Longwell, "with Huanatha. Await me there." To her, he said, "I will locate Tanukke and bring her back to you."

She nodded. "My thanks."

Longwell returned a curt smile.

Then they parted.

Jasen and Huanatha strode through the ship's interior, he in a kind of daze. It was happening—it was happening *now*.

"You are troubled," Huanatha said.

"I'm accustomed to a little more planning than this," Jasen said.

She laughed, a quiet, deep chuckle. "Life is not always so kind as to allow you to plan. But this is a blessing too, for it does not allow you time to fear, either."

That was true, although Jasen felt the fear there, lingering in the back of his mind in a dark corner. If he fed it—and he could—then it would quickly grow and overpower him. A strange thought to have, for he hadn't felt the same fear inside of him at battling Baraghosa. But then, Baraghosa had been one man, and Jasen's fear had been overpowered by his furious desire to do what was right and avenge the people of his village.

The Prenasians needed to be defeated as well. The *Lady Vizolans* should be set free. But here, Jasen felt room for doubt. Baraghosa *had* to be defeated, *would be*. The Prenasians, these warmongers from another land … they were like the scourge: viciously cruel, spreading like a plague to consume and overtake the lands they set their sights upon—and numerous. Almost more numerous than the trees, it felt, at times.

Ah, there it was, the fear.

Stop it, he told himself.

It is happening now.

He hadn't the *time* to fear.

Huanatha had memorized the ship's layout impressively, featureless and repetitive though its walls were. It was part of being a warrior, Jasen supposed, particularly one so accomplished, having an attention to detail that most men did not possess.

She led them to the stairs up to the top deck, pausing only once to check Jasen and Alixa's shared room. Alixa still was not there. Scourgey—Niamh—remained, lying on the bed in a curled, misshapen heap. Her head rose when Jasen opened the door. Coal-lump eyes regarded him blankly. She didn't make any move to follow though.

"She knows what is coming," said Huanatha quietly when they'd closed the door and moved on. "She senses it."

Jasen wondered how. He did not ask though. Some things in this world, he did not think he could understand.

"I hope Alixa is somewhere out of the way," Jasen murmured.

"She has kept to herself much of these past days," said Huanatha.

"How do you know?"

"I see her, here and there—we pass each other. She is very wrapped up in the things that cloud her mind. It is written, very clearly, upon her face."

"Do you know where she goes? I hardly see her."

Huanatha shook her head. "Somewhere else. I have not asked." At Jasen's furtive look, she added, "Do not worry. She will not be caught up in this."

Would she not? But what if Longwell was detected? He could not kill an entire ship by stealth. If he were caught, and things below the deck went south, and Alixa were nearby … as one of his wards, she would surely be punished, perhaps snatched up by the Prenasians and held captive until he stood down. Or worse, Longwell could become an example, the way Hamisi had—and Jasen and Alixa would both be examples with him.

He could die today. Both of them could. Perhaps all of them.

He was feeding it again.

It is happening now, he told himself again, as he and Huanatha clambered the steps leading topside. *It is too late to fear. All I can do is hope for the best.*

The sunlight streaked across the deck, painting long shadows beneath the masts.

No land in sight. Jasen was, quite suddenly, acutely aware of that fact. Because if this went wrong, if they were cast out into the waters, there was no one in the world to help them. Longwell, Huanatha, the *Lady Vizolans*, Jasen himself—they were alone and perilously outnumbered.

The *Lady Vizolans* were out already. Their chains spilled out around them, coiling like great steel snakes. There were a good couple of meters between each of the clasps around a man's ankle—enough to maneuver and to spread out. It gave them the space to work on the tasks the Prenasians foisted upon them: this morning, scrubbing the deck under the watchful eye of a brutish troll who held a cane. Even as Jasen strode past the line, the troll cracked it across Chaka's back with a noise like lightning cleaving the air.

Chaka yelped. The strike of the cane between his shoulder blades caused him to stumble, and the broom he had been holding clattered upon the deck.

He fell victim to the pain for only a moment—then he was scrabbling onto his knees, grabbing for the broom—

The troll grunted something in whatever language it spoke—if indeed if had the capacity for language at all—and cracked the cane across him again.

Chaka jolted. In that moment he seemed not just to arch his back but turn elastic, like the force of the whipcrack had caused all his bones to convert to fluid, the strike rippling across him like a wave.

"*Akh-huna! Ren akh-huna!*" he cried, snatching up his broom.

The cane cracked across him again, curving so far it was hardly believable that it did not snap. Chaka staggered, pulling the chains forward. Beside him, Kuura was yanked forward—

Beads of red liquid danced in the sunlight like a handful of tiny rubies thrown skyward.

"*AKH-HUNA!*" Chaka cried.

Rakon, upon the top deck, overseeing proceedings from where he'd spoken with Jasen this morning, chuckled. So did the small handful of Prenasians out here. Enjoying their morning's entertainment.

Jasen's blood ran hot.

Huanatha gritted her teeth as the cane cracked yet again. "Stop apologizing, you fool," she muttered. "It only fuels their cruelty."

Another crack.

Jasen's fists clenched. His jaw too.

Chaka stumbled again. Kuura was dragged—

Kuura whirled around. His teeth gritted and his fists tight around a broom of his own, which now he brought up between him and the troll, he was an impressive sight.

He brandished his broom at the troll. "*Un-de no Chaka! Taliss un-de!*"

Chaka began, holding up a hand to wave him off. "*Enh, Kuura—!*"

Then the troll grabbed the broom in Kuura's hands and shoved, so hard and fast that the rod slammed Kuura across the forehead.

He staggered backward.

The troll wrenched the broom from his grasp and flung it aside.

Before it had even hit the deck, the troll grabbed Kuura about the shoulder. He lifted him, in front of his face—he loosed a roar—and then he threw him.

The chains stopped him traveling far, but he slammed the deck, hard, on his back.

Jasen started forward—

Huanatha stopped him with a hand to the shoulder. "No."

"But Kuura—"

"You would be slaughtered." Shaking her head, lips pursed, she went on quietly, "Stay back. I will have words with Rakon. Let me defuse this. Do not move from here, do you hear? It will be over soon anyway." And across the deck she strode, past the *Lady Vizolans*, toward the upper deck where Rakon watched with undisguised relish.

"Ah, the former queen," he greeted as he caught sight of Huanatha passing the men of the *Lady Vizola*. "Come to watch this morning's theater, have you?"

She replied, though what she said, Jasen didn't hear. He was utterly, entirely focused on Kuura and the troll—the yellow-skinned beast was not letting up. Kuura had hardly risen from his near-back-breaking impact before the troll grabbed him up again, by the neck this time, then shoved him down, hard, face into the deck like a man might punish a misbehaving dog.

The troll rumbled something.

Kuura winced.

Chaka, alongside him, looked terrified. So did all of the men from the *Lady Vizola*. How much had they endured these past days already? Raking eyes across them, Jasen saw plenty of bruises, great welts running along their backs and across their shoulders where the cane had struck them. Burund had taken a lashing across the chest, two red, blistered streaks of skin forming an oozing cross on his sternum.

The troll was barking at Kuura, something Jasen couldn't understand. But Kuura seemed to, for he lifted his head, pushing back against the grotesquely large fist pressing down upon his shoulder blades, and retorted something through gritted teeth.

The troll sneered. He spat, a fat glob of phlegm that landed on the side of Kuura's face. It was disgustingly thick, more like half-solidified oil—and it had the same greasy, yellow-ish sheen, as it dripped down Kuura's cheek.

In Kuura's place, Jasen was sure he would have vomited there and then.

Kuura, though, recoiled, eyes wide, then the disgust set in, and then, hot off the back of it, rage. A fury like none other crossed his face, as he lay pinned there in the post-dawn sunlight, a vast troll holding him down, a gaggle of blue-skinned Prenasians looking on with amused interest.

Kuura bellowed a great roar. Shoving himself clear of the troll's fist, he rolled, chains clanking, out and onto his feet—

Jasen would never have thought the trolls, large as they were, could move very fast, but he had seen them mobilizing upon the rocky shoreline of Baraghosa's isle. They were swifter than they ought to have been, and this one was no exception. Before Kuura had even righted himself, the troll was turning, bringing the cane around to strike. It whipped through the air, cutting it with a whistle—

Kuura caught it with his hands. The cane bent into an arch.

Then Kuura snatched it totally free. It slid from the troll's fists—

Kuura bared his teeth. He brought the cane back, then swung—

The few Prenasians upon the deck were watching with greater curiosity now. Not one of them moved, even to step forward, let alone touch the hilts of the blades sheathed at their hips.

The cane streaked across the troll's forearm.

Kuura drew it back—

The troll's fist drove into his head.

Kuura reeled backward, pulling on the chains, dragging Chaka with him. Chaka cowered on the deck, eyes almost perfectly round. He scrambled clear as the troll, with no compunction for the feeble creatures at his feet, lumbered over him.

Kuura had hardly regained his footing when another meaty fist drove into him, this time from above. How the blow didn't cave his head in, Jasen didn't know.

Kuura took it—

Then he lashed out with the cane again, striking the troll's legs, low, barely above the ankle.

"Oho," chortled Rakon, drawing closer to the action upon his deck. "*Now* we have ourselves a show."

Huanatha was stoic beside him. Features tight, she caught eyes with Jasen.

He pleaded with her—*We need to stop this.*

A minute shake of the head, so small he could have barely discerned it if they were an arm's length apart, let alone across the war galley's top deck. But saw it he did.

But Longwell, he thought.

Huanatha could not answer, could not hear it. She must have thought it, though, because she shook her head again, even more clearly this time.

The message was clear: she could not act, and nor should Jasen. They must wait for however long it took for Longwell to complete his work inside the war galley.

But waiting did not appear to be an option. As Kuura slashed with the cane again, the troll dodged it. Then he swung out a kick—a low one, which for a man of regular height would sail across the bottom of Kuura's shins. The troll's kick came in across Kuura's knees though. He dropped, landing sideways—

There was a *crack*. For a second, Jasen believed the cane had finally snapped.

Then his brain untangled the fall. It had happened in a moment, but Kuura's arm had twisted at an impossible angle, and the *crack* had come just as it gave, the forearm buckling as the bones there snapped.

Kuura loosed an agonized, throaty howl.

The Prenasians cackled.

Rakon joined them. Whatever conversation he'd been having with Huanatha was forgotten. She stood in tight-lipped silence at his side. Jasen could have sworn her hand twitched over the place where Tanukke had once been.

If it were still there, how easy it would have been to unsheathe it and to bury it in Rakon's side now, while his attention was elsewhere. The stub of a blade would not penetrate far, but it would tear a hole in his gut, one not easily repaired. And should Huanatha drag it upward, opening a wider, more gaping crevasse of gore …

She could not, of course. No Tanukke to do it—and Longwell was still below.

Jasen urged him on. *Please*, he thought, *be swift.*

The troll was not done with Kuura. He snatched him up again, shaking him. The chains rattled, a chaotic wave running in either direction through them.

Kuura was drawn right up to the troll's face.

It leered into him with a yellow-toothed sneer. Jasen could practically smell its breath, fetid and hot, rotten, the way a scourge smelled in the heat of high afternoon.

He clenched his fists.

"*Vermin*," the troll growled.

Jasen was caught off guard at the word spoken in Luukessian—

Then Kuura spat a fat wad of phlegm into the troll's eyes.

"Payback, you son of a bitch," Kuura grunted back.

It was as though the scene came back in a reversed echo. For a moment, the troll was stupefied. Then his face twisted with disgust— and rage.

Kuura looked victorious—

And then the troll screamed, a cry like no sound Jasen had ever heard in his life, except for perhaps the mountain that loomed over Terreas when it finally split asunder and spilled its contents in a devastating rain.

The troll grasped the chain that dangled from Kuura's ankle cuff. Then it *pulled*—and the chain snapped clean off the cuff.

It threw them down and then strode past the *Lady Vizolans*, Kuura held in his fists, across the deck—

Jasen had a moment to begin thinking, *Where—?*

He realized the answer barely before that first word had formed.

The troll was taking him to the edge.

Like Hamisi before him, he would throw Kuura in.

Jasen's heart rate spiked. He stared in dawning horror.

His eyes found Huanatha.

She, too, watched. Her bottom jaw had fallen. It was the first time Jasen had seen her look shocked.

She didn't meet Jasen's eyes. He, like Rakon and the other Prenasians, and in fact everything aboard the ship except for the troll and Kuura—all of it was forgotten. Huanatha could only stare—and so Jasen had no answers, not the first clue of what to do—except his instinct.

He turned back to the troll and Kuura. They were almost at the deck's edge now. The troll seemed to be moving slow. It couldn't be, of course it could not—that was the adrenaline. Jasen was suddenly filled with it. It flooded his veins, coming in waves but not in them too, so it surged and rose but did not recede with each pulse. It filled him, moved him—

He was running.

Across the deck he moved, picking up speed.

The *Lady Vizolans* did not see him until he was past. Nor did the Prenasians—their focus was entirely on the troll and Kuura as they neared the edge of the boat.

Huanatha—she *did* see. She turned her head, and Jasen saw it, somehow, in the corner of his eye as he barreled forward, the lone white boy against an onyx-black deck, covered in men with skin almost as dark, tattooed blue men, and this grotesque, behemoth troll, the color of a filthy daisy—

"*PUT HIM DOWN!*" he bellowed.

The troll twisted.

Kuura came around with him, enclosed in two massive fists. Face bloody, greasy with the remnants of the troll's spit, his eyes widened in surprise at Jasen, tiny Jasen, hurtling toward them—

The troll dropped Kuura, who hit the deck, hard.

Then Jasen realized that the troll had the cane again.

He'd picked it up at some point during the fight and shoved it into the fabric around his waist. Now it came out in a blur—and how it would hurt, streaking across his chest, his face—

Jasen hadn't the time to think of it. He was carried by momentum, no time to arrest his sprint, or to dodge, as it blurred through the air toward him—

Kuura grasped the troll's leg and yanked.

The troll gasped. True shock registered on its face now. He stumbled, for Kuura had latched hold of his rear leg, supporting rather than fully bracing him as he swung for Jasen—and the cane snapped backward, missing Jasen by inches. He felt the whipping motion, felt the air streak past his face, heard it whine as it cut the air in two—

Then he leapt, hurtling forward with all the energy he could muster—

He hit the troll in the chest.

Its yellowed eyes widened.

Jasen seemed to hang there for a moment before rebounding. Face to face with the beast, he could see every awful thing about it—the way its skin was gnarled and thick, like animal hide. How yellow those teeth were. And how broad and sharp they were, narrowing to points designed for ripping through flesh and pulverizing bone.

He could feel its breath upon him, just as rancid and hot as he had imagined.

Then he rebounded—and the troll teetered, back, back, back—

Kuura pulled his leg hard, with both his good arm and the broken one—The troll's leg came out from under it. Now its arms were spinning, wheeling in the air as it tilted farther, over the section of the ship's side where no railing existed—

And then it fell beyond the edge of the ship with a splash like a rock dropped into a pool of water.

The next moment, too, seemed to last far longer than it could have. Shocked silence draped the deck like a smothering blanket. The *Lady Vizolans* stared. The Prenasians stared. Huanatha, too, stared, as did Rakon, whose mouth hung open.

Then—

The *Lady Vizolans* roared a battle cry. They rose, chains clanking about them.

The Prenasians pressed inward, drawing swords—

Huanatha rounded on Rakon, screaming her own battle cry as she grabbed for his sword before his hand could fly to it—

And the mutiny began.

13

The Prenasians drew swords and flung themselves at the *Lady Vizola's* men. They were outmatched four to one but far better positioned—they had swords, for one thing. For another, they were not clamped together with chains.

But the chains around their ankles were not enough to completely hobble the crew—and even if they had been, the men of the *Lady Vizola* had finally reached their breaking point. The Prenasians surged forward, swords drawn high, ready to cut the *Lady Vizolans* down, but the men who served Shipmaster Burund were furious and determined. They threw themselves into the battle, clutching at whatever was nearest, brooms, a pail of water—even the chains themselves, bunched into a heavy steel loop and clasped between wide hands, so they could be swung like a hammer.

The first of the Prenasians, one of the captains who'd come to the isle of Baraghosa, with inky black tattoos resembling the wings of a bird across his shaved temples, met them. He swept with his sword—

Jasen saw a streak of red as it found its target.

But where this *Lady Vizolan* fell, another took his place. Medleigh shrieked a war cry as he barreled forward, chain tight in his hands. He swung out with it, the steel python snaking through the air—

It slammed the Prenasian captain across the mouth.

The blow exploded both of his lips in a shower. His head was jerked backward—

His sword fell from his grasp.

The man he'd cut still had enough wits about him to snatch the sword up from where he lay. His side had been split open, a pool of deepest red rapidly spilling out around him—but he grabbed at the sword's hilt nevertheless, gripping it in fingers coated in his own blood—and he drove it into the Prenasian's leg, right behind his kneecap.

"*Dogs!*"

Rakon's cry cut over the chaos suddenly unfurling upon the deck. It had been—how many seconds now? A dozen? No more than that, surely, since the troll fell over the edge of the boat. Huanatha had grabbed at him, and though Jasen did not know what had happened in the moments since, he saw them now: Huanatha two arm-lengths away from Rakon, circling with him slowly. Her teeth were bared. Crouched low, she was ready to spring. He, like a bear, pivoted too.

His blade was in his hand, clasped so tightly that his knuckles were almost the same pale blue of Huanatha's armor.

"Aligning yourself with low-lives," Rakon growled. "You have fallen far, *queen*." He spat her former title. "I should have thrown you into the waters the moment we were on the sea—you and that bastard *Lord Longwell*. He is with you on this, is he not?"

"More than with me," Huanatha growled. "He is slitting the throats of your men below deck as we speak."

An enraged panic spread across Rakon's face. For a moment, he seemed uncertain of whether to fly at her—or do as he did, which was to turn to one of the Prenasians doing battle with the *Lady Vizolans* on the lower deck.

"*Santos! Dué—*"

Huanatha sprang at him.

Rakon slashed—

A roar from beside him twisted Jasen's neck.

Kuura was up on his feet. Cradling his broken arm close to his midriff, he grasped for Jasen by the shoulder. "Get away!"

"What was—?"

"The troll! His feet tangled in the nets!"

Jasen's eyes drew wide with panic. "Is he climbing?"

Kuura did not know. But his own panicked look was enough of an answer: if the troll hadn't gone into the sea, if it was still lashed to the war galley, it could, given time, clamber back aboard.

Against this small cluster of Prenasians, the men of the *Lady Vizola* stood a chance. But if the troll were to clamber back on board, or worse, if somehow the lower decks were to hear of the mutiny and come to help before Longwell had finished subduing them, the *Lady Vizolans* would quickly find themselves beaten.

Jasen shot a panicked look across the deck.

The first captain was down. Whether dead, or just out of action, Jasen could not be sure. There was a lot of blood, he was certain of that—but it was not all his. At least two of the *Lady Vizolans* were down too, bleeding heavily.

The other Prenasians were taking more careful steps. They hung back, out of reach, swiping with their swords at hands or brooms or pails or the single stolen sword, taken from that first Prenasian casualty. With the *Lady Vizolans* in shackles, they could keep their distance; the captured men had little agility, only brutish violence and thirst for vengeance to their advantage—besides, of course, their numbers.

One of the Prenasians had broken from the rest. Streaking past, he ran for the door leading into the ship.

"He's going to warn the others!" Jasen cried, pointing.

Kuura followed. Then he nodded. Releasing Jasen, he snatched up the cane and hurtled across the deck.

The Prenasian turned just in time to see a glimpse of Kuura, and no more, for the man leapt at him—and collided, sending the two of them tumbling in a blur of black and blue skin.

And then there was a jolt, just shy of Jasen's heel.

He turned—

The troll had clambered back up. Its ugly head reared over the side of the ship, one long arm stretching onto the deck. Its fingers were curved into claws and were gouging long canyons into the deck, sending onyx splinters flying, as it found its hold.

"*Boy!*" it growled.

Jasen shook his head. "Get off this ship!" And he stamped down hard, digging his heel into the troll's fist.

It rumbled a hiss, drawing its hand back—

Only it was not pulling back, as Jasen first thought—it was reaching for him. Its fingers wrapped about his ankle—and he was *pulled*, the world twisting sideways—

"*BOY!*"

"*GET OFF OF ME!*" Jasen roared back.

But it dragged him hard and fast. He yelped, the deck spinning, then his head slammed the gouges the troll had ripped in the deck. He saw stars—felt splinters—only those stars were actually white spots, and there were so many of the damned things, all clouding his vision like spores from mushrooms—

He grabbed wildly, raking with claws of his own—

They found something hot and wet. The troll gasped and let go.

The moment the pressure on his ankle left him, Jasen rolled free.

The hand swiped out for him again—he saw it coming, a streak of ugly yellow, but he threw himself clear of it.

Scrambling back to his feet, he had one single moment to assess what was happening on deck—Huanatha dodged a swing of the sword from Rakon, twisting her body at an angle that her armor could barely allow; Kuura and his Prenasian foe grappled for a sword sunk into the deck a few feet from them; and the *Lady Vizolans* were spreading around the Prenasians, using the chain binding them to herd the blue-skinned men into tighter and tighter quarters—

Then he was eye to eye with the troll again.

Eye to *one* eye. His fingers had dug into the troll's left eye. It was screwed up and bloody; deep crimson liquid glued his eyelids together.

Looking down at his hand, he saw that it was covered to the knuckles.

He took a moment to thank his ancestors that he hadn't seen it happen, then he steeled himself to push in again.

"*SCUM BOY,*" the troll roared. "*LOW, NOTHING BOY!*"

"I *said,*" Jasen began—"*get off this ship!*" And he surged forward, swinging a boot—right into the troll's flat, swollen nose.

It roared back, swing blindly for him.

Jasen ducked and rolled clear this time, then he was back up on his feet.

But he was tiring—tiring so quickly. His breaths came hard and fast. Damn, he hadn't even exerted himself that much.

One dying boy.

Baraghosa's words came back to him, but he locked them out. However close he was to the veil between this world and the next, however exhausted he felt as that skulking darkness came closer and closer, he had to fight here and now. He could not let this troll back onto the deck, onto the ship. It would be the death of all of them.

Steeling himself, he surged in again, ducking another fist. The second came down, the cane streaking with it—

Jasen grabbed for it.

It struck him across both palms—and it was more painful than he could have imagined. One instant he had his hands open, fingers splayed; the next he hissed as white hot pain erupted, jolting through his arms, so strong that it blocked out everything else. All he knew, for long seconds, was the screaming agony that had once been his hands, a huge cloud of pain that stretched outside of him, so he could not free himself from it.

It hurt—oh, it *hurt.*

He needed the cane, though. It was his only weapon.

So when the troll drew back, prepared to swing again, Jasen gritted his teeth, and prepared himself for it.

THWAP!

There was no preparing himself for it, none at all. The pain drew to a crescendo as the cane came down between his fingers again—

But he grasped it, tight, like a wrench around a nut—

And he stumbled backward. Trusting his muscles to do what they needed to—they didn't seem to be responding at all, in truth—he pulled away from the troll, hoping that, though its grip was undoubtedly stronger than his own, he had caught it off guard—

And he had. The cane came free, brushing past gnarled, thick skin, the only true resistance—

The troll's eyes—its *eye*—grew wide. It groped for him—

He was already clear. Grimacing at it—damn, this *pain*, it was like he'd been slapped with the sun itself—he grasped the cane tight, bent it into the shape of an arch—

It snapped into two jagged points.

Jasen gripped either end—his improvised spears, probably two feet long each—in one hand.

"I'll say it one more time," he wheezed. "Get off of this boat."

"*VERMIN BOY!*"

Jasen gritted his teeth. "Have it your way, then."

He flung himself at it.

The troll grabbed for him, but

Jasen ducked. He dodged. He weaved, sidestepping every blind thrust of an arm, a fist—

He shoved into a blind spot.

The troll glared at him with its one good eye—for a second. Then Jasen plunged the spear into it, hard.

The troll roared—not a boom of rage, but its own agonized cry, belted from a haggard throat. Jasen was entirely forgotten as it grasped for the spear, now buried a good four inches into its face—

Jasen dodged backward, releasing it.

No longer holding itself onto the deck, now both of its hands were occupied, the troll tilted backward again.

Jasen took his chance. Sprinting to close the short distance again, he leapt, sailing a hard kick straight into the troll's chin—

"*ARGH!*" it boomed—and over it went, backward, a flurry of mad limbs.

Still connected to the netting by its feet, it fell backward in an arc. It slammed into the side of the war galley, and its head and shoulders landed in the water with a deep *splosh*.

It pulled itself out though, the muscles of its stomach tightening.

Damn this.

Jasen took a second to peer around. The *Lady Vizolans*—Kosi was down too now, lying sprawled against one of the masts, his head twisted in the wrong direction and a crimson slit running from his throat down to his navel. Not far distant from him was a Prenasian man—and the angle of his head was wrong too. A pool of blood spread from under him, one glazed eye looking across it like a man across the sea.

They'd managed to find a key, the *Lady Vizolans*. From one of the downed Prenasians, Jasen assumed—maybe that first captain. A handful of them were free, Medleigh among them. They wielded swords, striking out at the three Prenasians who were left.

The fourth was still engaged with Kuura. He loomed over the *Lady Vizola*n man with the sword poised at his neck—Jasen felt a bolt of renewed panic—but then Kuura rolled, the sword missed him, and he swung out both of his legs, striking his adversary about the knees. The Prenasian yelped—then he was not just tipped but *thrown* sideways, the sword flying loose—

Huanatha pressed against the rail enclosing the upper deck. Rakon had his sword pointed at her throat. He was speaking—and his teeth were bloodied. She'd got a good hit in, maybe.

She swung out a foot. Tall and long-legged as she was, it was long enough to shoot straight into Rakon's balls.

He half crumpled, half staggered forward, stabbing out with the sword—

Huanatha ducked it, kicking it out of his grip. It spun in the air, landing farther up the deck—

They scrambled for it, both of them.

Jasen turned back. Everyone was engaged, everyone occupied. And still no sign of Longwell—though he must surely be finished soon; killing all the men on this boat could not take so long, could it? But of course it could—there were dozens of them, probably over a hundred. And this battle upon the deck had not taken very long yet. It was still early into the mutiny, above and below deck.

So Jasen was on his own against this troll.

Well, fight it alone he would.

Stepping to the edge of the boat, he clambered down into the nets, his one remaining spear held tight.

The troll glared up at him—or at least it would have if it had any eyes left to do it with. The spear embedded in the bloody crater that was its right eye was gone, perhaps fallen into the water. The troll, at least, did not grasp it.

It must have felt Jasen upon the nets, the way a spider does when a fly entangles itself within its web, for it aimed its head right in Jasen's direction.

It said something in a low rumble. Must be speaking in its own language, whatever that was—Prenasian, Jasen assumed. Perhaps it was not as dumb a creature as it looked.

It was about to be a dead creature, though.

Jasen staggered down the netting. It was a sheer drop, perfectly vertical—although if he did fall, he would land atop the troll, he supposed.

He did not intend to drop.

He descended lower.

The troll rumbled. It was flailing about, trying to right itself. Its hands groped for the netting, so that it could lever itself back up.

Jasen wouldn't permit it.

He got to within striking distance of the feet. Both were trapped in the same stretch of net. How, Jasen could not imagine. But they were a tangle about the troll's ankles.

Holding himself in place with one hand, he brought the cane down amongst the tangle.

The troll jerked as the sharp end dug against its skin. *"BOY!"*

"I told you to get off this ship!" Jasen said through gritted teeth, sawing at the knotted netting with the cane's jagged tip.

The troll lifted its great hands, levering itself up by its midriff, its abdominal muscles tensing. It swung for Jasen, who ducked, then another fist blindly groped for him. It closed around the netting just a few inches from Jasen's shoulder. Not finding him, its fingers probed, grasping—

Jasen paused his sawing and stabbed the troll in the palm, driving the pointed tip of the cane hard into the softer flesh there.

The troll howled and pulled back its hand. The spasm of pain caused its whole body to swing backward again, slamming the side of the ship. Its head and shoulders again splashed into the water.

Jasen tightened his hold on the net and began to saw again.

But it was not going well. The ropes were thick. The cane's jagged tip had worn a small groove—or rather Jasen thought it had. Looking at it again now, trying to find his place, he realized he hadn't made the slightest dent. And with a great knot to cut loose, the cane would blunt long before even slicing through the first rope, let alone the full tangle.

The troll rose again, roaring, spitting water from its mouth and nose. Its face was bloody, a smear around each of its ruined eyes. But a blind troll was still a troll, one more than capable of wrecking the

Lady Vizolans—however many of them remained; Jasen was far below the deck, and with the mad bucking of the troll he could not very well hear what was going on above.

He craned his neck up to look at it, and his eyes grew wide.

The net was affixed to the side of the ship by metal rings, looped around them in knots.

He could climb back up and loose the entire thing.

A desperate look down at the troll—it was righting itself again, raising its body in a mammoth sit-up, its sharp yellowed teeth bared, fingers spread out like claws.

Jasen stabbed with the cane, sinking it into the webbing between two fingers.

The troll roared again, but its momentum was not arrested. The hand swung for him, homing in—

Jasen yelped as it smashed into the war galley's hull just above his head. A quaking vibration rocked through him, threatening to dislodge his hold.

The troll's fingers probed again. It mashed its hand back and forth, blindly grabbing everywhere it could reach to try to find him.

Jasen rolled clear of the fist, grabbing for a hold of his own as he dodged.

A hand came down at him again, and he jabbed up again with the cane, putting as much force as he could muster into the strike.

It sank deep into the troll's palm, a good couple of inches, the sound it made tightening Jasen's stomach—even more when the troll pulled back roaring, and Jasen saw the cane had gone right through, the tip of it pointing out of the back of the troll's hand, just below the knuckle of its middle finger.

It reeled back, and Jasen took his chance. Practically throwing himself up the netting, he climbed up the ten or so feet to the top, where the metal rings hung.

There were eight of them in all, spread across a span of maybe a dozen feet. The net hung down between two of the angry faces, leering out from the galley's hull.

Jasen cursed the pure dumb luck that the troll had gone over here, of all places, where it could get tangled, and he got to work.

The first two knots came undone easily. The third was stiff. His fingers strained against it—but—*there!* It loosened, and he pulled the rope free before moving over to the next.

But the troll, of course, was still below. It knew that something was happening. The boy who'd stabbed him was gone now, he could tell even without groping. But the net was also dropping. As the fourth loop came undone, the net flapped, sinking the troll deeper, so that its chest right down to its nipple was submerged.

It rose up again, fighting, spewing water mingled with greenish blood from between its lips. *"BO-O-OY!!"* it bellowed.

It grasped for the nets—but this time, instead of groping for Jasen, it found itself a hold. And now it began to pull itself up, lifting its upper body past its tangled legs.

Jasen stared for one single alarmed moment. Then he yanked at the fifth knot, pulling it apart—then across, to the sixth—

The net jerked down. Now held by only two rings at one corner, it sagged, much of it hanging in the ocean. The troll was becoming more tangled as the free netting coiled and wrapped about it,

but it fought on, blind and determined, teeth gritted, climbing fist over fist, closer—

The seventh—

Jasen yelled as the net dropped. Now he hung on it too, a couple of feet from the single ring holding it to the side of the boat. Held on by a corner only, it hung down in overlapping folds. There were so many handholds, all one atop the other, the footholds just the same—

The troll rumbled, *"KILL YOU, BOY?"*

And it would. It was just a few feet below him now. If not for the net wrapping about it, entangling it, the troll would be upon Jasen already. He had only seconds.

Scrambling for holds, he found a twisted purchase and climbed to the last ring. He pulled—

The weight of the troll, and the entire net, had pulled the knot too tight, though, dragging it down against the war galley's hull. Jasen prised, with desperate fingers from below—but it wouldn't yield.

He forced himself up, past it, onto the deck—

A momentary glance to see that the Prenasian was down and Kuura victorious, but the other Prenasians were still fighting, and Rakon and Huanatha were engaged in battle with their fists now upon the smaller deck to the fore of the boat—then Jasen pivoted, looking down into the angry face of the troll, wrapped in black netting, but climbing.

"BO-O-OY!!"

Jasen pulled at the last knot desperately.

Too—damned—tight—

The troll lifted itself higher still. Almost within reach now—and in just another two great lifts like that, it would be back upon the deck—it would overpower them by sheer force and might, even tangled and blind as it was—

Jasen found the place where the knot turned in on itself. In one desperate last attempt, he plunged the cane into the tight crevice, using its pointed tip to force the binding to loosen it.

The troll slammed another fist down, rattling Jasen's bones. It was barely a foot under that last ring now.

Nearly out of time.

He shoved the cane with all his might, so it was through at its widest, then he grasped at the rope, pulling hard—

The knot gave.

Jasen recalled what Longwell had said to him—that killing would blacken his soul. He would be tainted by it for as long as he lived—and beyond.

So be it, he thought, and he released the net.

The troll fell, net and all, in a wild tangle that finally pinned its arms as tightly as its legs. It landed in the water, sinking like a rock, until the deep ocean blue had swallowed all traces of its rough yellow skin.

Jasen breathed. His vision was spotty, he realized now, absolutely covered by the white patches, like the fine, snow-white ash that had fallen from his house in Terreas when it burned. He blinked against them fiercely, sucking in steadying breaths. He could collapse now—and he would, he was certain; all the energy ran out of him, leaving him shaking. He'd held himself up on his hands, but now his arms gave out. The world turned over-bright, washed out.

He pulled himself away from the edge, lest he go into the sea after the troll he'd worked so hard to dispatch. Then he closed his eyes, head between his knees, focusing on each breath as they came, in and out, in and out. The pendant around his neck pressed to him, and he gripped for it, slipping it out of his tunic into a sweaty, aching hand.

Breathe. Just breathe.

Then a hand was upon his shoulder.

He jolted up—the battle!

But it was Kuura. Bloodied and exhausted, covered in welts from the troll's cane, and his broken arm held carefully to his midsection, he looked at Jasen with a grim kindness.

"It is over," he breathed. "We have won." He, too, was out of breath, and he pulled it into his lungs with a rattle. "Thank you."

Jasen nodded. He hadn't the air for words. Just the shock of Kuura's touch, the fear that he'd have to thrust himself into a battle anew, had taken it out of him even more than ever. So he rocked back on his heels and took in the picture that was the war galley's deck.

It was not a pretty one. All but two of the Prenasian men were dead. At least five of the *Lady Vizola*'s crewmates had gone with them. Jasen felt a pained spike at that—and then a guilty one as relief came over him when he saw that Burund was among the survivors. He was tending to Medleigh, who bowed below a mast, blood running down his face. His bottom eyelid had split, by the look of it. If it was the worst he had suffered, he had gotten off lightly.

The two Prenasians left alive were a slight, rat-faced man who now found himself bound in chains and cuffed to the mainmast—and Rakon. Huanatha had finally overcome him, although not without plenty of cuts and bruises of her own. Now she stood over him, his sword in her hand, pointed right between his eyes. She did not thrust at him with it though, just stood poised—an act of courtesy in return for the favor shown to her, Jasen supposed.

Were it him who stood over Rakon with his sword, though …

Just then, the door to the deck below was kicked open.

It splintered and cracked as though one of Baraghosa's own bolts of colored lightning had struck in the middle of the deck, the door slamming against the wood in an aftershock of thunder. Jasen felt a quiver of fear run through him, tensing at the sound.

Jasen turned, the *Lady Vizolans* too, to see. They tensed, grabbing for their stolen swords or their improvised weapons, ready to do battle again with another wave of Prenasians.

But it was Longwell who stepped out, spear in hand, armor drenched in red. Only a step behind, walking slowly, her dress damp with stains at one of the sleeves, came Alixa.

Jasen's heart leapt. Thank the ancestors, she was safe.

Bloodied, practically soaked in it, Longwell glistened in the early morning sunlight. Tri-point spear in hand, he tramped across the deck. Bloody footprints followed him behind.

His expression was grim … and perfect silence greeted him.

Burund stepped out to meet him.

"Shipmaster," Longwell finally said, reaching him. "This vessel is yours."

14

The *Lady Vizola II*, a much more poetic name than *Prenasian War Galley 324*, was en route to a port at Nonthen. The plan there, said Shipmaster Burund, was to release the Prenasian captives into the port city to be about their lives. Jasen was not sure how to feel about that; it was certainly more merciful than anything the Prenasians had intended for the crew of the *Lady Vizola*.

After that, their course was undecided.

It was five days after the bloody battle that had wrestled the boat from the Prenasians, and Shipmaster Burund held court on the war galley's command deck, the sun shining overhead and the breezes pleasant as they ruffled the sails. He was joined by Kuura, Longwell, Huanatha, Jasen, and Alixa. They discussed their course aboard the top deck, looking out at a late morning ocean, bobbing gently with waves. No sign of land masses out there yet—but they'd appear before long. Jasen wondered whether it would be as majestic as the Aiger Cliffs.

But it didn't matter. Whatever happened next, Jasen already knew he would not remain long at Nonthen.

He hoped that Longwell still felt the same. It had been over a week since their conversation on the shores of the isle of Baraghosa. That was plenty of time for him to have changed his mind.

"We must discuss our next course," said Burund. He spoke in the slow, measured way he always did—as though the course of events five days prior had not changed him in the slightest. And perhaps it had not. Jasen did not know what Burund had seen during his many seafaring years before this. Violence might be something with which the shipmaster was intimately familiar.

If that were the case, would Jasen think less of him?

No, he decided, for the same reason that he could not think less of himself for sending the troll overboard. The beast never had emerged from the seas again, and Jasen felt himself curiously empty at the thought.

Some things were necessary, and Burund was an honorable man. If he had killed before setting foot upon this war galley, it would surely have been only if it were absolutely necessary—to save his own skin, or the lives of his men, for instance. Not for proving a point, the way these Prenasians and their trolls had.

"It will come as no surprise to you," said Longwell, standing proud and clutching his lance, "that I petition you to allow us to track Baraghosa, that we may do battle with him once more."

Alixa snorted. Arms folded tight across her chest, she made a great point of looking away from Jasen, Longwell and Huanatha.

After the mutiny, Alixa had quietly disappeared and found a cabin of her own. She'd relocated with Scourgey, and as a result, Jasen had hardly seen them. He'd gone looking for her, but she seemed determined to avoid him and made haste in escaping him on the rare occasions where they did run into one another.

Burund sighed and rubbed a bruised hand across his jaw. "You are correct. This does not surprise me."

"The sorcerer must be eradicated," Huanatha said. "He is a threat to all men."

Another snort from Alixa. She shook her head. "You are obsessed, the lot of you."

Huanatha rounded on Alixa, but it was Longwell who stepped in to answer her. "Baraghosa is a vile serpent of a man, a monstrosity made flesh, who sows dissent everywhere that he treads. He must be stopped—"

"And the three of you must be the ones to stop him," said Alixa. "Of all the souls in all the world, it must be my loon of a cousin, a high-strung former queen, and a clanking suit of armor to do it."

Huanatha looked furious, but

Longwell took her insult with better grace. "There are others who feel as we do."

Burund looked at them from under hooded eyes. "You have faced this Baraghosa twice already. Failure has been the end result both times. Why would you consider pursuing him again?"

"It's folly," Alixa added.

Huanatha opened her mouth, but Longwell stilled her with a touch.

"Baraghosa is—" he began, but Alixa cut him off.

"A serpent," Alixa repeated. "I know. He came to my village and took children from us year after year. He took them away to die. He left families broken. But he is stronger than us. I have thrown myself into this battle, and I understand your desire to go after him. Yet it is madness, and it has gone on long enough." She turned to Burund. "I will not be following these people to their deaths. I request instead that you help me find passage to Emerald Fields, so I may reunite with my countrymen, my brothers and sisters of Luukessia."

"Your brothers are dead," said Jasen, words coming unbidden and sudden, and very hot.

"And Baraghosa had nothing to do with it," Alixa said, with a surprising calm. "Baraghosa said as much—the mountain was not his doing. I have no score to settle with him." She turned again to Burund: "I am not a part of this deranged quest any longer. Nor should you be."

Kuura, whose broken arm hung in a cloth sling around his neck, nodded. Thus far he'd been quiet, watching from the sidelines. Now he made his voice heard. "I am in agreement with Alixa."

Huanatha gasped. "Kuura—!"

"I'm sorry," he said, and he really did look it, though maybe it was partly out of fear that she would turn her fury upon him too. "I have fought alongside you—an honor—but I am not as young as I used to be. This fight is above me … and it is not mine." Looking sheepish, he went on: "I was dragged into this as I was looking out for the well-being of these young Luukessians. If you go after Baraghosa again …" He looked pointedly at Jasen and shrugged, "… there is no aid I can give that will make you safe."

Huanatha snarled. "You coward. All this time, I thought you a man of honor, with the spirit of a warrior, and it was all deception."

Kuura held up his hand, the one not hanging limp at the end of a sling. "I did not mean to deceive—"

But Huanatha would have none of it. Striding for him, she jabbed at him with a finger. "You think this battle is not yours? So you have heard nothing of Trattorias, the king of Muratam? The one Baraghosa replaced me with upon the throne?"

Kuura's eyebrows knitted. "Yes, but—"

"Muratam now rains war down on its former allies, sends foot soldiers into their lands, even as we speak. It cuts the heads from the leaders of villages, kills the men who would threaten to usurp them, and makes slaves of the people who they conquer. All of this is sown in Trattorias's name—and who brought him to power? *Baraghosa.*" She said it with such utter contempt, such pure hatred, that her accent grew thick and the 'r' and 's' in the sorcerer's name curled richly. "*He* is the cause of this bloodshed—bloodshed that may one day destroy your own people, Kuura of Nunahk. Your land is not so far from my own. Think of it—your own family, your own children, their heads cleaved from their shoulders, your wife held down by soldiers as they—"

"This is quite enough," said Burund. He did not raise his voice, but there was a firmness to his words, the way he issued commands, that cut over Huanatha and stopped her before she could say anymore.

Kuura's lips were pressed together in a thin line.

"Baraghosa creates chaos wherever he travels," said Longwell, his words quieter and more measured than Huanatha's. "He causes harm to all who he comes across, at least all who cannot further his own goals, anyway, whatever they may be."

"Surely you know this," Huanatha said to Alixa.

"I do," she answered. "He came to our village every year, trading seed for a child. And now there are only two children from Terreas left." She looked pointedly at Jasen. "So why should we sacrifice ourselves, if that is what it takes, when we are all that remain?"

"Because it is *right*," said Huanatha.

"He has not killed us, even though we challenged him," she said. "He has shown some degree of mercy, for all his misdeeds."

"But you have shown no great threat to him thus far," said Burund thoughtfully.

Alixa's face twitched. "Regardless," she said, "it would be lunacy to squander our lives now, when he has at least made efforts to spare us."

"You think he has made efforts to spare us?" Huanatha asked. "To spare *you*?" She bared her teeth like a wolf. "You forget how close he came to sinking a knife into your belly? To goring you there in front of all of us? Do you forget the feel of the blade pressing into your skin, a millimeter away from cutting you open and spilling your lifeblood until your veins ran dry? *Do you forget?*"

Alixa, like Kuura before her, had paled. She swallowed, and Jasen could almost see, in her eyes, her mind replaying those awful moments there in Baraghosa's tower, where by his magic he had held her aloft, like a puppet ... and that blade, glinting and sharp, sailing toward her, gripped by an invisible hand ...

"I remember vividly," she said quietly. "And it is not an experience I wish to repeat—or to goad Baraghosa into repeating. I will not be going with you."

Huanatha opened her mouth to argue.

"My word is final," said Alixa, cutting her off before she could begin. "I will not be moved on this. I have seen enough violence, enough death, for this lifetime."

Burund nodded. "I have heard your thoughts—all of you, very clearly. Now I must weigh them."

"Wait," said Longwell. "Before you do … Alixa, I understand you do not wish to reconsider—but Shipmaster, Kuura, perhaps I can convince you."

The dragoon's eyes narrowed. "I was Lord Protector of a city called Reikonos. Perhaps some of you have heard of it. I have shepherded that place for many years—from the scourge, when they came upon our shores—" he glanced at Scourgey here, tucked as she was behind Alixa, her head rising as Longwell spoke, listening, "—and from other threats, both internal and external.

"In facing these threats, we were united. But when Baraghosa came …" Longwell's lips pressed into a thin line as the memory came back over him. "He sowed division, and from it began an insurrection, my own people turning against me, all for the purposes of placing his own pawns in command of the city. Men I had fought alongside, men I had dedicated so many years to protecting, to guiding, they rose up and forced me from my post—because of him.

"It is a familiar story. And it will be the same the world over. Wherever Baraghosa goes, he does this again and again, finding the weak spots of those who stand in his way and exploiting them. He is one man, and one man alone, and yet he is capable of so much … Much that we know … and much that is beyond our comprehension."

A flash of the storms Baraghosa had caused flickered across Jasen's mind's eye—the strobing, unnatural colors of lightning, the way the ocean swelled into blisters where it struck, then sloughed off into great waves …

That he could do even worse than this, Jasen had no doubt.

"It happened to Huanatha, just as it happened to me," Longwell went on, "and so it has happened to many more, and will happen to even more still. It is happening even as we speak, I am certain. He lived in my city for decades before he pressed his scrawny fingers into the cracks and split them wider, first advising us …"

"Where does he come from?" Jasen suddenly asked. It had been eight full days now since Longwell had promised him this answer.

Longwell's lips thinned. "He comes from a place called Saekaj Sovar." A hesitation. His tongue ran across the very tip of his top lip momentarily—considering just how much to say, perhaps, or how to say it.

"When not covered in spellcraft and illusion," he went on, "he does not look so dissimilar from these Prenasians, really. His father is descended from their stock, originally—the ancient, Arkarian variation, at least."

Another hesitation. This one was longer. His features tightened.

"His father was one of the gods of Arkaria. His name was Yartraak. Baraghosa is a bastard of his, one of the last alive. He is learned in spellcraft and possessed of strength not normally found on our continent, and he is a keen fighter. He helped keep Reikonos free during the coming of the scourge … and he helped nearly destroy us when his purpose turned. His machinations left people dead, left my honor amongst my own citizens compromised. So I left to pursue him, giving my advisors charge in my absence." His knuckles turned white as he tightened his hold upon his lance. "I will not return until I have settled this score with him."

Baraghosa, bastard child of a god—so that was the cause of Longwell's hesitation. He was not weighing up what Jasen should know; rather, he weighed up just what he should tell Burund, lest the knowledge sway him from Baraghosa's pursuit.

Whether Burund was influence by this last bit of information or whether his mind was already made up, Jasen would never know.

"You can, perhaps, find a ship in Nonthen that will carry you on this errand," he said. "Both of you, if you wish it," he added, looking to Huanatha—and then, turning his gaze upon Jasen: "Or all three of you, should you desire to pursue this foolishness to its conclusion."

Foolishness. The word stung even more at the victorious look that passed over Alixa's face as Burund said it.

But Jasen pushed it aside. This was not the time to feel hurt. The shipmaster had made his decision, and Jasen would respect it. Burund had done much for him, after all, far more than Jasen had had any right to wish for. It was not right to keep dragging him, or the men of the *Lady Vizola*, into danger when they did not wish to follow.

"You will not take us," said Longwell—not a question, but a statement.

Burund looked out over his men, working furiously upon the deck to maintain control of a vessel that required so many more to man it.

"I can only see what these brushes have brought me close to; what they have cost me." Pain flickered in his eyes—after these long weeks, he was tiring. "My responsibilities are elsewhere. So no, I will not take you. I will take the wiser course …" He looked to Alixa. "And stay away from Baraghosa."

15

If Alixa had been scarce after their arrival aboard the war galley, she vanished entirely after Burund's decision was made. Jasen did not see her at mealtimes, not in the mornings or evenings. He asked Longwell, Huanatha, and Kuura if they saw her. None had, and none had time to walk Jasen through the bowels of a ship that still confounded all sense of direction to search for her room by room.

He wondered if perhaps Scourgey—no, *Niamh*, the name was so difficult to keep in his head—he wondered if she could sniff Alixa out, like a dog.

Or perhaps she knew where Alixa was already, in that strange, mystical way of hers that Huanatha could tap into. Alas, it was foreign to him, and Huanatha was distracted. She had sharpened what was left of Tanukke's shattered blade and practiced with it from dawn to dusk, swinging and stabbing, learning the weight of her new-old weapon. Why she did not trade it in for something more complete Jasen could not fathom, for there was a well-stocked armory available to her.

He joined too, him and Huanatha and Longwell upon the deck below the mizzenmast. Huanatha and Longwell blurred as they moved. Jasen, by comparison, was clumsy. The lessons he'd learned upon the *Lady Vizola* had mostly deserted him. Perhaps it was the way his brains had been rattled when he swam out to rescue Hamisi. Maybe it was connected to those white spots that kept clouding his vision, and the fog that had begun to precede them these past few days. He knew what that augured, and that most likely, both things were connected.

He tried not to think of it. That would only open other questions—like how long he had left. That he was declining was unquestionable, but at what rate, he could not be sure.

Scourgey might know, could perhaps smell it on him. And so Huanatha could too.

He wouldn't ask. Better not to know. He needed only live long enough to see Baraghosa faced justice. After that ...

Well, nothing else would matter, would it?

*

Jasen awoke just before dawn on the morning of their announced arrival at Nonthen, his head light and a sick feeling in his stomach. It seemed to always be with him in the mornings when he awoke, along with that weak feeling that lingered throughout the day. He struggled upright, ignoring the lightheadedness. It would pass. It had to.

It would be mid-morning when the *Lady Vizola II* pulled into port, so said Kuura the day before, perhaps a little earlier or later depending upon how the ocean currents and the wind carried them.

Scourgey—for crying out loud, *Niamh!*—lay at the foot of the bed. Although he did not recall it, going by the tangle that was the bedcovers, he'd not slept particularly well. The only part that remained in place was the oblong Scourgey occupied.

She raised her head to peer at him through the dim light from the lantern. It was burned down almost to a nub. Jasen didn't especially like to keep it lit—the war galley was, after all, a glorified wooden box, and therefore flammable—but without a window in these quarters for the pre-dawn light to come in, better the slim risk of a lantern on very low than tripping in his sheets and knocking himself out on the bedframe.

He patted Scourgey's head idly, using the heel of his free palm to wipe the sleep out of his eyes.

Oh. That was—damn it, another white spot. But no headache this time.

He blinked at it, Scourgey forgotten.

It didn't disappear. But it did seem to dislodge, after maybe seven or eight hard blinks, slipping down his vision like a mote of dust falling in a sunbeam.

It lowered to the bottom fourth of his vision, to one side ... and then it stayed there.

He shook his head. Damn it.

Well, they were drawing in to Nonthen today. He, Longwell and Huanatha could be in pursuit of Baraghosa before midday.

"You coming?" he asked Scourgey as he stepped from the bed.

Her answer was to lower her head. She'd not gone far at all the past week and a half, restricting herself almost entirely to this room, with only the occasional foray up to the deck with Alixa or himself. In the end, Jasen had needed to bring water and food to her, she was so unwilling to move for it. Today was apparently going to be the same again.

"I'll get you breakfast," he said. "Back soon."

He left the room.

On the *Lady Vizola*, breakfast for the scourge had been scraps of meat from the mess, which she'd eaten happily. Now that Jasen knew that she had once been a person, though, he made an effort to fetch finer things for her. Of course, on this vessel, "finer things" still amounted to cured meats and dry crackers, although the Prenasians also travelled with barrels of oranges and limes and an overly sweet pink fruit with barbed points across its skin.

Jasen stepped into the mess hall and made for the serving station at its far end.

Like the rest of the war galley, the mess hall was a utilitarian affair. A vast oblong, it was split into rows by tables with benches, bolted to the floor. A handful of windows provided light, streaking in faint bars across the onyx wood. This time of morning, it was dim, very dim. And empty.

Jasen meandered across the hall to the serving station. He stepped around it, thinking still of Scourgey, how unpleasant it must be to go from being a human to being an animal, subsisting off scraps and entrails. Which of those was worse, he wasn't entirely sure.

Nor did he get to make a decision, for as he rounded the serving station, he saw, bent low over a barrel, head and shoulders fully inside of it—

"Alixa!"

She straightened so fast he almost thought he heard her spine crack like a whip.

Accusing eyes stared at him.

The oranges she'd been retrieving bounced out of her hands and rolled away.

"Jasen," she said after a moment's panicked look.

He stooped to pick up one of the oranges. It had gone a bit soft here at sea—no telling how long it had been in the barrel for—and the fall had split the skin. Juice, sticky and sweet, had leaked out and left a trail on the floor where it rolled. It coated his fingers.

"Now I know why you're never around at mealtimes," he said.

Alixa snatched it off of him. "I don't want to eat with you."

She made to pass him—

Jasen wheeled about, following quickly behind. "Wait!"

"No."

"Alixa!" he called—she was marching down the central aisle, an orange in each hand. An unevenly broken wedge of hardtack stuck out of one pocket, wrapped in a thin square of fabric.

"I don't want to talk with you either," she said, without looking back.

"Why not?" For goodness' sake, she was being so—"*Why not?*" Jasen repeated, catching up to her. "I'm your cousin, for crying out loud."

She snorted sarcastic laughter.

"What is so *funny*?" Jasen demanded, getting right in front of her.

She stopped, but only long enough to give him a dark look. Then she sidestepped and was past again.

"What's *funny*," she answered, not looking back, "is that you think that I owe you some sort of duty by being your cousin, when you yourself don't show the same duty to me—or any of our ancestors."

"I *do* show my duty to them," Jasen said. "I've been searching for Baraghosa for over a month now."

"And in that time you have learned that he had nothing to do with the fall of Terreas," Alixa said, "but you still want to pursue him. Is that duty? Not to our families, it's not."

Jasen's lips thinned. He couldn't help himself from clenching his fists. Damned Alixa—when had she started to frustrate him like this?

"Baraghosa is evil," he said.

Alixa whirled. Jabbing him in the chest with a finger, she said, "Admit it. You know Baraghosa did not destroy Terreas. Go on, admit you're just being bullheaded and stubborn."

"He did not destroy Terreas," Jasen said.

"Hah!" And she spun on her heel and marched away.

For someone so small, she could certainly move when she wanted to. Jasen hurried to catch up. "Just because he did not destroy Terreas does not mean he is innocent of sin. Or absent malice."

"So let Longwell and Huanatha deal with it," Alixa said. "Ancestors know they're foolish enough."

Jasen caught himself before he could retort. Longwell and Huanatha, foolish? They were the least foolish people Jasen had ever met. Perhaps there was a touch of arrogance to Longwell. And Huanatha certainly had an abrasive streak to her.

But foolish? Absolutely not. No, they knew what was right. They knew their *duty*, a duty to an entire world Baraghosa threatened.

"Baraghosa must be stopped," said Jasen.

"By men," Alixa answered, "not a boy." She laid her own venom into that last word—*boy*—and combined with the sidelong glance she shot him, it stung, enough that Jasen was close, again, to losing his temper with her.

Somehow, though it took muscles he didn't know he had to do it, he kept himself in check.

"You agreed with me," he said, "before our last battle. You said it yourself, you agreed that we should stop him."

"When you're surrounded by imbeciles for long enough, you start to think like them."

He gritted his teeth, but instead of speaking, he let himself think for a moment. There had to be some other way to make Alixa understand why this was so important, why he had to do it—and why she should too. Because, no, Terreas had not been Baraghosa's doing ... but Baraghosa had meddled in it for decades, disrupting lives—

"You say I have no duty to my village," Jasen said, "but what about Pityr? He was our friend. Baraghosa took him—took him to die."

Alixa flinched at the mention of Pityr's name. When he had been taken, it was like a part of Terreas had died, at least for them. Some of the joy had left it, never to return.

That was Baraghosa's doing. And Alixa had surely felt it, as deeply as Jasen. It was, after all, what drove them together—a bond forged in sadness.

"There are more Luukessians than Pityr," she said. "I have a duty to all of them."

Jasen shook his head. "I cannot believe you'd say that."

"And I cannot believe everything that comes from your mouth these days."

"Pityr would want him stopped."

Alixa spun. Her nostrils flared. Her eyes were fiery.

"What Pityr would *want* is for both of us to continue to the Emerald Fields—to carry on surviving, rather than dying for ... for this poxy *stupidity*. If you have any sense of duty to him, any at all, you would come to the Emerald Fields, instead of letting yourself die at the hands of a man who has already shown himself capable of crippling you without even a touch."

They stood like that for a moment, at an impasse. Jasen realized that they'd come to the stairs leading out to the top deck. He could hear, through the door at the top of them, a little hubbub, conversations and shouts between the *Lady Vizolans* as they tended to the vast galley.

"I am absolutely certain in my conviction he must be stopped,"

Jasen said quietly. "That stopping him is more important than anything else right now."

"So try to stop him," Alixa said. "But know that it will cost you your life."

He came close to telling her, then and there, that whether Baraghosa did him in or not, his life was already lost, the sands of it slipping through his fingers with every passing second—

But there came a shout from the deck, a cry that was not conversation, but a noise of alarm.

Jasen and Alixa's eyebrows knitted. They looked up the stairs—

"Something's up," said Jasen.

"Brilliant," Alixa muttered, already climbing the steps two at a time. "When *isn't* something up?"

Jasen followed, taking the steps two at a time for the first half of the stairway. But fatigue suddenly gripped him. The world's colors went wrong, and there seemed to be a shadowed tunnel between him and it.

Visions lingered about its edges—silhouetted forms, hardly visible against the murk pressing in at the corners of his sight. Like shadows in the light. Familiar ones, at that.

His mother? His father?

They were gone as soon as he'd spied them. By then he was a full six steps behind Alixa. So he hurried, gripping a handrail carved from a single wooden beam for support; he no longer trusted himself not to trip.

Up they went, then out the door, which Alixa threw open—

Nine, maybe ten men were arrayed on the deck.

Another was in the crow's nest, at the very top of the mainmast. It was he who was shouting down, alarm filling his voice.

Already, another man was mounting the mast, and the steps up it.

The man in the crow's nest was looking forward. So were the *Lady Vizolans*, all focused on something on the horizon. From here, the sails were blocking it—so Alixa and Jasen headed forward, striding in lockstep, past the lowest of the sails to see—

Alixa began, "What the—?"

Smoke rose in a dirty smear from a thin sliver of land very far ahead. It was a big billow, too, much larger than a chimney or a signal fire. Too big to be normal ...

It struck him at once that what waited ahead was not unlike the smoke that had loomed above Terreas. There, too, black had plumed into the sky in great clouds, far darker and heavier than any chimney or oven could ever have put out. This was something significant,

104

something out of the ordinary.

It was ... destruction.

It was ...

"Nonthen," Jasen murmured, a spike of fear in his chest.

16

Nonthen might once have been a grand port city. Now, though …

There was almost nothing left of it. Where a city once stood now lay a smoking crater, a vast piece of the earth just *missing*, like a child had sunk its fingers into the wet mud beside a pond and scooped it away. Seawater had flowed into the cavity, leaving a great bay where the city had once stood.

Only what had once stood at its edges remained: small shanties and buildings that now wobbled, their foundations shaken by the devastating event that had rendered the city such a hellscape.

People were left though—and there were plenty of them. Most were the dark-skinned men and women native to the coast of Coricuanthi, but there were plenty of sailors from other lands here, too. The boats they had sailed in on were utterly broken too, their fragmented pieces scattered upon the seawater, a huge mass of floating debris that mingled with bits of broken buildings and docks on the surface of the water.

As the *Lady Vizola II* drew nearer and nearer, the horror became worse as the picture became more distinct. The full span of the devastation was apparent as they entered the crater, which was easily several kilometers across. Terreas could have fit comfortably into this space, probably even two or three copies of it, neighboring fields and all—if, of course, there had been no detritus to block it. Debris utterly covered the ocean's surface, an endless carpet of it.

There were bodies too. Lots and lots of bodies.

Men and women waded out. They called, in many languages, for loved ones. Jasen heard names, as the *Lady Vizola II* gradually carved a path through the debris for the newly forged shoreline: *Bradley, Noah, Yeshua, Amit, Ru Shi* … The two calling that last name, a man and a woman, he with dark skin and she with light caramel, threw themselves into the wet, loping out at an awkward run. Their eyes were on something that floated nearby, and Jasen saw it with horror just as they got there: the body of a child, a girl, who floated with her face under the water and her back to the sky. Her skin was exposed, but Jasen did not realize at first, because where the fabric of her clothes had been burned away, her back was an awful black, as if she'd been seared in a fire.

They dragged her up, calling her name, wailing it. Her mother grasped at the child's face, tilting it skyward, pleading as she looked into dead, empty eyes.

Her father clutched her to his body. He cried, a pain like none other, into the sky.

The child did not move. She only hung, limp and scorched, oblivious to the agony that tore through her parents.

Jasen touched the pendant about his neck.

And it was the same all around. A few people were pulled from the waters, gasping for breath, groping for a hold on those who wrestled them free. But many more were totally still, all those bodies just floating there, waiting for someone to fish them out.

"What happened here?" Jasen murmured.

Alixa swallowed hard, averting her eyes from the parents of Ru Shi. "I don't know."

Burund watched from the deck with the rest of them. Almost all the crew had come to the top deck, to look out at the ruined city. They chattered here and there, in quiet, tense pockets—but mostly there was only silence between them, broken by the hubbub of what remained of the city.

When the *Lady Vizola II* had come to perhaps a couple of hundred meters from the new shoreline, it stopped. It had crept in ever slower up to now, so at first Jasen did not even realize the vessel's movement had ceased.

Kuura joined Burund. He spoke to him in their own language, face serious.

Burund listened. Then he nodded, and said just a couple of words back.

Kuura made off. A handful of the *Lady Vizola II*'s crew followed.

"What's the problem?" Jasen asked, joining Burund with Alixa in tow.

"The waters grow shallow," said Burund. "This vessel can get no closer. They are taking a longboat out instead."

"Let us go with them," Jasen said, decision coming instantly. "We can help."

Burund's lips thinned.

"Please."

"Fine," said Burund after a moment. "Go. I am no longer your keeper now." He watched Jasen carefully. "You understand?"

Jasen nodded. "You've watched after me long enough, Shipmaster. Thank you." He stepped past, heading for one of the longboats being unlashed from the war galley's side.

Alixa moved toward the hold.

"Where are you going?" Jasen asked.

"Scourgey will want to be on solid ground again." She disappeared into the ship.

Jasen was not entirely sure just how much of what was left of Nonthen still qualified as "solid," but he did not argue, just joined the queue, waiting for Alixa's return.

She was back soon with Scourgey. Scourgey did not seem to be too happy about it, though; she kept her head down, creeping along very close to Alixa's heel. Alixa patted her gently, trying to soothe her with words. But they did not placate her, the black eyes carrying a vacant, sickly look. When it finally came time for Jasen, Alixa and Scourgey to descend the side of the *Lady Vizola II* and climb into the first boat, with Huanatha, Longwell, Kuura, and Chaka, she whined madly, her claws clattering on the deck where she shook.

"Come on," Alixa pleaded, poised upon the net leading to the boat. "It'll be okay. I promise."

She reached up to take Scourgey by the paw.

Scourgey whined louder still.

"Let me," said Longwell. Climbing back onto the netting, he scaled it fluidly, even in his armor. Reaching over the deck, he very gently coaxed Scourgey forward.

"I have you, Niamh," he murmured softly, pulling the scourge onto his shoulders. "Shh. I have you."

She relaxed. Draped over Longwell's shoulders, she allowed him to descend with her upon him. Half coiled about his neck, she seemed to stare into his face with her dark eyes, all the way to the boat. There, Longwell released her; but she didn't go far, taking up position by his heel and resting against him. He favored her with a grimace-like smile, then, when Jasen and Alixa had completed the company, took up a pair of oars.

Rowing toward the shore was slow. The oars seemed less to be moving water and more to be shifting debris. Even finding a gap in which to lower the oar for each stroke between broken wood and fabrics and—bodies—was a challenge.

The water grew shallow quickly, though. People were out here, wading and shouting, crying out for their loved ones. A young girl on her father's shoulders was crying, pointing at the lumpen body of a tabby cat heaped on a board. Huanatha called out to him as they passed by, but the man gave only a blank, shell-shocked look before moving on, wordless.

They moved quietly. Huanatha, Kuura, and Longwell all exchanged murmurs. Jasen listened, but it was all speculation, wondering aloud what might have happened here.

When they were perhaps a hundred and fifty feet from the shore— which, Jasen saw now, was an oozing wet clay, its reddish color leaking into the water like a dye—Alixa cried out. She dropped her oar—

Jasen was behind her. He scooted forward, trying to grab for it, but it went over the edge.

Huanatha turned. "What—?"

Longwell gripped her shoulder. "A body."

Jasen saw it at the same time as Huanatha did. Alixa's oar had dislodged debris in its sweep—and a body had floated up to the surface, no longer stuck under wooden boards and mangled metal framework. It came up face first ... only what was left did not exactly resemble a face, anymore. The skin was almost entirely seared off. His, or her, eyes were gone, but what took their place were sunken, red raw patches of gore. The nose had been razed too—as had the full bottom jaw.

Jasen turned away, fighting the clench of his gut. No wonder Alixa had dropped her oar.

"It's okay," Longwell murmured to Alixa. "He is not in pain now."

She refused to look out to the water or row. Cradling herself, she said in a whisper, "I don't want to be here anymore."

Jasen leaned forward. He slung an arm around her momentarily. But with two rowers no longer rowing, their slow pace drew even nearer to a crawl, so after only that moment's comfort, he took up his oar again and resumed its stroke, taking great care not to look at the seared visage that bobbed at the water's surface as they left it behind them.

"What sort of event could level a city like this?" Kuura asked.

"A storm ..." Longwell said, although it was plain on his face that he did not believe it.

"I have seen no storm before capable of gouging a hole in the earth," said Huanatha. "Have you?"

"No." Longwell shook his head. "I have not."

Closer inland, Jasen began to recognize parts of boats. That curving panel of boards, that must have once comprised a hull. There was a crow's nest, or at least part of it; it was still round, and still possessed a couple of the wooden beams that had once been its meager railing, although they were smashed in half. A captain's wheel lolled atop the water beside the half-risen stone remains of whatever building had once been here. Fully whole, it looked almost comical among a sea of near indistinguishable wreckage.

Most of the survivors were spread out here. There were plenty upon the shore, but dozens and dozens fanned out into the waters. So many were shouting, crying … the cawing of carrion birds over their cries made the whole event seem like a feast for vultures, their voices joining one loud chorus.

Already, though, people were organizing. Small clusters had arranged themselves upon the shores, or close to them. They waded out in ones and twos, sifting through the detritus for bodies. However broken they were, however blackened, they pulled them from the water, dragged them back to land … and then they went out again, searching for the next.

Huanatha called out to an elderly man with a bent back. Skin the color of burnt sugar, he had been guiding someone else, another rescuer, out to something that had caught his attention a little too far for him to go.

He turned at the sound of Huanatha's voice. His face was frail, as was the wispy white beard hanging down to his Adam's apple.

He called something back to her, a question.

Huanatha responded.

The rowers ceased so they might speak.

Jasen listened intently as they talked. He could not understand any of their words, and they seemed to be different than both the *Lady Vizolans'* native tongue and the language spoken by the Prenasians.

The man grew grim. He spoke at length, shaking his head.

"What's he saying?" Longwell asked.

"It was not a storm that did this," said Huanatha darkly. "It was a man—with ghostly white skin and sunken eyes and a malevolent smile—a man trailed by glowing orbs, following him wherever he went."

Jasen's stomach clenched, as his eyes took in the wreckage around them as if seeing it for the first time.

Of course. The name bubbled from his lips, and he knew in his heart, in his guts, what—who—had happened here.

"Baraghosa."

17

"I don't believe her," Alixa muttered.

She and Jasen were ashore. With every step, the clay beneath their feet crumbled a little more, dyeing the waters a reddish brown that overpowered the near-black of churned silt.

The entire place smelled of sulfur. The smell pressed against Jasen's throat, reminding him of the mountain that had split open, the terrible fumes that had suffused the burning ash cloud when it laid Terreas to waste.

Three boats had come down from the *Lady Vizola* II, almost all hands throwing themselves into the rescue operation. One of those boats remained occupied, rowing carefully through the debris and fishing out bodies, then ferrying them to shore. Only once did someone come up spluttering. A fervor gripped the men then, fighting to bring the man in to shore, to men and women calling, providing their own help. But he was too scorched, and Jasen saw, as he was lifted out, Medleigh rushing to assist, he had only one arm. The other was just a stump, totally blackened.

He lasted only a few minutes before death took him.

Alixa could not stomach it. So she and Jasen, and Scourgey with them, retreated to where the survivors grouped in wailing clusters around the crumbled brick and warped metal and exploded wood beams that had once been the great buildings of this city. They tended to the wounded as they could, not understanding the language of the men and women who spoke to them, but understanding their gripping hands, their tear-streaked faces, the blisters on their cheeks and foreheads and the blood oozing down them.

They couldn't help. Not really. Not even a dozen Medleighs, two dozen, could turn around a fraction of these people's injuries. There were just too many, the city's ruin too vast. But Jasen and Alixa did what they could, scavenging fabric and tying it about wounds, helping people up and guiding them farther from the muddy, collapsing shoreline.

"Why would Huanatha lie about Baraghosa having done this?" Jasen asked.

They were escorting one of these people now, an old woman with arthritic hands and grey hair. She wasn't even as tall as Alixa. Clearly in pain, she gripped the base of her spine as best as her twisted fingers would permit, wincing and whimpering with every hobbled step toward safety.

"To further her own agenda?" Alixa suggested.

"Why would she do that?"

"To convince the rest of us to continue this mad chase."

"Mad chase?" Jasen echoed. "Do you not see what's around us? Baraghosa has killed—again. This devastation … it's his doing."

"If Huanatha is to be believed."

Jasen clenched his teeth. His frustration was very close to the top again.

So was his exhaustion, though, and as he clambered up a stump of brickwork, guiding the old woman between them, he stumbled, canting forward.

The old woman came down with him, shrieking—

Jasen's knees hit the edge of the brick. They stung, a line of searing pain.

He rolled, old woman forgotten.

"Oh—for goodness—" Alixa began. She darted for the old woman, grabbing for an arm.

The woman waved her off. Practically howling, she crawled forward and away from the foreign children with pale skin, and the foul-smelling beast that loped alongside them, who'd pitched her into the dirt and a carpet of fragmented brick.

Jasen lay on his back. Damn, his knees hurt. And his chest.

Scourgey pressed her nose to him. She whined.

"I'm fine," he murmured, not sounding remotely convincing.

Alixa loomed over him. "Can you get up?" Her irritation seemed to be giving over to concern.

"Give me a second," Jasen wheezed.

This was getting worse. It had been bad enough in Luukessia, on their last fateful mission to Wayforth, coming in waves. He thought back, remembering how he'd believed, then, that he was tired or undernourished. The Aiger Cliffs were worse. Scaling the path up to the clifftops and the field of lightning rods … but he'd believed it just fatigue then, too.

If Baraghosa had not told him the truth, that he was dying, would he be suspicious now? Would those white spots in his eyes give him greater cause for concern? Would these episodes of exhaustion have caused him to query Medleigh, instead of brushing his ailments off?

Bizarre, to have taken the word of a man he hated, one who sought to levy destruction everywhere he went, at face value.

And yet Jasen felt it in his heart, that in this one thing, at least, Baraghosa spoke true.

Still, there were so many unknowns. And for a moment, he saw them all, a strange kind of tangle, many possibilities, all out of reach but each of them just as real as any other.

He blinked it back.

Scourgey lowered her nose to his skin again. Her nostrils opened wide, breathing in his scent, and she whined.

What did he smell like to her, exactly? Did he have a rotten smell of his own, clinging to him like a mist? Was it sour, rancid, like meat turning in the hot sun, besieged by flies?

He closed his eyes. Breathed. In, out. Just focus on that, he told himself. In and out again.

He held his mother's pendant in a loose grip.

"Do you need Medleigh?" Alixa asked. Her voice seemed to come from very far. There was even more worry in it now, all traces of their arguments this morning—these past weeks—evaporated.

He opened his eyes, shook his head.

Alixa was blurred. Her anxious expression was visible to him, though.

Jasen levered up, eyebrows knitting.

White spots crowded his vision. They clustered in corners, where the world had gone darker than it had any right to be. But they danced all over too, like cataracts, floating on a pool of oil. And where they swept, he saw Nonthen—but not the Nonthen of today. This was a living city, unbroken. He saw grey stone buildings rising where now there was a sea of brackish water and debris. He saw red everywhere, banners of it, fabric hanging down from windows, fashioned into awnings to keep the bright sunlight at bay.

And he saw people, caramel-skinned, in long robes, all of them moving, moving … Others were among them, people from different lands. Men and women and children with darker skin, Coricuanthians; lighter-skinned people filtered by too, from lands like Longwell's Arkaria, standing out not just by color but by their dress, which was much more like Luukessian fare than the people of Nonthen wore.

There were smells, too, and Jasen caught them in the back of his throat: the bright scent of seawater, the fleeting tastes of seared fish, not burnt, but crisped on a coal fires out at the docks.

It flickered—and then there was the crater that Nonthen had become. But if he moved his head … if he followed the flow of the white spots in his eyes, it peeled away again, it was there, the city, a ghostly, ethereal overlay.

He gasped.

Alixa's eyebrows drew close. "What is it?"

"Do you see it?" he asked.

She turned in the direction he stared. "The ruin?" Her frown deepened. "I see it."

Jasen shook his head. "The shining city," he murmured.

Scourgey pressed close to his shoulder. She whined, a baleful crooning noise, unlike the fearful whimper she'd given out when faced with the rowboat ride from the *Lady Vizola* II.

Alixa turned back to him. "Jasen? Is something …?"

He heard little more than that. Her words, already coming from some distance, stretched, getting farther away from him. The white spots clouding his vision grew more frenzied, and suddenly there was a screaming pain in his head—*actual* screaming, a thousand voices rising in his ears, shrieking at horrors no mind should know. It threw the world's colors out again, the overlay of the old city turning wickedly bright. Nonthen as it stood now, spread underneath, the brightness warring with darkness—and the darkness won, pitch black consuming all the light, and into it, Jasen fell.

18

It was dark when he woke again. For a few seconds he was unsure if he was still in the black place he had fallen. It was peaceful there, quiet, away from all the screams …

Then a match was struck. A lamp was lit in the corner.

Huanatha stood by it. She waved the match to put its flame out, then deposited it just inside the lamp.

"Hello," she said, her voice quiet.

"I'm … on the ship?" Jasen asked. His voice was hoarse, tired.

Huanatha nodded.

She lowered her lithe body onto a stool. Elbows on her knees, she leaned forward, peering at Jasen with a peculiar expression made stranger still by the flickering candlelight, caressing one side of her face in its soft amber glow.

Jasen moved to rise. But his body wouldn't obey. His arms, still weak, struggled to straighten. And there was another weight upon him, across the bottom of his legs. Had he hurt himself worse in his fall? No, he couldn't have, and it had been his knees, anyway, that he had struck, not the bottoms of his shins.

He lifted his head to see that

Scourgey lay upon him. She watched him, the same as Huanatha did, the candle's gentle wavering reflected in her black eyes. Rarely did she appear to display any readable emotion at all, at least by those dark orbs. It was all in her body language, the way she moaned, or tensed, or crept close.

Now, Jasen thought he could see sadness in her.

"She can feel it, you know," said Huanatha.

Jasen's eyebrows knitted. Now that his place in the world was concrete once more, he could feel the soft undulation of the boat. It was cool in here. The ship got warm during the day, its black wooden exterior baked by the sun, keeping the heat close. It bordered on uncomfortable, which was why Jasen stayed out of the confines of his quarters when he could.

He felt just a hint of that latent heat in the room now.

"It's night?"

Huanatha nodded.

"Where is Alixa?"

"In Nonthen still," Huanatha answered, "helping how she can. Her heart cannot abide the suffering of others. She was not made to fight—but she learns. She will learn more. It is her destiny."

"Learn more? You mean how to fight?" Jasen's throat felt raw, words coming out in a croak.

"And other things."

"No." Jasen shook his head. "Not Alixa."

"She did not have to fight Baraghosa before," Huanatha said, "and she took up weapons then."

"She felt she had to."

Huanatha regarded him for a quiet moment. Finally, she said, "Perhaps," and no more.

Jasen eased himself up. His arms shook, trying to take his weight.

"Do not rise," said Huanatha. "It will do you good to rest."

"I need to help."

Huanatha chuckled, a very low laugh that made the hairs on the back of his neck rise in a way that was strangely sort of pleasant. "You are determined as always. But rest now. Your body needs it. Alixa, she is fine, assisting where she can ... That is where she belongs, for this moment."

It was Jasen's turn to laugh, although his came with no amusement at all. "Alixa belongs in the Emerald Fields. There is no other place in the world for her."

"Perhaps. At the very least, she has other places to go along the way."

Scourgey shuffled against Jasen's legs, moving her forelegs, crossing one paw over the other. She lifted her head for only that, then settled it against Jasen's shin. And still she watched him with the same singular focus that she had settled upon Longwell when first he was brought aboard the *Lady Vizola*.

There was definitely sadness in her expression now, though; none of the bounding joy that had overtaken her at the sight of her former ... companion, friend, whatever he was.

Niamh, he reminded himself, for the umpteenth time.

"Why are you here?" Jasen asked Huanatha.

"Someone needed to be." She licked her lips. "I believe we should discuss some things."

"Discuss what?"

Her face creased with a ghost of a smile. Crow's feet, just as faint, radiated a short distance from the corners of her eyes, thrown into relief by the candlelight flickering behind her.

"What would *you* like to discuss?" she asked.

Jasen frowned. Why did she insist upon speaking in riddles?

He considered, for a moment, that it was all a dream, that he was still in the dark place after all, in that blessed quiet where the screams ceased.

It was not a dream. Dreams did not feel so real, so mundane. He remembered the dream he'd had—how many nights ago now?— where he walked between his mother and father, in the grasses sprouting in the fields lying between Terreas and the wall the scourge were afraid to across. It had been over-bright, the details blurry and inconsistent.

This, on the other hand, was his room, and his bed, on a ship that gently rose and fell with the tide. It was Scourgey's real weight upon him; and it was Huanatha's real face, her real eyes, fixed upon him in the twilight of the candlelit cabin.

"Where do we pursue Baraghosa next?" he asked.

Huanatha answered, "That, I do not know. For now, there are only mists."

At Jasen's disappointed expression, she said, "Do not look so dejected, Jasen. We know he has been here. We know what he has wrought. And we will find him."

"And find none to take up arms with us," he muttered.

"Perhaps not," said Huanatha. "More than likely not, in fact. We can still challenge him, though."

"How?" The image of Nonthen—the Nonthen that once had been, and the cratered rubble that it was now—came back to him. "If Baraghosa could do *that*, how will the three of us ever hope to fight him?"

"We have righteousness on our side."

Jasen felt the strength leave him, and he sagged weakly upon the thin pillow. "Righteousness is not enough. Not for this fight."

Her expression faltered. For just a moment, her determination flagged.

But she recovered herself. When she spoke again, her voice was low. "We will defeat him. And we will not be only three. This I can promise."

"Who else will join us?" Jasen asked. "Not Shipmaster Burund, or Kuura. And not Alixa. I said to you before, she will take up arms only if forced. Otherwise, she will never touch a weapon. She detests it."

"Why?"

"It is … not *proper*," said Jasen. "She was always so concerned with propriety in Terreas." He recalled the way she took those pointless weaving lessons, the way she listened to her batty old Aunt Sidyera prattle on, shielded from all the world in a house she rarely left. She had hated those lessons immensely—but it was the proper thing for her to do, and so she'd spent many an afternoon in front of the loom, listening to the old woman drone on.

"And yet she drew a dagger upon Baraghosa," said Huanatha. "She will come around."

"She won't."

Huanatha watched him. "You seem very sure."

"She will get no closer than she has. It's too … ingrained in her, I suppose."

"Hmm."

"The woman who is responsible for our being here—Shilara Gressom; her name was Shilara Gressom," he added, because it was very important that it be known, "she was a soldier, once. She was capable, and experienced, and she saved our lives, and yet she was cast out of Terreas because women could not be warriors." He shook his head, and for a moment, he hated the home he had known, or that part of it anyway.

Huanatha bared her teeth. "The closed-minded—I would like to see what your people would have thought of *me*," she bit off, looking as if she were ready to take the closed-minded villagers on right now.

"Little good," Jasen muttered. "But they are not here anymore … so you cannot ask them."

Huanatha's lips pursed. The fight hadn't gone out of her—Jasen didn't truly believe it would ever leave her until she took her last breath—but she remembered where she was, and what they were talking about, that this was Jasen's home, now wiped from existence, buried under a mound of slag and refocused her attention on him.

"Alixa did not like Shilara," Jasen said. "Not until the very end … and maybe not even then." He tried to recall their last days together, but it was such a blur. The small moments, there had been plenty of them; how *dull* that trip had been, in hindsight, how few scourge they'd run into to cause their hearts to beat in a frenzy. The bigger moments, though, those were seared in Jasen's mind forever: almost being lost in the river; the devastating eruption that had destroyed

Terreas; the mad rush to the beach, the cart dragged by Scourgey after Milo died; and Shilara's final stand, throwing herself to the scourge so that Jasen and Alixa could live for another day …

"She looked in the mirror," said Huanatha, "and did not like what she saw."

Jasen lifted an eyebrow.

"You don't believe me," Huanatha said, nodding, "I see it in your face. But it is true. It is true of all of us, at one time or another. What we hate in others is often what we hate most about ourselves."

Jasen considered this. "I don't think Alixa is much like Shilara."

"No? Well, you are the expert." Huanatha grinned at him. Then, slowly, her grin faded.

More softly, she said, "She will be fine, you know. When you are gone, I mean."

A spike of horror drove itself through Jasen's chest at that. He'd been about to say, "Of course she will," before Huanatha's clarification. Now he stared at her, heart suddenly in his throat, the words dead on his lips.

But of course she knew. Scourgey knew it, and Huanatha could read Scourgey.

Jasen swallowed. The lump in his throat was dry and stayed where it had lodged itself. "How long have you known?"

"Long enough," she said.

His heart drummed.

He could ask her so much.

"And … and how long," he began, careful, fighting back the tremor that threatened his voice now he was addressing it head on. "How long do I …?"

"Not long."

Only two words. And Jasen could have guessed as much himself. The onset of those headaches, the spots in his vision, his growing weakness … it was all happening much more frequently now. Death was racing ever closer, picking up speed like a pebble falling down a mountainside.

But to hear it spoken aloud … it hollowed his chest.

"Baraghosa …" he began.

"Will be ended," said Huanatha, "and you will see his end, one way or another, before we see yours."

His heart skipped again. "You're certain?"

Huanatha nodded. "I think so."

So he would see Baraghosa die. The fear that he wouldn't, that the pursuit of the sorcerer alone would outlast him, had weighed him down like an invisible weight this past week. Now it lifted—but only slightly, for new questions came. How would Baraghosa be defeated? And would Jasen—that was to say, would it be Baraghosa who ...?

He swallowed again. That infernal lump, so dry, refusing to move.

"How will it end?" he croaked at last.

"That I cannot say," said Huanatha quietly. "No one can. To know would mean your choices mean nothing. And this life is not meaningless. We make our decisions ... and our decisions then make us."

He felt hollow again, at that. It would be easier to know, surely it would.

"But I have no decisions left to make," he said.

Huanatha frowned. "You have nothing *but* decisions to make." Straightening again, a mad look glinted in her eyes. "You could follow your cousin to these Emerald Fields she is so dead set upon. You could sail to the ends of the earth, away from Baraghosa and all of us, to forget him and let him do his will. And when you die—and die you shall—you may choose whether to do it on your back, with your arms thrown over your head ... or you may do it standing tall, fighting to vanquish an evil greater than you have ever known." She shook her head. "You say that you have no choices left, but the truth is that you have chosen not to do these things. You have chosen this path every day until now, and you will choose it every day until Baraghosa is defeated. You are ... chosen."

Jasen stared. "I'm ... chosen?"

"You *have* chosen. The chosen one—not in the sense that some specialness has fallen upon you. If anything at all, the fates have been especially cruel to you. You are chosen in that you have chosen to be here. Your choices led you away from your village before its end, and your choices have led you to challenge Baraghosa when you saw him do evil. Those choices will lead you farther still, Jasen. That is," she said, her expression suddenly dark, "if you continue to act with courage, and do not choose to run. We are all chosen, all of us here. Not just you and I, and Longwell, but your cousin too, the shipmaster, Kuura ..."

"But they will not fight," said Jasen weakly. "They have said so themselves—they wish to be clear of this battle."

"They may yet reconsider."

"Is that your answer for everything?" he blurted. "They have had their time to think, and they have chosen not to continue, just as Alixa has done. For all the pain Baraghosa has wrought, we three appear to be the only ones willing to stand against him. Hoping that those people will reconsider is like ... is like hoping that your people will just give you your throne back."

Huanatha appraised Jasen for a long, long moment. He'd offended her, he was sure—the issue of her throne was undoubtedly a sore subject—but he had to make her see how dire their situation was.

"My throne," she said at last, "is a debt that I will settle with Baraghosa, and the usurper he put there. I will take it back, with their blood upon my hands."

There was rage in her face now, but it was a different one than Jasen usually saw. She did not bare her teeth, like a snarling wolf. Nor were her eyes wide and deranged, her eyebrows arched so high they almost touched her hairline. This anger was a quieter sort, more contained. But she seethed—oh, yes, she seethed. It boiled behind her eyes, a blazing inferno a hundred thousand times more powerful than the meager candle that reflected, flickering, in her iris.

"What happened?" Jasen asked. "You said Baraghosa turned your people against you—like Longwell's?"

"He spent long years worming his way into our people," Huanatha spat. "He brought gifts, made trades; he advised; our council consulted him. He was useful, it has to be said, although he pushed, relentlessly in later years, for Muratam to go to war."

"With who?"

"The Prenasians," said Huanatha.

Jasen's eyebrows drew together. "Why?"

She shook her head. "I do not know. His reasons were vague. Said they posed too much of a threat, that we should unite against the enemy." She pursed her lips. "I resisted for a long time." She took a steadying breath. "And then, when I was on a royal visit elsewhere, he goaded my cousin, Trattorias, into killing my relatives while they slept and assuming the throne himself." Her jaw was tight. "They came to me in spirit, one by one, as he slit their throats. Their cries ..." She shook her head. "I will never forget their cries. They pleaded for me to intervene, but I was too far away. By the time it was done, I had hardly unfurled my sails."

Her eyes had glazed at the memory. Now they came back to Jasen, in the room, Scourgey resting upon his legs.

"You know how this feels," she said. "You know the pain of losing your loved ones, the pain of being unable to prevent their deaths."

And it came back as an echo: the sight of the mountain split open, spilling molten rock over Terreas. Scorching rock, ash pouring down upon the village in a second, burying every man, woman and child alive under it—if they had been alive in the seconds after it happened.

He hoped they were not. He hoped, again, that his father had just been sleeping, hadn't had even the time to rouse as magma demolished the walls of the Weltans' house and encased him in it ...

"It is no coincidence we are drawn together in this," said Huanatha. "The dead guide us."

"The ancestors," Jasen murmured.

"Yes. Our forebears. They watch. The veil grows thin between you and them, the closer you get to your end. You see it—as I do, all the time."

Jasen's gaze had fallen somewhere past Scourgey, out into a far infinity, as he thought of all the awful things he fought so hard not to think of—those last moments of everyone he had ever known, before this. Now, though, he found himself staring at Huanatha.

The veil grows thin. You see it.

Flashes came to him: his mother, looming behind the rocks on the isle of Baraghosa; the spectral silhouettes flickering, for just a few seconds, in the cabin with Longwell and Huanatha before the mutiny; and this morning, the old Nonthen on top of the ruined crater that it had become, all its people—

"You will hear them, too," said Huanatha, "as it comes closer."

So that screaming noise ...

Those were the people here.

Those were the souls who Baraghosa's attack had ripped from their bodies, thousands of them.

"They guide us," said Huanatha. "They can do little ... but a little can be enough. A ship a few degrees off course, over the period of days and weeks, gets farther from its destination by many miles. Their pushes, so subtle, from beyond the veil ... over great spans of time, they bring us together. And now, here we are. Together, we are chosen. And we have chosen for ourselves."

Chosen? But how, if they were pushed?

Could you be pushed and still choose?

"Something is happening," said Huanatha. "I, and the dead, do not know what Baraghosa is planning. But it will shake the foundations of the world—that much is certain. So we choose. And now you must, again, decide: whether to let it go, as the shipmaster wishes to, as your cousin wishes to. Or do you fight, with what little time and strength you have left?"

And here she rose. Stepping forward, she ran an idle hand across Scourgey's haunch; then she bowed low over Jasen, and pressed her lips to his forehead.

"It is your choice that will see us through," she said, "or see us gone. It is in your hands, a big fate—the fate of all of us in this world, perhaps."

She left.

The door closed with a soft *click*, and but for the scourge resting softly on his shins, watching him through black eyes, he was alone once more.

He lifted his hands.

In the dim light of the candle, they looked so terribly pale.

His hands shook.

Whatever was killing him … whatever illness … its roots penetrated deeper all the time. Today, they had found a great cleft inside of him which they could burrow into—and now, like the roots of a tree through stone, it would grow and grow until it finally broke him into pieces.

A white spot, in the corner of his right eye, opened. It lowered, like ash falling through the skies—and he saw, again, for just the shortest moment, a flash of people. A man, a woman—his father? Mother? They were gone before he could be sure.

He was tired again. And he'd not moved—only talked.

His hands quivered.

It is in your hands, a big fate—the fate of all of us in this world, perhaps.

But how, when he was so weak, could Jasen carry the fate of anything … let alone an entire world?

19

A knock at the door brought him out of the dark place once more.

He blinked, confused. The lamp had gone out, the small pillar candle poked into it had burned down. There was just enough light coming from the hall outside, under the door, that he could make out the very edge of the bed where he lay, Scourgey upon him still.

A shadow broke the narrow beam of light.

"Come in," he said, trying to push himself up. He had more strength for it now, and he rose to sitting easily … at least, more easily than before.

The door opened.

Alixa stood beyond.

She was past weary. Dark circles hung under her eyes, and her whole body was limp. Almost every inch of skin and her clothes was coated in a thick layer of reddish-black clay, soot, and congealed blood, none of it her own.

She hesitated a moment, and Jasen hesitated with her. Then he was pushing to stand—

"Don't," said Alixa, rushing in to still him with her grip on his shoulders. "Huanatha said you should rest."

"I have been resting."

"No, would you—*would you bloody stay still?*" Alixa cried, pushing him down. "You hit your head. You're supposed to be recovering."

Hit his head? But he'd been lying upon the ground already before blacking out, hadn't he?

"I thought I passed out," he said.

"You did," Alixa confirmed, taking a seat at his hip, and resting a hand on Scourgey's head. "But you were staggering around before that, going on about—screaming noises, people dying …" She shuddered. "It frightened me. Even more when you fell."

He touched his head, rooting his fingers through unruly black hair, looking for scabbed-over wounds.

"You didn't bleed," said Alixa. "Medleigh said you didn't crack your skull open or anything. But you just—you went out like a snuffed candle, and nothing I could do would wake you." She added in a small voice, "I was scared you were gone."

So he'd been conscious for longer than he recalled. Strange—he could have sworn he lost consciousness before rising. Had the impact to his head stopped the memory from being recalled? Possible. Medleigh might know, at any rate.

Then again, it was hardly important now, was it?

Nevertheless, he was curious: "How did I get back to the ship?"

"Scourgey carried you." Alixa looked at her fondly, gently running her fingers across the few wiry hairs atop the beast's head. "She just sort of shuffled herself under you and picked you up, and she ran, before I could go to pieces in my panic. Good girl," she said gently. "She took you to Longwell first. He was just leaving, to go find out … where *he* has gone, I suppose. Longwell took you to Medleigh, who checked you over, and Huanatha brought you back to the ship. Both of you. I would've come too, but she said I would be more use in Nonthen." Rolling her shoulders, either in a shrug or to banish some ache, she finished, "That was yesterday morning."

Yesterday—he'd been out almost the entire day, and much of the night too, after Huanatha's conversation.

"What time is it now?" he asked.

"Just after dawn."

"Have you been there all night?"

Alixa nodded. "They've set up camps now, with fires. Aid is starting to trickle in—real aid, more than we could give. But some of us are still out there." Suppressing a sudden yawn, she said, "Shipmaster Burund relieved me."

"How is it?" Jasen asked. "Nonthen."

"You saw it," said Alixa. "There are still bodies being dragged out of the water—too many to deal with. I don't know how many I pulled out myself …" Closing her eyes, likely to blot out the images seared into her brain, she went on, "Help has been flowing in all night from the nearest settlements, but with so many injured … it's going to be weeks before anyone can even think about rebuilding. *If* they think of it. I don't suppose they will, now—not the shape it's in. More shore keeps falling into the water. Last I saw, boards were being put down to create more solid walkways, but … the whole thing is a wreck, Jasen."

The ghostly image of Nonthen as it had once stood came back to him. Nowhere near as majestic as the Aiger Cliffs had been, it was still a bustling city, full of so much life. What was left now was more completely destroyed than any army or even the passage of centuries could have managed. Now the clay layer had been revealed, the two, three, maybe even five meters of solid soil above it washed away; Jasen doubted anything could be built here ever again. It would be just a bay, shallow, perhaps totally dry when the tide was at its farthest out—and littered with the rotting detritus of what once had been.

"It was Baraghosa," Alixa said quietly.

Jasen nodded. "I know."

"I doubted it—all the way until maybe midnight. But the more I heard, especially as others came from the neighboring villages ... his description came back again and again, his name. It was him, Jasen—he destroyed Nonthen."

"Why, though? And how?"

"The city's council ... 'resisted his overtures,' someone said. He'd been pressuring them for a long time, wanting some kind of pact against the Prenasians. They refused, and so he unleashed a storm upon them—and this is what he wrought. All because they wished to maintain their independence."

"A pact against the Prenasians? That's what Huanatha said too," Jasen murmured. "He wanted Muratam as some kind of ally."

Alixa hugged one knee to her chest and leaned her head on it. "Any idea why?"

Jasen shook his head. "No. But it cannot be for good."

"No," Alixa conceded sadly.

"I have to know what he's doing, Alixa," said Jasen. "And I have to stop it from happening."

She sighed. "I know." Closing her eyes, she rested her forehead on her knee where her chin had just been. "Is there no way to talk you out of this?"

"No," Jasen answered, as kindly as he could—because now there would be no argument, and whether or not Alixa would come along with him or forge her own path to the Emerald Fields, this was the point where finally she would understand. It had to be, with his time running short.

"I have chosen this, Alixa," he said. "I have chosen this because stopping Baraghosa is right ... and because, even if he had nothing to do with the mountain destroying Terreas, he did meddle in our village, the same way he meddled in others the world over. He took children from among us, took them off to die."

"Pityr," Alixa whispered.

And as she spoke his name, Jasen saw him: that boyish face again, smiling—here in this very room with them. He was ghostly, faint—but it was him. Jasen would remember his face clearly even if he lived another eighty or a hundred years, he would remember it. Pityr was here. Pityr was with them.

He was gone as soon as he'd appeared, before Jasen's heart gave a mighty thump in shocked acknowledgment.

But he'd seen him. He'd seen their friend, beyond the veil.

"Yes," said Jasen, "Pityr. And others like him. Baraghosa destroyed families, year after year."

"But why?" Alixa peered at him again, over the top of her knee. Sadness and confusion warred in her eyes. "Why take children?"

"Why usurp Longwell and Huanatha?" Jasen asked. "Why destroy Nonthen? Why seek pacts against the Prenasians? I don't know. I suspect the only person who knows the answer to those questions is Baraghosa himself."

"And you intend to ask." It was not a question, but a statement.

"I will ask if I must. Maybe I will only have to listen. Whatever the case, I will know."

"You think he'll just tell you?"

Jasen's conversation with Rakon the morning of the mutiny came back to him. He'd spilled much, so easily, simply for the sake of talking. And Baraghosa had done the same—he'd told Jasen more than he needed to. Why else would he reveal that he was dying?

"He likes the sound of his own voice too much," said Jasen. "He will talk."

"And then?"

The resolve ran heavily through Jasen. "And then I'll kill him."

Alixa shook her head, back and forth, eyes fixed on him but wide, oh so wide. "It doesn't have to be you."

"I know. But I choose this. I choose it today, and I choose it tomorrow, and I choose it every day until it is done."

"But—but—but *why*? Why, when you could leave this madness behind? You know there are other Luukessians out there. Longwell said so himself—they live on, in the Emerald Fields. We could be with them, and carry on our family names."

"Every Luukessian I have ever known is dead. One day I will face them again." He did not add, *One day very soon*—but he did think it, and it only cemented his decision even more. "I could not stand eye to eye with our ancestors if I did not at least try to stop him again."

"He will kill you."

127

Perhaps. Very likely, in fact. But nevertheless: "I must do this."

Alixa watched him in the dim light for long seconds. Scourgey's eyes shifted in their sockets, a slight side-to-side movement between the cousins' faces.

"Who will take you?" Alixa asked. "Ships arrive, but most of them see the destruction and turn back."

A fair question. Jasen had hoped that, with Longwell and Huanatha, he could charter passage here in Nonthen. That did not seem likely now, which left him with only one option.

Pushing up, he unfurled his legs from where they rested under Scourgey's chin. He swiveled to the edge of the bed, and pushed up—

His arms shook under his weight. And his legs shook too. No sooner had he stood than he toppled backward, landing on his backside.

Hard though the mattress was, that fall should not have forced the air out of him as though he'd been punched.

"What's wrong with you?" Alixa asked in alarm.

"Nothing," Jasen wheezed. But there were white spots in his eyes again.

He tried again. This time he stumbled forward. But he caught himself by placing a hand upon the wall, arresting the fall before he crashed headlong into the floor.

Hand upon the wall, he walked to the door—no, staggered. His feet could not rise.

Scourgey whined.

"What's wrong?" The alarm was clear in Alixa's voice. "You can hardly stand up!"

"Not now," Jasen answered, opening the door and stepping out into a corridor that seemed far too bright, those lamps glowing with such ferocity that he winced.

"Where are you going?" Alixa asked, following behind, her voice high.

"To speak with Shipmaster Burund."

20

"We have discussed this," said Burund. "My answer remains the same: no."

He strode away from Jasen, who was propped up on Scourgey, and Alixa, across the deck.

The light of dawn streaked across them. The sun hadn't long risen, but still it cast a glorious gold upon the onyx deck of the *Lady Vizola* II. The day was shaping up to be a warm one, and only a gentle breeze came in on the sea. Today, it carried the scent of seawater, but that stink of sulfur and burning had not been dispelled. Nor would it leave for a long time, Jasen supposed—like a taint had befallen the place. It was just something else, with the ruined earth, that would keep the city from being rebuilt for decades, perhaps centuries.

Little had changed since yesterday morning. The flooded crater was still filled with debris, though less than there had been when they'd arrived. Whether that was due to the efforts of the people on shore or simply to the tides as they washed in and out, Jasen could not be sure.

Encampments had been set up on shore. The people were very small from here, but he could see where they clustered and bustled around torches. Pyres lit the landscape, glowing brightly in the shadows the sun had yet to banish. They breathed out a thick, constant plume of tar-colored ash.

Grimly, Jasen realized these were bodies. Too many to bury—they had to be burned; it was the only way to dispose of them before decay set in.

For all of Jasen's despair at the destruction of Terreas, seeing Nonthen was something else. Terreas had been blanketed in ash and molten rock, banished from existence in seconds, all the life in it crushed—hopefully before anyone within it knew what was happening. But Nonthen had survivors, men and women and

129

children who were broken, who had seen the power that Baraghosa unleashed and lived through it, but whose lives were now in crumbled tatters. Most of them had lost loved ones, loved ones who were now converted to soot and carried away from the crater by the wind. Many others would never find their dead—they had been utterly vaporized in the blast that felled this city, no trace of them left.

Jasen had lost his family, his home, that much was true.

These people, though … they had it worse.

And Shipmaster Burund, who saw the very same scene of devastation that Jasen did, who knew that it had been Baraghosa's doing, now turned and walked away.

Jasen hobbled after him. Ancestors, it was so difficult to walk …

Scourgey braced him. She made a soft noise as he clutched her, digging in with his nails to stop himself from falling down.

Alixa stumbled along half a second behind him. Eyes on him instead of where she was going, she held her hand out, mere inches away from grabbing him should he teeter, threaten to bowl over.

"Jasen," she began, "you should be—"

"Please listen to me!" Jasen called after Burund.

Burund did not look back; just kept on.

"Please—Shipmaster, please would you—"

"*I know where he is!*"

The cry cut through the morning. Few hands were on deck, only Kuura and a couple of the *Lady Vizola*'s men comprising the small outfit. They all turned as one, though, to see Huanatha raising herself up onto the deck, her blue armor and muted grey breastplate gleaming in the early morning sunlight.

"The dead have spoken to me!" she cried. "They tell me where to seek him!"

Longwell's head appeared after. "I'm not sure I would shout that to everyone," he muttered.

But only the shipmaster and Kuura understood, of course. The other two *Lady Vizolans*, who had been working with Kuura, only exchanged curious looks.

"Where who is?" asked Burund.

"Baraghosa," said Huanatha. She strode across the deck to meet him, eyes blazing upon him with a steely focus.

Burund's lips thinned. He cast a look back at Jasen, mouth downturned. "Well, the three of you had better find yourselves a vessel to travel there in." He stepped past—

Huanatha blocked him. She was taller than he, but even if she had not been, the fire in her face would have been enough to give the shipmaster pause. Teeth bared, she growled, "Do not bury your head in the sand again, Shipmaster."

"I do not bury my head," Burund snapped back. "I protect my men."

"You protect nothing but your own hide."

"Huanatha," Longwell warned. Joining the growing congregation about the shipmaster, he inclined his head in a wary greeting to the shipmaster. "This conversation requires diplomacy."

"This conversation?" Burund asked. "I assure you, Samwen, there will be no conversation. I have heard all of you many times. You wish to pursue the sorcerer. *I* wish to keep my men alive—a task, I should not need remind you, I have already failed at because of this foolish quest of yours."

"Your men lost their lives to the Prenasians in battle," said Huanatha. "There is no higher honor—"

"*Huanatha.*" Longwell stilled her with a hand to her elbow. "Shipmaster Burund, please, hear us out."

"Yes," said Jasen. "Please listen."

It was as though the three of them only just realized Jasen were still there. Burund frowned at him over his shoulder. Longwell gave Jasen a curious look, confusion flickering over his face for a moment, wondering, perhaps, why he seemed to be gripping Scourgey to stay upright. Only Huanatha did not react with any surprise.

Burund rounded on him. "I have listened," he said, "to all of you, many times. Now it is your time to listen to me.

"Because of you, I have lost my ship. I lost five of my men because I chose to entertain your ambitions. That falls to me—and it falls to you too." He stared down at Jasen with steely eyes. There was no hatred in them, nor in his words—but looking back at him, Jasen believed he deserved it, he almost wished that the shipmaster did hate him. He was worthy of that. He'd dragged innocents into this, gotten them hurt.

He had gotten people killed.

"So why," said Burund, "would I consider partaking in this foolishness any longer?"

"Because you know that Baraghosa must be stopped," said Jasen.

"He did nothing to me personally, before this," Burund countered. "A cruel man though he might be, it is not for me to have any part in his justice."

"A cruel man?" Jasen repeated incredulously. "A cruel man? There are bodies burning out there—" he pointed, back to the shore and the pyres spilling soot into the pale blue sky "—bodies turned to dust, but which were already black and scorched, because of Baraghosa. He is more than a cruel man. He is a vile, evil, nefarious villain who poses a threat to all of us, you included—and *he must be stopped.*"

"Listen to the boy," said Huanatha. "Let his sense into that thick skull—"

"*Huanatha.*"

Burund stared down at Jasen. He had a sense that he was probing him, looking within.

"You have a death wish. The sorcerer will kill you."

"I am dying anyway."

The words were out before Jasen could stop them. But would he have stopped them? No. He was too far gone. He could not hide it any longer. And he had to find a way to get Burund to really, truly listen to him.

There was a long pause. Burund's expression flickered with confusion. Longwell, too, started, looking at Jasen with his eyebrows drawn low.

Alixa sidestepped, coming around his side to face him from the front.

"Jasen?" she whispered, eyes moving back and forth between his, searching. "Is it—are you—?"

"It is true," said Huanatha. "I have sensed it in him, as did Baraghosa … and as has your scourge."

Alixa reeled back. Eyes wide, she clapped a hand over her mouth. "No … No!"

"It's true," Jasen told her. "It's why Baraghosa picked me to go with him. He knew I was dying, even then—before the signs."

Burund watched him with flinty eyes. "And now you wish to die at his hand."

"No." Jasen shook his head. "I wish to stop him, before there are more Nonthens. Before there are others like Longwell and Huanatha, forced from their thrones as Baraghosa pulls strings in their courts for his own ends."

"You are one boy," Burund said. His gaze flicked down him and up again. "One dying boy."

"I *will* fight him," Jasen answered. "I do not wish to die at his hand—but I will die, and if I have to die fighting him? Then so be it. And if you will not take me, then I will commandeer my own Prenasian war galley, and I will take the fight to Baraghosa."

Burund studied him, unmoving. "You are determined."

"He must be stopped. I will do whatever it takes. I will fight with every breath I have left in me to stop him. Even if it kills me … even if it breaks what is left of me to do it … I *will* stop Baraghosa." His gaze shifted to Huanatha. "I choose this."

The warrior nodded. The ghost of a smile lifted the corners of her lips.

"I am with you," she said.

"And I," said Longwell, standing forward. "You are the very courage I have come to expect from my countrymen. You do Syloreas, and Luukessia, proud."

Jasen's heart swelled at that. Suddenly, the backs of his eyes were burning.

"Thank you."

"I will go too."

This was Alixa. She said it in a soft voice, so quiet that it took Jasen off guard. He turned to look at her—these were the last words he would have expected her to say—and saw her resolution as she gazed at him. Her eyes were glassy, but she nodded, the tiniest little up-and-down inclination of her head, more to herself than to him, or anyone else present.

"You will?" Jasen breathed.

"I will." She took his free hand in both of hers. "Until the very end … whatever it may be."

"See?" said Huanatha quietly. "I knew she would come around."

Alixa glanced inquisitively between them, but she did not say anything.

"So, you see," said Longwell, turning to Burund, "we are more determined than ever. We have been beaten by Baraghosa, yes, I will concede that to you. And true, all of us can see behind us, looking over Nonthen, that he is growing in power. But we all know, in our hearts, that Baraghosa stands only for evil—and we know that he must be stopped, even if it means our death, because not acting against him may mean the death of *all* of us."

"You are but four," said Burund.

"Actually …"

They turned to see Kuura, all their eyes landing on him at once. He grinned, an awkward and uncomfortable but wide and toothy smile.

"We are five," he said, joining Huanatha and Longwell and Jasen and Alixa. "Gods, how mad … but no. I cannot sit idly by." He took a long breath, steeling himself. "I stand against Baraghosa too."

Burund appraised them all through unreadable eyes. He was outnumbered, well and truly. If this were a battle of fists, he could be beaten into submission. But he was not Rakon, or the Prenasians, to be overcome by force. They could argue with only their words and their wills and hope, *hope*, to get through.

Jasen held his breath, waiting.

"You are mad," said the shipmaster at last. "Every last one of you."

"Aye," said Kuura. "But this, you already knew, at least of me." He flashed another smile. "These people are right, Shipmaster. Baraghosa sows destruction. You may think he has no ill will to us personally, but he is a threat to us all."

"So you wish to battle him a third time."

"I can think of nothing I wish for *less*," said Kuura. "But his evil deeds are spreading. We can run from it ... but for how long? Everywhere we go, we run into the debris left in his wake. What we see of Nonthen, the sheer show of power he has demonstrated, it is beyond comprehension. If we run, if we allow him to grow stronger for another week, a month, a year ... he may well grow unstoppable. We must act now. If we do not, we may never get the chance again. He may destroy our ship from across the sea next time, perhaps without even intending to. Ours was hardly the first we had come across that he'd done it to, after all." Kuura gave him a look of great significance.

Burund listened.

Then his gaze swept past them, to Nonthen—the crater that was left of it, its buildings turned to rubble if not wiped off the face of the globe entirely, thousands dead and thousands more injured. Heat from the pyres lifted the ash of the dead skyward.

At long last, Burund sighed. "So be it."

Jasen's heart leapt. "You'll take us?"

"I will provide your passage," said Burund, "no more. I will not see more of my men die because of this folly." His gaze crossed Kuura. "Not any who do not throw themselves into harm's way, at any rate."

"Thank you, Shipmaster," said Longwell, extending a hand to shake. "You are truly one of the greater men I have ever known."

Burund shook wearily. "Thank me after this is over." Sighing, he turned to Huanatha. "You say the dead have told you where he is?"

"They did," she said. Here for the first time, Jasen saw something new in her eyes. They were ...

Alight?

"So where am I to sail?" Burund asked, a little wary, for he must have seen it too.

"To the land I am exiled from," she answered, and then the gleam dancing in her gaze made sense at last. "Muratam."

21

"Why didn't you tell me?"

They were back in Jasen's quarters, him and Alixa and Scourgey. He sat at the pillow end of the bed, his back to the wall. Scourgey sat beside him. He leaned on her just as much as he leaned against the wall. They were all that kept him upright.

Something had definitely changed in him after his episode in Nonthen.

The end was coming now. There was no denying it.

But they were moving. Nonthen falling behind ... and Muratam ahead.

With luck, it would be their final stop in their pursuit of Baraghosa.

Alixa sat a little farther down the bed. Her knees were to her chest, her chin resting between them. Her eyes shimmered in the lamplight, faintly pink. But she'd not cried. She had been shocked, her voice had shaken, yet she'd held herself together. For that, Jasen was thankful. If she fell apart now, he did not think he possessed the energy to console her.

"I didn't know how," he answered.

"And you've known since ..."

"The isle of Baraghosa. Two weeks, more or less. But the signs were there before. I just didn't see them for what they were."

She nodded. She'd seen them too, hadn't she? That was why she accepted it so easily. That whispered *no* on the deck ... it been fear, not denial. But she knew, even without Huanatha's confirmation, that this was happening. Jasen was dying.

He was *dying*.

And now it was said aloud—now that he could really, truly feel it, eating away at the inside of him—he felt ... *hollow* was the only word he could think of to describe it. His lungs and heart surely remained

135

in his chest—he still breathed, and he could feel his heart, counting down the last beats of his life—but he just felt so … empty.

His pendant resting upon his chest was like a weight. He reached into his tunic, took it in hand, held it.

His mother had given him this. It was all he had—

And yet it was everything.

I will be with you soon, he thought, to his mother and his father, wherever they were—perhaps in this very room, like Pityr, watching, hidden by a veil he could glimpse through from time to time. *I just have this one last thing to do.*

Alixa bit her lip. There was something on her mind, something she wished to ask, Jasen thought. He waited for it, but it didn't come. He could not read it from her expression, only that she was troubled.

She breathed.

"What is it?" Jasen asked.

Alixa shook her head, lips clamped tight. She rested her forehead upon her knees again.

And then she laughed.

"What?"

When she looked up, tears sparkled in her eyes. But she was smiling. "Do you remember when Hanrey found out Josef had been picking the strawberries from his hanging baskets?"

Jasen frowned, half because the sudden shift in conversation had caught him off guard and half because though he racked his brains, he could not recall it. "No?"

"You must," said Alixa. "You were there."

"When?"

"It was three or four years ago, now," said Alixa. "You must remember. I do, because it was one of the funniest things to have happened that whole summer. We were sitting together, all three of us, near the assembly hall, you, me, Pityr. They were just finishing a meeting, I think, because the door opened and out came Hanrey and Euonice, arguing like always. She must have been particularly irritating that day, because he stomped off before she could follow—it was after she twisted her ankle, remember? She hadn't been back on her feet very long, and she wasn't managing very well."

The barest skeleton of memory came back to Jasen. Eyebrows drawn, he forced all of himself into picturing it. "I think so," he said.

"Pityr kept saying it was like she forgot to use the cane while she was resting up, you remember? He used to do that stupid impression of it—waggling an invisible stick around, wobbling on it like he was infirm. You remember that, surely?"

Jasen did—it brought a wide smile to his lips.

Alixa grinned back. "You do remember."

At first it was just a brief thing, Pityr pretending to stumble about, his whole body shaking, his back bowed low like the invisible cane was the only thing keeping it up. When he saw just how it made Jasen and Alixa laugh, though, it had grown into a routine. He'd stagger about for longer. He'd pull the stupidest faces. He'd put on a gravelly sort of high-pitched voice, nothing at all like Euonice's, which made it even funnier, and berate Terreas: "Why's everything shaking all the bloody time? Can't you keep still?" Up pretend steps he'd climb, huffing and puffing, accusing Hanrey of putting an extra inch onto them while she was off her feet. Then it became two inches, three ... Eventually it was a full six inches. By that time Euonice was long healed, and the routine mostly retired in favor of other things ... but it never failed to make Jasen laugh. Alixa too, though she kept back her snickers as best she could—properness and all that.

Actually, come to think of it, that had probably been a factor in the death of the routine. Aunt Sidyera caught her laughing out of place somewhere around then, and from that moment on Alixa had allowed the joke to amuse her for all of a few seconds. Then it was, "Oh, stop that, Pityr. She's all well again now. It's not funny to laugh at an old woman." He'd obliged, though not without a wink at Jasen when Alixa's back was turned and one last pull of that ridiculous face he put on.

"I remember the impression," said Jasen. "I still don't think I remember Josef though."

"Right, so Hanrey left Euonice behind. He was really fuming—he was so red-faced—and he marched past us muttering, and then who should come round the corner but Josef. He had a handful of strawberries, big fat red ones, and one in his mouth, and Hanrey saw him and just—that's it, you remember, don't you?" she asked as a slow dawning washed over Jasen's face. "He *exploded*. Shouting down the street, so everyone in the entire world could hear it. '*So it's you who's been stealing my strawberries!*'" She did her best imitation of the gruff old councilman. "'*Every ruddy day I come back to see someone's been off with the things! Do you know how long those damned seeds took to take?*'"

Jasen could see it now. Josef was a couple of years younger than he and Pityr, so at the time he must have been nine, maybe ten. He was a skinny little boy, quite runty actually, but he had, for want of a better description, a damned big pair of balls on him. Authority meant very little to Josef. Jasen saw him around Terreas here and there, often getting into trouble, but no matter how many tellings-off he got, he never changed, never stopped causing trouble, never ceased his back-talking. He was a law unto himself. And on that day that Hanrey confronted him, he reacted in a way that only Josef could: instead of denying the charge—because Hanrey couldn't know, really, that it had been Josef who did it (though he almost certainly did)—he grinned right back at him, with a mouthful of half-chewed strawberry.

"You cheeky little—!" Hanrey had roared. "I'll have words with your mother! Now give me those strawberries, you thieving little—"

And he snatched out with a liverspotted old hand for them.

Two things happened at that moment.

The first was that Josef pulled backward, so instead of grabbing the strawberries out of his hand, Hanrey slapped them from it instead.

The second was that Euonice rounded the corner too.

"What in the blazes are you doing to that boy?" she cried, and she hurried up with a burst of speed she hadn't shown since probably three decades prior.

"He's a thieving little blighter!" Hanrey responded. "He's been stealing my strawberries!" And he whipped his hand out again, presumably to grab Josef by the wrist so that he could march him all the way back home and have words with his parents.

Euonice was there first. She whipped out her cane in a streak that would make Huanatha proud, and rapped Hanrey hard across the knuckles. "Don't you dare lay a finger on him!" Euonice brandished her cane, which was apparently utterly unneeded at this point.

"THAT BOY HAS BEEN STEALING MY STRAWBERRIES!"

"Leave the boy alone," she said, "you crotchety old fart."

Hanrey's lips pursed. He glared, from Euonice, to Josef, and back again. Then, without another word, off he stalked, back toward the assembly hall, disappearing with a *bang!* as the door slammed closed behind him.

Yes, Jasen remembered it very well. It came to him vividly, the image of all their faces: Josef, grinning madly; Hanrey, eyes bulging, steam practically pouring from his ears; and Euonice, who let none of her joy show upon her face, though Jasen knew she was almost as happy in that moment as Josef. They were all so clear to him that he might still be there, in Terreas three or four years ago or however long it was.

"Hang on," he said. "One of the funniest things to happen that summer? As I recall it, you were mortified."

"I was. Josef had been *stealing*—and I was friends with him! I thought Hanrey would come over and lay into me next."

Jasen shook his head. "Typical Alixa. So concerned with what is proper that you were guilty by proxy." But he smiled too. "And look at you now."

"Covered in blood and mud and ash. At least these are your bedcovers I'm dirtying."

He laughed—and oh, how good this felt. It felt as though he hadn't laughed in years. Perhaps he hadn't. He'd not laughed properly since Pityr was taken anyway, not like this. And if it hadn't been for Pityr, he might not have laughed with such mirth since the day his mother died. It had been Pityr who had been able to cut through that grief, giving Jasen the semblance of a boyhood he would never have had otherwise …

Jasen wished he could thank him for that.

You can. Soon.

He ran his middle finger along the back of his pendant, feeling the polished stone upon his fingertip.

"I miss home," he said softly.

Alixa nodded, somber once more. "I do too."

He thought of it, his mind pulling away from that scene outside the assembly hall, like a bird aloft on the wind. He saw the village itself, nestled in the shadow of the mountains, below the cratered, smoking peak that would one day be its destruction. He saw the fields, the farms, where crops grew and sustained lives that refused to yield, to the scourge that had destroyed everything beyond this enclave. He saw the great stretches of grass, where no crops grew yet, but one day might, when the village grew large enough. He saw them, rolling down gently to the wall that kept the villagers in and the scourge out. He saw the grasses grow high, as spring gave way to summer, and dandelions and daisies and wildflowers grew amongst their green blades, and the rye fields beyond the wall grew taller than they had any right to be. Then he saw them cut back for straw, bundled into bales tied with twine. He saw the grass rise again, but then autumn came, slowing its heavenward reach, and finally a frost gripped it, turning the village into a beautiful, blue-white idyll, almost the same color as the snow at the tops of the mountains.

He loved the summer, but winter was better, in a way. Perhaps that was because of his childhood memories—he and his mother and father, clustered together at home in front of a warm fire, listening to the crackling of the wood, its occasional *pop*s … drinking hot soup, warm and spiced … long evenings, the sun low, the village lit by lamps, the glow from windows, behind curtains, and, on clear nights, a sky full of stars.

Best of all, winter had been the farthest they could ever be from Baraghosa.

Home.

Jasen missed it so, and thinking of it, thinking of what he had lost, he felt an even greater hollow inside his chest, one that put the sadness at his looming fate to shame.

Terreas was gone.

Perhaps Alixa thought of this too. For a time, both of them were quiet. The only sounds were their breathing, Scourgey's, and the boat, shifting on an ocean as they moved once more, perhaps for the last time, after Baraghosa.

Finally, Alixa broke the quiet. "I almost don't want to ask, but ... do you have a plan to beat Baraghosa?"

Jasen answered her honestly. "No."

Alixa nodded.

There was more she wished to say. Jasen could see it. But this, he could guess at. How did he even plan to fight, exhausted as he now was? How could he, when he would grow only more and more tired as the days passed?

He did not know the answer to that either—only that he would.

22

Jasen vomited.

He hung over the edge of the deck. One hand gripped the railing, keeping him from going over. It was a limp hold, though, and if the boat happened to give a particularly powerful lurch, his fingers around the wooden post would not save him from sliding into the sea—a sea full of bright orange vomit.

It hurt coming up, hurt dreadfully. More bile than anything else, most of its volume came from the water Medleigh had instructed he drink as much of as possible.

It had been four days since they'd left Nonthen behind, their Prenasian captives left upon the crumbling clay shores. To say that Jasen had deteriorated was an understatement. For the past two days, he'd been unable to keep food down. Since yesterday, the water he forced into his stomach seemed to just stay there, sloshing about unpleasantly. Now it was coming up again every few hours.

"You must keep drinking," said Kuura. "It is important that you remain hydrated."

Jasen did. But it was so hard to force himself to swallow it, knowing it was only coming back out of him again before too long, and not easily. The spasms racked his body. Every shuddering heave was like a bruise that grew inside of him, always aching.

The vomit coursed through his nose on its way out of him, burning.

He coughed, spitting it out over the side of the ship. It streaked the side of the boat, hot and foul.

"Jasen!" cried Alixa.

She'd been practicing with a pair of daggers, taken from the armory below deck. Huanatha and Longwell both conducted lessons, intermingling their own practice with guided instruction to Alixa and Kuura.

141

Jasen had joined them on the first day. Fatigue cut his efforts short, though.

Energy rapidly deserting him, he hadn't been able to do more than watch since. Just lifting the sword was too hard. He'd suggested, breath wheezing out of him, *Maybe a dagger?* Longwell and Huanatha exchanged a glance. She told him, with her kindest look, to just rest for now. He needed to conserve his energy for their last battle with Baraghosa.

As the days passed, and he slipped closer to the veil, he wondered more and more often, *what energy?*

Alixa dropped her daggers now with a metallic clatter and rushed to his side. Landing heavily on her knees, she grasped him by the arm.

"Are you okay?" she asked, alarm high in her voice.

He vomited again. Little was left to come out of him now. Just empty retches and flying spittle. That and pain—a lot of pain.

"Is he seasick?" asked Longwell, lance placed aside.

Lying beside Jasen, Scourgey whined. Apparently the disease had eaten enough of him that she was scared to touch him. Rather than lie with her head upon his legs, she curled up beside him, close enough that he could reach out and touch her, that she could slip under an arm and brace him as he moved around the ship, to the deck and back—but she would not place her weight upon him anymore.

"Of course he's not seasick," Huanatha murmured. "He is dying."

"Have a little bit of tact," Alixa hissed. "He can hear you."

"It's … fine," Jasen breathed. "I know I'm dying. It's no secret." He wiped his mouth and let his arm drop like a leaden weight.

"You're not gone yet," said Alixa. She said it as though speaking the words would anchor him here for longer. "And we are close."

"How close?"

"A day." This was Longwell. Bowing low over Jasen, he rested a hand upon the boy's shoulder. "We will see this through. I promise you."

Jasen nodded and closed his eyes. The sun was bright. And the deck hurt. But he needed to stay out here, if only because, in case Huanatha was wrong, he did not wish to die alone in his cabin.

No. She could not be wrong. He would make it through to see Baraghosa's end.

"Go ready yourselves," he said. "I'm fine."

Alixa's frown, though he could not see it, was clear in her voice. "Jasen, you are not—"

"Time is short," he said. "You need to practice."

He could see her, in his mind's eye, her lips pursed together, preparing an argument.

"He is correct," said Huanatha.

For a moment, Alixa did not rise. She squeezed her cousin's arm gently, and although that small touch hurt, it brought comfort to him too. He could feel the creeping blackness now, wending farther inside, its snaking tendrils devouring the life inside of him.

If not for Baraghosa, it would be so tempting to just give in to it … to just close his eyes and let it take him, so that he could reunite with his mother and father and his ancestors …

But he had made a pact, to them, and to himself: he had this one last thing to do. And he would do it—somehow.

"I'll be right here if you need me," said Alixa softly.

He nodded weakly. "Thank you."

She kissed him on the cheek. Then she rose and was gone.

Tomorrow. Muratam would come tomorrow. Their battle with Baraghosa would come. And he would still be alive to see it.

He told himself this as he lay there, waiting as the blackness pushed deeper, deeper, deeper still, blotting out a little more light with every inch it grew.

*

He was sick again.

"Easy." This was Kuura. He rested a large hand on Jasen's shoulder.

Evening had come. The sun was moving low to the horizon. It had come down right in Jasen's field of vision. Bloated and reddish-orange, it had been blinding, painful even through closed eyes. So he'd moved, to put it behind him—which meant he now vomited over the other side of the deck.

He emptied his stomach. Nothing solid at all to come up—it had been how long since he last ate?—and hardly any bile either. What did come out of him was watery, a very pale orange color. Insubstantial though it was, it still stung the back of his throat and his nose as it came up, and it did not stop him from feeling utterly exhausted.

When he was finally empty—again—Jasen moaned. "Ohh …"

"Drink," said Kuura. He pressed Jasen's flask into his hands. His fingers wrapped around it feebly—and then tried to push it away. "No, drink. You need to stay hydrated."

"I'll just be sick again."

"You will be sick anyway," said Kuura, and though Jasen could not see his face, there was a hint of a kindly smile in his voice. "This will help you keep the little strength you have left. Drink."

Reluctantly, Jasen obeyed. Swallowing hurt too: his throat was raw, and the muscles that controlled it were tired. The water should have soothed some of that ache, but his body was long past soothing now.

He drank. It probably wasn't much, but his stomach felt uncomfortably bloated. Then he dropped the flask. The cap was tied on with twine, but he hadn't tightened it, so water spilled out across the deck, pooling around his chest.

"I see that," said Kuura, picking it up and turning the cap tight. "You c'not fool me by tipping it away. I may be getting on in my years, but I am not completely stupid."

"Could have fooled me," Jasen said.

Kuura laughed, his traditional great big belly laugh. Though Jasen had his eyes closed, and his head turned out to sea, he could picture the man very clearly, sat beside him, with his head thrown back and every single one of his teeth visible. It brought a faint smile to his lips too.

"Your humor has taken a cruel turn in these days," said Kuura when his laughter had ceased.

"I just say what I think now."

Kuura boomed a laugh again. It felt good to hear.

"Of course," he said. "Why worry who you will offend when you will be rid of all of us soon?"

Jasen smiled. "Exactly."

They sat in quiet. The war galley gently rose and fell upon the sea. Wind blew through, caressing Jasen's face. He could smell the salt constantly now, subtle but tangy, just as he could also smell Scourgey. Her scent was not overpowering, as it had once been. Why he could detect both smells now, when he thought he'd grown immune to them, he did not know. He could only guess that the filtering system that had sorted sensations for him was giving up too.

The black roots of death crawling through him had found it, then. And now they worked on breaking that, too.

But they had not made it to his core yet. Jasen knew that. He hurt, yes, hurt terribly when the sickness came. He could hardly bring himself to stand. Yet the darkness had not eaten down to the deepest parts of him. And awful though that pain was, every second that he felt it was another second he knew he was alive, and he came another second closer to the final—he prayed—confrontation with Baraghosa.

After a long time of quiet between them, Jasen asked, "Why did you change your mind?"

"Hmm?" said Kuura.

"About fighting Baraghosa again. Why did you reconsider?"

"Ah ..." Kuura rearranged himself, letting loose a long sigh. "I suppose the answer to that," he said slowly, carefully, "is that I listened to you."

"What do you mean?" Jasen asked.

"Your speech, to Shipmaster Burund—it was so ... impassioned, so certain. You have believed that stopping Baraghosa is right ever since I laid eyes on you, of course. But to see you reduced to this ... to see you dying ... and still willing to stake the last of your life, the final days you could spend far, far away from this fight ... how could I not listen?"

"I see."

"There are reasons more than this, of course," said Kuura. "Baraghosa has worked his way along the coast of Coricuanthi, sowing the discord Huanatha and Longwell and others speak of. And the destruction he laid upon Nonthen? I cannot deceive myself about that. Nor can I fool myself into believing that his cruelty will not spread. That endangers my family."

Of course—the family he had back home. A wife, children ...

"Baraghosa would kill them," said Jasen.

"I know. Perhaps not tomorrow, perhaps not even a year or two or five from now. But whatever his machinations, his malevolence is growing, spreading. I must do what I can to stop it before it reaches those I care about most."

Jasen nodded. Then he turned. Damn, but it was difficult, pushing himself up and over—Scourgey scrambled up, claws clacking on the deck, to use her body to help ease him over.

Though the orange disc of the sun was blinding and bright behind him, just a half-inch from finally kissing the horizon, Jasen looked Kuura full in the face.

"You might die," he said flatly.

Kuura nodded. "I might."

"Doesn't that frighten you?"

"Of course," Kuura said. "But we all must die sometime, mustn't we? Yet I ask you this: is there any better time to die than standing for what is right, protecting your loved ones, that they may live on another day without fear of evil? I don't think so."

"No," Jasen agreed. "I don't think so either."

"Then we understand each other."

"Thank you."

Kuura grinned. And in spite of the way Jasen hurt, despite how the muscles ached just to move—he grinned right back at him.

*

He was in a village. It spread ahead of him, and there in the distance was a peak, all but the very tip of it obscured from view by the rows of buildings leading up a gentle rise to the village center. Out here, the houses were fewer … As he turned his head—he was in a chair, apparently, one positioned on grass strewn with broken wood—he saw there were hardly any buildings at all out here: this was the village's very edge. Just behind lay a long stretch of grass, a carpet of it that came to knee height, rolling down a hill to a wall …

He was in Terreas.

And beside him, in this debris-strewn front yard—

"You've come a long way," said a voice, a woman's. She sounded tired.

Liquid sloshed.

Jasen turned to see Shilara Gressom. She sat in a chair dragged out from the kitchen, leaning against its high back. She didn't look at him, just looked straight out at the village itself. In her hand was a ceramic flask—whiskey—and she gave it a little shake before upending it and taking a nip.

Then she looked over to him and held out the flask. "Want a drop? You've earned it, by now."

He stared at her. How—?

"I don't understand," he said. "You died."

"Yep." She withdrew the flask and took another swallow from it. "And it bloody well hurt. Damned scourge." Another drink, her wrinkled neck rising as she swallowed. "But it was worth it though, wasn't it?" She glanced sideways at him again. "My, oh my. Look at what you've become. Jasen Rabinn, commandeered a war galley."

"I didn't … the war galley isn't mine …"

"Pfft. Not in name. But that shipmaster's following you, ain't he? Vessel's more or less yours. You might not be at the helm, or giving orders to all those men you've found yourself with, but that war galley is under your charge, I'd say." Her beady eyes lit on him, a sparkle in them. "I'd call that pretty damned impressive for a little villager boy from Luukessia."

Jasen could not think of what to say to that. It was not true, of course, but once Shilara got an idea in her head she could not easily be dissuaded of it, and so he kept silent, turning his gaze out into Terreas instead.

Was this a dream? It must be. He recalled having retired to his cabin last night, not long after the sun went down. His bucket, the one

Medleigh had fished up for him to puke his aching guts into if he awoke in the middle of the night, had been cleaned since the morning. Good—it meant his cabin did not stink of bile.

He'd gone to sleep clutching it, he remembered, one arm looped around the metal bucket like he was cuddling a toy from childhood.

So this was a dream.

Only it had none of the wrongness of his other dreams. When he came back to Terreas in his sleep, the village and its surroundings were not quite right. It was as though the place had been rearranged, and he walked through a place that was familiar but not quite right, all of its edges out of focus, like his eyes were smeared and blurry.

This Terreas was just as he remembered it. The village was sharp, the mountains in the distance clear.

There were only two small problems.

The first, and largest: this Terreas was not buried under a layer of solidified magma.

The second: the incomplete mountain, the one with the crater at the top, the very same mountain that had unleashed the explosion of lava that had crushed Terreas—it did not breathe even a single puff of smoke.

"Am I dead?" Jasen asked with sudden alarm.

Shilara chortled. "Not yet."

"Then how—?"

"You ask too many questions. How? Why?" Shilara sipped whiskey again. The flask was down to its last quarter, Jasen would guess, because she had to tilt it way up to get her nip of the fiery liquid. "Some things, you can't know. Some things don't have answers."

He frowned at that. But he shut his mouth.

There was an amiable quiet between them, for a while. Shilara sipped at her whiskey, on and off. When she was between nips, she looked out at Terreas—the little portion of it she could see, anyway, from her ramshackle cottage with the misted windows, right at the very terminus of the village.

Jasen looked out too.

A couple of fires were burning. It must be summer, going by the warmth, but nevertheless there were still at least two fires burning, smoke pluming out of chimneys and rising in high, pencil-thin streaks in this breezeless day. One must be the baker's; Jasen could taste warm bread in the air, sweet pastries and savory ones all cooking at once, their flavors intermingling and spreading across the village, mouth-watering and oh so inviting.

This was home.

And perhaps, if he rose from this seat and walked away … maybe, just maybe, he could find his father; embrace him; tell him that he was sorry for having left without telling him, sorry for bringing him such fear in his final days—and, most of all, sorry for the fate that would befall him—that *had* befallen him.

He was just about to do that when:

"You have the heart of a warrior, Jasen."

He peered at Shilara. "Huh?"

"You—" she pointed with the neck of her flask, "—have a warrior's heart."

Jasen stared.

"Oh, don't look so bloody baffled," said Shilara. "It's simple enough. You've heard it, I can see you have, and you're not stupid like that old codger Hanrey, so don't ask me to try and explain it."

"I don't—" Jasen began blankly. "I'm not sure …"

"Oh. I see what this is. Fishing for compliments. Putting on a dumb face so I stroke your ego."

He looked more blank than ever. "Uhm …"

Shilara chortled. "No, I'm wrong. This *is* stupidity. What's happened to your brains since we last saw each other? I know you had 'em. The sorcerer rattled them so hard that they've pissed out of your ears?"

She took another swig of whiskey. Closer to empty, the flask came.

Jasen had a very sudden thought: the moment that flask was empty, the dream would end. He was certain of it, so totally sure.

He needed to see his father, now, before it was too late.

He gripped the arms of his seat, pressed, lifting—

"Sorry," said Shilara. "You're not going anywhere."

And he was not. He was stuck fast, unable to leave the seat, like he'd been glued by the backside to it. But, no, it was more than that. He could move—but his body wouldn't obey. He could shuffle, could shift—but his arms would not straighten, and nor would his legs.

He was a prisoner.

Panic did not come, as it might have. Disappointment, though … that washed in.

"Don't be so down about it," said Shilara. "You'll see them soon—all of them."

Jasen's heart skipped. "My father?" He dared to add: "My mother?"

Shilara nodded. "Ayuh." She took another swallow of whiskey. Damn, but she was putting it away. She'd always sipped at it in life, whittling down a flask's contents slowly. But she at least paced herself. Here, now, it was like she had one destination ahead of her—drunkenness—and she jogged toward it steadily.

"As I was saying," she went on, "your heart. A warrior's. No one's really got one, not in this village." She shrugged. "Maybe one other, but she's a got a lot of work ahead of her to become what she's meant to be."

"Uhm ..."

"Would you shut your mouth and listen?" Shilara said. "Didn't your parents teach you to listen to your elders?"

They had ... although the village outcast was not necessarily what was meant by 'elder.'

"We don't have all the time in the world," Shilara went on. She drank again, a hearty swallow. Lowering the flask, she ran the back of her hand across her lips, coating it with a thin sheen of liquid. "Now, as I was saying. No one in this village really has a warrior's heart at present—no one but you."

"I—"

"You're interrupting again."

"But I don't understand," Jasen protested. "How is that?"

"How *isn't* it?" Shilara pointed at him. "You went after adventure when your whole life you'd been told to stay within these boundaries. You showed courage when your whole upbringing, you were shadowed by the fear of the wider world, and what lay out there for you. That is what makes you a warrior, inside." She nipped her drink again. "You didn't grow into it, like your cousin is. It was in you all along."

Was it?

He searched inside, looking for this—this *warriorness* that Shilara said he possessed. Surely he would feel it, surely he would know it when he touched it. He felt it exuding from Huanatha and Longwell, so he knew the sensation of it ... but no matter how he looked, turning the inner parts of himself over, he could not locate it.

"I don't—" he began.

"Of course you don't," said Shilara swiftly. "But you are. The people around you recognize it, I can guarantee it."

Huanatha? And Longwell?

Shilara seemed to read his thoughts: "Those two see it best of anyone."

But how did she know—?

"A warrior's eyes are always open," she went on. "They are always seeing, always looking for their foe's weakness. They search, constantly, for what is different about them—and they utilize it to stop them."

Baraghosa.

Jasen frowned.

"But he does not have a weakness," he said finally.

"Of course he does," Shilara scoffed. "He is mortal, not a god. He is strong, yes, he has powers many mortals know not—but he has a weakness."

Jasen racked his brain. "So what is it? How is he different?"

Shilara swallowed. Very close to empty now, the flask.

She peered at him, her lips wet. "You already know."

Jasen balked. "I do?"

Shilara nodded. "Yes. You just don't know that you know."

He was about to ask her how, about to question how she could be so sure … but she took one final swallow, tilting her head all the way back to empty her flask of whiskey.

"Would you look at that," she said. "I'm all out."

She held the open flask upside down.

One drip of caramel liquid hung at the neck. The drop elongated, gravity pulling at it.

Then it broke free. It streaked down, a tiny ruby.

It landed upon the earth at Shilara's feet—

Jasen awoke in his bed.

Longwell stood over him, Alixa silhouetted in the corridor behind him.

"Rise," said the lance-carrier. "We are here."

23

The country of Muratam lay on the beach-lined coast of Coricuanthi. Its heart, the place where Huanatha had ruled until Baraghosa had usurped her, was a city called Tarratam. A port city, it lay right where Muratam kissed the azure blue waters of the sea.

Arranged upon a great, steady rise inland, the entire city was built from brown stone, but banners and parapets and rugs in rich shades of blue, green, and red hung from slit windows, like jewels scattered in sand.

At the outskirts of the city, near the port, the buildings were smaller. These were homes rather than businesses, although the city certainly had its own collection of stalls, with vendors cooking in the early morning sunlight, the scents of warm, exotic spices warring for supremacy in the air. But they were far fewer than there had been at Aiger Cliffs, even though the cities both were similar in size.

There were hardly any boats docked, too.

"This port thrived when I ruled," Huanatha growled. Her grip tightened on Tanukke's hilt. "Trattorias will feel my vengeance for this."

They rode a boat out, several of the *Lady Vizola*'s crew manning the oars. Alixa grasped them too, matching their steady cadence as they put the war galley behind them and approached the docks. Longwell lowered his lance to take up oars too.

Jasen had tried, feebly. But he was dissuaded by Kuura and Alixa, who told him just to sit, and by Shipmaster Burund, who rode out with them, in a long shore coat—and with a sword belted in a sheath at his hip.

"You're joining us?" Longwell had asked in muted surprise.

"I, too, have listened and heard," the shipmaster answered. "I cannot deny the truth: Baraghosa is a threat to all. I will not risk my men, but I will help to stop him, in any way that I can."

Longwell nodded. "Thank you, Shipmaster."

Jasen breathed a thank you too, nodding.

Burund appraised him with a steely eye. "No. Thank you—for helping me to see what my eyes and my heart were blind to. Now, let us see this done."

Huanatha did not row either. She stood at the very tip of the rowboat, looking out over the city. Though her back was to Jasen, he could see that she was shaking her head. She wore her anger like a cloak, and it seemed to grow longer with every stroke of the oars.

Aiger Cliffs had been a ceaseless bustle, even into the night, ships still pulling ashore and vendors at stalls cooking long into the night by lamplight and the coals of their own fires. Tarratam, conversely, was almost painfully quiet—literally. As the rowboat came nearer to the dock, Jasen realized there were hardly any people. Those who moved about hurried from place to place, as though they were afraid to be out in public.

They docked in silence.

Huanatha leapt from the boat before they'd finished tying it to the piling. She marched across the empty deck, her armor clanking, her footsteps one of the few noises cutting through the day.

There were trees here, thick ones with heavy, rubbery leaves unlike those in Terreas. Jasen spied birds, perched high in them, wildly colorful creatures with long, hooked beaks.

Even they seemed afraid to sing.

The party clambered off—those of them come to fight Baraghosa, anyway. The rowers who'd come from the *Lady Vizola*'s crew held back, anxiety etched on their faces. They kept hold of the oars, as if they might need to use them at any moment to propel themselves and their boat back out to sea.

Shipmaster Burund parted their company with a short goodbye in their own language, perhaps a promise to return. Then he turned on his heel and stepped across the dock and into Tarratam proper.

Huanatha led them, looking surprisingly relaxed, though she swept the docks with an intense, unwavering gaze. Longwell strode after her. Kuura was next. Then came Alixa. She had a dagger tied to her belt. It looked unwieldy hanging from her hip, and unwieldy in her hands when she practiced upon the *Lady Vizola* II's deck. But she had taken to it as well as she could with the time they had.

Alixa kept pace with Jasen. He leaned on Scourgey, stumbling through the city.

"You should remain at the boat," she murmured to him.

"No."

"At least ride on her."

"I can walk."

Scourgey loosed a very low whine, encouraging him upon her back, perhaps, in her own way.

But he would walk. He would not ride in to a final battle with Baraghosa, unable to hold himself high.

The few vendors in stalls seemed more than surprised. Their wide eyes were almost comical, staring at the party clambering from the rowboat and pushing toward the place where Tarratam reached its apex ... staring at Huanatha, leading the procession.

The peak of the city, at the top of a high, rolling hill, was a huge, sprawling building complete with many high towers. This was the castle that Huanatha had once ruled from, and where Trattorias now sat upon the throne, Baraghosa whispering to him. It looked less like the castles of his imagination, though, than a fortress, blocky and unbeautiful and

utterly imposing.

Looking upon it, Jasen had no trouble believing that this was where Baraghosa could be found.

The few Coricuanthians out this morning were as shocked as the vendors at the docks. Most stared in open-mouthed wonder before creeping back into the shadows. Though their eyes alighted on the exiled queen, they dared not hail her.

So Huanatha hailed them instead.

She shouted something in her own language, to a woman swaddled in a dark blue cloth, the bottom edges of which had gone to rags. The woman spun, a look of purest horror on her face. A baby was swaddled close to her chest, and she clutched it tight, as though afraid the exiled queen would steal it from her very arms, and she hurried into the nearest open doorway and out of sight.

Huanatha growled.

"Why do they run?" Alixa asked.

"Trattorias has them living in fear," Kuura said. "Once Huanatha was exiled, he positioned guards to police the people. If any were even to mention the former queen, they were ... 'removed from society.' At least, that is how I heard it was put." Kuura's lips thinned into a narrow line. "One can only imagine the punishment for speaking to her."

"But there are no guards out here," said Alixa, peering about. "There's almost no one at all."

"It does not matter. Fear is a very powerful thing," Kuura said.

Huanatha hailed a pair of men. But they just as quickly went scurrying off.

Huanatha growled. "What has my cousin done to these people that they are terrified to speak to their former queen?"

"With Baraghosa at his side, it is likely he has only sown more discord while you have been gone," muttered Longwell. "Relent with your shouting; it will only drive them off further."

Huanatha held her tongue at that. She stalked silently up the dusty roads cut between buildings, many stone—but many more, Jasen saw now, only wood. These little hovels were nested amongst the sturdier buildings, with fat, dried leaves stitched together to form walls and awnings against the sunlight. From the sea, they'd been well hidden, either by the blocky stone buildings, or just by blending into the ground's dry brush.

Jasen peered into the little hovels as they passed. Despite the brightness of the sun, they were dim inside. At first, Jasen could not make out the interiors of the small, single-room homes they passed by. But the more they passed by, the more his eyes were able to adjust. And he saw they were all empty. Plenty of them were littered with rags and other odds and ends, yet none were occupied.

The ground seemed to eat up the heat and radiate it out, so even though they had traveled hardly any distance south these past few days, the temperatures had soared. Jasen felt himself baking, less from the morning sun and more from the warmth beamed up at him from the dry, cracked earth underfoot. Which settlers had decided to make a toehold here, Jasen hadn't the faintest clue. Certainly they were not around for him to ask them.

"Where is everyone?" he muttered to Alixa.

Her answer was grim: "I don't know."

Up the hill they went, and the higher they went, the fewer people they saw. Even the guards that Kuura mentioned were nowhere to be seen—although Jasen had a sinking feeling that as they came closer to their destination, that would change.

At least, he hoped so. Because the sheer quietness, so still and eerie, raised in him a fear that Trattorias's usefulness to Baraghosa had passed. If the king was not here, if Baraghosa had moved on, then Jasen did not know what he would do; he wasn't sure he had it in him to stay alive many more days, let alone fight.

Though, to be fair, the question of how he would fight Baraghosa was still unanswered anyway.

The roadway wound through blocky buildings. All the windows were slits, tall and thin, and Jasen realized whatever purpose they served in the day-to-day of life in Tarratam, these stone buildings were built for defense. And dry and cracked though the earth was, the vast hill on which the fortress was built made it a veritable stronghold, positioned right on the coast for maximum access to goods via trade.

On and on, up and up …

His eyes tracked past empty hovel after empty hovel. So many were in disarray. At first, Jasen had believed their occupants had simply left in a hurry. But the more he saw, they more he began to think they'd been ransacked.

On closer inspection, some of the hovels themselves had been damaged. The wide open entryways had been pushed wider. The roofs hung a little lower where wooden beams had cracked. The dried leaves were ripped and battered, as if a storm had come by. But storms did not affect some huts and not others.

No, people had done this.

He was just about to say so, when—

Something stirred in the hovel he was peering into.

"Huanatha," he said, voice rising.

She pivoted, eyes wide.

"Someone is in there."

She followed his pointed fingers, stalking past him to look through the empty doorway Jasen indicated.

Whatever had moved had ceased. Damn—a false alarm. Possibly an animal, or a trick of the eye.

Then Huanatha strode in, reached down to a bundle of dark blue cloth piled against the interior wall of the hut. She gripped it in a hand, lifted it clear—

And there lay a woman.

She cowered, her eyes closed, one arm thrown over her head. And though Jasen could not understand the words she spoke, he understood the meaning: "*Please do not hurt me!*"

Huanatha spoke to her, her tone kind.

The woman slowly opened one of her closed eyes.

She stared in amazement at Huanatha's face, for a long, long moment, her eyes wide. Jasen thought it was another level of terror entirely that now gripped her at the sight of the queen.

Then she burst into tears and gripped Huanatha into a fierce embrace.

Huanatha jerked, taken aback. But she wrapped an arm around the woman nevertheless, holding her as she cried and talked and cried in her ear, words flowing in a mad flood. They appeared more like a mother consoling a child than an armored warrior comforting one of her countrymen.

The woman, who could not have been much older than Jasen, at most twenty, was youthful, with beautiful brown eyes and hair the shade of deepest night. She spoke in a quick, heady stream. Huanatha interjected, asking questions, and receiving long answers.

"What is she saying?" Alixa asked Kuura. He, Jasen, Burund, and Longwell remained outside of the hovel, looking in.

"She speaks of Trattorias's reign since Huanatha's banishment," said Kuura. "The king has been ... 'unkind,' she says, but to call his cruelty that is no justice."

"What has he done?" asked Longwell.

"First thing he did after Huanatha's exile was build a contingent of guards. They have policed the city into a fearful silence. All mentions of Huanatha are punishable by solitary confinement or beatings, to start with. But there is more. Rumors of Trattorias's rise to power, and Huanatha's exile, spread in whispers, and when they made their way to the king, he ordered his guards to silence any talk of it. Any citizen found murmuring was taken away ... 'removed from society,' she says, as I heard in my own village."

"Did he kill them?" Alixa asked.

"It seems to be the implication, yes. She mentioned ... pyres, I believe, but she did not say exactly what for, just that they burned at night ... she moved on too quickly. So ... it would appear so, yes."

Jasen looked up at the fortress on the hill. He had flashes of Nonthen and the great fires erected around the devastated city as the dead were disposed of in the only fashion that was available given the great numbers of them. It was a gruesome way to dispose of the dead. And to think that this supposed "king" had willingly built those pyres, had given the orders that loaded the fires with bodies converted to ash and dust ... it was sickening.

Of course, the king did not rule alone. He had Baraghosa at his elbow, whispering advice, commanding Trattorias's actions more than Trattorias did himself.

It was just another reason why the sorcerer needed to be wiped from the face of the earth.

"It became a crime to speak ill of Trattorias," Kuura went on. "By then, the population of Tarratam had been halved, and another half of all who remained had either fled or were making preparations to leave. But Trattorias did not like that either, and so he ordered his guards to ransack houses like these ones, wresting anything of value from the people so they could not charter a boat from the city. Of course, that was not how he put it—he called it 'confiscating illegal paraphernalia.' But the people knew the purpose behind the ransackings."

"Why is he so desperate to keep the people here?" Alixa asked.

Kuura shook his head. "I do not know. And I do not believe she does, if Huanatha asks her."

"She will not," said Longwell. "She will challenge Trattorias on that directly."

"If all these people had their possessions taken from them," said Jasen, "then where is everyone?"

"Many simply fled on foot," said Kuura. "Others swam out at night, hoping to be carried by the current to the next city along the coast. And others sought refuge in the boats that docked here, swimming out and hoping that the sailors upon them would take them away. But word of Trattorias's attacks on his people spread, and so the boats came less and less frequently—and now, the only people who remain are those too terrified to leave."

"That's awful," said Alixa.

"And so you see," said Longwell grimly, "why it is imperative that Baraghosa be stopped."

"How can he have so much power? How can he twist people so?" Jasen asked.

"He finds a weakness, and he pushes upon it until it yields," Longwell said. "It may take years, decades even … but that is what he does. It is simple, almost too simple to work over and over, and yet it does. He is far too cunning."

"But *why*?" Alixa asked. "What purpose does all this serve?"

"I do not know," said Longwell. "But we will find out."

The woman's tears had petered out now. She'd released her hold on Huanatha and pulled back so the armored warrior could speak to her face to face. And now it was Huanatha's turn to speak, quick words that the woman nodded along to, over and over. Her eyes were glazed—but there was a hope in her face that hadn't been there before, a hope that Jasen suspected she had not felt for quite some time.

Finally, Huanatha took her by the shoulder. She squeezed it, said one final thing, and then the woman rose. She bustled past Jasen and Longwell and all the others, her eyes sparkling, then she was off, her quick walk turning to a jog, then a sprint as she hurtled down the hill toward the port—and she shouted, her voice rising into the hot, dry sky.

Huanatha strode out the hovel. She hardly glanced at the woman's receding back before moving past, sights set on the fortress. Her stride was so quick that even Longwell had to hurry to keep up.

Jasen gripped Scourgey, moving along as best he could, fighting against the aches deep within him and the pressing fatigue to reach Huanatha's side.

"Where is she going?" he asked.

"To alert the people who remain here," Huanatha growled back, "that the rightful queen has returned to take back her throne."

24

They went up the hill, the earth so dry and cracked that it was almost impossible to believe there an ocean just a mile or so away. Closer to the fortress, the hovels were replaced with defensible stone buildings, orange-brown and square, their only decoration the rubber-leaved plants around them or the fabrics hanging from windows, making awnings above the doorways.

Here, there were people. Not many, and like those near the dock, they stayed mostly out of the open. But they watched, with wide eyes and open mouths, as the former queen climbed the rise with death upon her face.

But as the number of people increased, so too did the guards. Clad in partial armor, with deep blue fabric showing in the places where metal did not cover them, they were milling about idly in the streets. As Huanatha led her group closer, though, they stopped to watch.

When they were close enough to make out expressions, Jasen saw fear upon many of them. They exchanged glances. Hands went to the hilts of swords. None were drawn though; a man slightly taller than the others waved them off with a hand, and they released their grips.

He had a look of great alarm upon his face too.

If Huanatha knew him, she did not let on. The guards, she paid no heed at all. She just kept striding, up and up the rise, toward the fortress and the imposing outer wall separating its inner courtyards from the rest of Tarratam. Her face was set.

If sheer rage alone could be the death of a man, Trattorias and Baraghosa should be dead the moment she laid eyes upon them.

"Why aren't they stopping us?" Alixa asked. "They can't want Huanatha to get close to the king."

Longwell pointed behind her. "That is why."

Jasen and Alixa both turned.

159

Alixa gasped.

A crowd had gathered. The remaining men and women of Tarratam, and even their children, massed, spurred on, Jasen suspected, by the woman to whom Huanatha had spoken. Dozens and dozens of citizens came up the hill, an army in the making. Though they lingered a couple of hundred feet back, it was clear they were there in support of the former queen.

And with every step, more joined them. Word had spread. The former queen was back, come to take her throne again—and to free them from a cruel man who had brought them only fear and pain.

"The people rally to her," Burund mused.

"I can only hope I see the same," Longwell muttered, "on the day I return to Reikonos."

"You will," said Kuura. "I have no doubt of it."

"Thank you for your confidence."

Jasen couldn't help but watch, clutching onto Scourgey so he was guided forward even without turning to see where he walked. The massive crowd, all of them there to support Huanatha, was an awe-inspiring sight.

And for the first time, he really believed that this was the end. Today, Baraghosa would be defeated.

"How are you feeling?" asked Burund, from close behind him.

How was he feeling? There were all sorts of answers he could give to that. Afraid for what Baraghosa would do to them. Defiant. Uncertain, for he still did not know how he would fight—adrenaline, perhaps, could blot out those dark, rootlike tendrils weaving their way through him. This, though, he doubted: his heart was pumping hard already, yet the liquid energy it pulsed through him hadn't been able to cut through the growing fog. He could walk, yes—but he had had four days of conserved energy behind him to help with that. And he had Scourgey. She pulled him forward far more than his own legs could.

He chose to answer with the strongest emotion of all: "Determined."

Longwell gave him a sidelong look, a smile. "I would expect nothing less of you, Jasen Rabinn."

"You believe the sorcerer will be in there?" Burund asked, nodding ahead at the fortress, its huge outer walls, and the gate manned by guards who were steadily becoming clearer—and who, it appeared, were disturbed by the sight of the mob climbing the hill. They stared in clusters. Some of them seemed to bounce on their feet—preparing to engage, perhaps.

But the dozen or so of them were vastly outnumbered.

Trattorias's guards could no more stop this mob than they could a landslide.

"He may have moved on from Muratam already," Longwell mused slowly. "But do I believe that to be so? No. And sure as I am that he is here, I am also sure that he will be in that fortress. It is the center of everything—and that is always, always, where he can be found."

Jasen hoped he was right.

He is, a voice whispered.

His own?

He could not be sure.

The mob following Huanatha numbered in the hundreds by the time they reached the outer wall. Massive and imposing, it looked as if it had been hewn directly from a mountain. Guards stood behind the parapet that ran along the top, bows in their grips, looking down at the army arrayed before them.

Yet they did not nock arrows.

Nor did the guards about the gate draw their swords. They could only stare, a dawning horror on their faces, as the people of Tarratam drew nearer, led by Huanatha, Longwell at her side, Kuura, Burund, and Alixa close behind, with Jasen draped over Scourgey, all moving with purpose—to the gate.

Though Jasen and Alixa had overlooked the mob as it first amassed, there was no ignoring it as they drew closer to the fortress. The sound of footsteps on the earth grew. So too did the voices. Beginning with a quiet muttering, as if afraid to be overheard, the voices became louder with every step, and by the time the people had arrived at the fortress, they were shouting.

This was their land. The guards had been allowed to rule it—but no longer.

First, though: to cut the head from the snake.

Huanatha stepped forward. She surveyed the arrayed guards about the gate, her lip curled. Her gaze moved over the parapets too, to the guards who stood, in a nervous sort of limbo, looking down at the mob.

She shouted something.

Jasen did not understand the words.

His vision clouded with white spots. A stabbing pain ran through his head—

He buckled, clutching Scourgey.

She whined, from far away.

And suddenly there were more voices. The mob was louder than it had any right to be—as if not just hundreds stood out here, behind their rightful queen, but thousands and thousands, all amassed as one. He heard them, and he felt them, in the dark he had fallen into, the tunnel he found himself in the darkest parts of ...

So many voices, all vying for volume. So many languages, swirling about him. A veritable cacophony, his head would be crushed under the sheer weight of it all—

And then it eased. The souls were still there, these departed ancestors of people. Jasen felt them still ... but their presence was suddenly a comfort.

There were so many of them! They moved around him, and he felt them, knew they were there in the dark tunnel and outside of it, spread across Tarratam—and farther, too, a throng of souls that extended beyond the imaginary walls of this city, out of this country, across this entire world.

He had a sense of being dislocated in time. Many moments were overlaid, all at once, and perhaps if he had not been so exhausted already, it would have nauseated him. But he could unjumble them; if he picked out one voice among the others, it was as if that soul had clung on to some last remnants of the time they had left behind. He could see where and when they came from, could feel their stories, like dipping his toes into the cool pool that had been their lives, breathe in just a little of it. Here, this one—she was twenty-one, with long, dark hair, almond eyes, with a gap between her front teeth. She'd loved fishing, but not with anyone from her village; she went to a creek by herself, up near where the spring that fed it burbled out of the ground, on the side of a mountain of her own, gently sloped and green. The fish there were black, and she only ever fished them if she could count four dozen in each of the pools where the creek languished a while before rolling on down the slope to a bay where a man lived, a very handsome man, with a crooked smile and a turned-in foot—but she loved him, thought he was so beautiful, even if he did not see it himself ...

And then this one. An old man, close to eighty. His bones had been tired at the end of his life, almost four score years. When he was a boy, catching polliwogs and skipping stones, he'd wanted to live forever. But when his wife had died—there was something wrong in her breath, the doctor had said, and the illness ate her alive in less than a season—he had awaited death impatiently. It had taken so long to come, longer than his bones had been tired. He'd waited what felt like forever to find his wife again.

He had her now. Jasen saw her, just behind him, their hands

entwined. His bones weren't tired anymore, and nothing black ate her from inside.

Another and another and another. Jasen could pick out information about them all, as easily as if he were plucking blackberries from a bush. This person came from a far eastern land whose name Jasen could not pronounce. That person had been deeply unhappy, for a long time, too long. This person had had an affair, their air of conflict still hanging about them so many years on.

Why were there so many people? Why all here?

He could pick the answer out—but they were moving again, Scourgey was pulling him along, and though his feet were far, far away, he forced himself back to them, out of this dark tunnel and back to Tarratam …

The gates were open. How Huanatha had convinced the guards to open them, Jasen couldn't know. Probably the great mob of people she brought with her had been a deciding factor.

Alixa gripped Jasen's wrist. "Are you okay?" she whispered.

"I'm fine," he breathed.

"Just then, you sort of slumped. I thought …"

"I'm fine," he repeated, more firmly.

Alixa pursed her lips at him. She did not argue, though, just walked on with him through the expansive courtyard leading to the fortress, with its tall palm trees and scrubby, dry-looking bushes.

Her hand remained upon his wrist.

The fortress was entered via a huge pair of doors. Easily the size of one of the Prenasians' trolls with half of another stacked upon its head.

Guards, three of them, stared in muted horror at Huanatha's approach.

She shouted, raising her fists—

The guards leapt into action. Two ran for the mighty door.

The third bolted across the courtyard.

One of the guards shouted after him.

He did not turn back, and nor did he answer; he just ran, flat out, faint puffs of rusty dust kicked up by his boots as he pelted away.

The two remaining guards levered the doors open.

Huanatha surged in before they'd even come fully apart.

Longwell and Kuura followed. Alixa and Jasen were next, with Scourgey carrying him. Burund brought up the rear, a hand perched upon the hilt of his sword, just in case.

And behind them all, unstoppable, marched the massive mob from Tarratam. It flooded into the courtyard with shouts and cheers.

Jasen heard one of the guards bleat something. Then he was sprinting away; his partner deserted too a moment later.

Given the general squalor of Tarratam, the interior of the fortress was surprisingly lavish. Pedestals were arranged throughout the wide open corridors, with trophies from distant lands upon them. A vast, sparkling purple geode sat upon one; on the next was a carving of a man, cut out of a black rock with glittering silver sparkles within it. There were paintings of boats upon the seas, of tropical forests, of animals that Jasen did not recognize, with orange fur and black bands running across them. Enormous animal skins, which must have come from great beasts that required a dozen men to take down, were displayed on the walls.

Huanatha stopped at a podium with a fine glass vase upon it. It was blown superbly, with iridescent swirls all over its surface.

"My cousin's stolen trophies," she snarled. And she took it in hand and flung it, as hard as she could against the sealed doors at the far end of the corridor. It exploded in a vibrant shower.

"*I AM HERE, TRATTORIAS!*" she roared. "*YOU WILL NOT DEFILE MY THRONE A SECOND LONGER!*"

She broke into a run, flying down the corridor to the room at the end. Longwell burst after her, and Alixa and Kuura too. Burund hurried onward, and Jasen gripped Scourgey, who slipped fully under him so that he rode upon her back, and then she put on a frenetic burst of speed that carried him past all of them, to the fore, hurtling alongside Huanatha—

She leapt, as though she threw herself across an invisible chasm and smashed hard into the doors.

They burst open.

And here was the throne room. Expansive and grand, decorated with more of Trattorias's stolen treasures, it was almost empty of people; there were only a handful of alarmed guards, who must have come from the parapets or elsewhere in the courtyards, addressing a dark-skinned man with a chiseled face and curly hair. He wore a bold crown made of gold, inlaid with deep blue gemstones.

The guards whipped around as Huanatha hurtled in.

Their faces fell as they stared at her, their mouths agape.

The king stared too.

But Jasen looked past them all, past the terrified guards, surely about to abandon their posts just as their comrades already had, to the man at the throne's side. A spindly, spidery sort of man with two glowing orbs settled close to his shoulders, his expression showed no shock, no reaction of any kind. He looked toward this sudden intrusion with only a faint interest.

"Baraghosa," Jasen snarled, eyes beaming daggers at the sorcerer.

"My, my," the sorcerer murmured. "The dying boy from Terreas lives ... and he comes to fight me once more."

25

Trattorias rose.

"What is the meaning of this?" he barked. He had a somewhat high, reedy sort of voice, not entirely unlike Baraghosa's, which was just a mite higher than a man's ought to have been. He stood nearly as tall as Longwell. His broad chest would not have been out of place on the *Lady Vizola*.

And there was no missing the jewel-encrusted scabbard at his side.

Huanatha's eyes flashed upon it in an instant. They bulged. "You thieving snake," she hissed. "You have no right to my armory."

Trattorias rested his hand upon the sword's hilt. "I have every right. I am the king. And you, cousin, are exiled from these lands."

"Not anymore," she growled back—and she took a threatening step forward.

Trattorias called for his guards in his own tongue, voice rising with alarm.

They hesitated a moment, but they stepped in front of him, raising their own swords.

Trattorias's eyes flashed. "Tell me, cousin." His tongue flicked up and down like it was a serpent's, tasting the air. "How did you gain entry to my fortress?"

"This *castle* is *mine*," Huanatha growled.

"I asked how you gained entry," Trattorias snapped. "You will answer your true king."

Huanatha growled. Her teeth gritted, she rested her hand upon the hilt of her blade—

"Drawing a weapon upon the king? You traitorous wretch!" He snapped off something to the guards—ordering them to seize her, perhaps—and their nervous looks grew more panicked.

Staring with wide eyes at their former queen, they took their swords in shaky hands and stepped forward, slowly and carefully.

Longwell gripped his lance. He took a menacing step closer, standing at Huanatha's side.

On the other side of her came Kuura and Burund.

The guards stilled.

Trattorias's face fell. A dim horror swept over it, but then he regathered his wits. He boomed something to his guards—

And then came a thunderous noise from behind.

Huanatha and Longwell did not move. Nor did Kuura and Burund, poised and ready to throw themselves into the battle if the guards pressed.

Jasen, at the back, did look. He turned his head to see the mob surging into the fortress.

Now Trattorias paled, like a caramel ghost. He barked orders to his guards. They did not move. He shouted again.

The guards stared in terror, past Huanatha—

And then they broke. Sprinting away in a mad flurry, all three of them bolted in perfect unison toward a side entrance.

"Baraghosa!" Trattorias cried.

The sorcerer moved in a whirl. One hand, he thrust out toward the door through which Huanatha had come. It slammed closed, and a steel beam, on a hinge, fell down with a quaking *clang* across it, barring entry.

The other hand, he thrust out in the direction of the guards.

They jerked back as if a string affixed to the base of their spine had been yanked, pulling them backward in a spasm. They rose into the air, and with a subtle movement of his fingers, Baraghosa twisted them, bringing them before the king.

They struggled. Invisible bonds wrapped them. They could buck, they could squirm. But their arms were glued to their sides, their legs stuck together like they'd been sewn all the way from crotch to ankle. And their mouths were stuck shut.

Terror gripped them as they thrashed, silent.

"What would you do with them, my liege?" Baraghosa asked.

Trattorias glared up at them. "Their loyalty has ended. Kill them."

A faint smile lifted the corners of Baraghosa's mouth. "As you wish."

He straightened his fingers—

The heads of all the guards twisted. Three *cracks* came all at once, loud, like the bough of a tree snapping.

Their bodies fell limp.

Baraghosa discarded them, a casual wave sending them to the side of the room where they dropped in a heap.

And now he stepped before the king. Unnaturally long fingers pressed together, steepled before his chest.

His eyes were always so flat, so black, no depth to them whatsoever. He raked his gaze over them.

When Jasen had stood before him, in the assembly hall when he made his choice for the year's trade—the year's sacrifice—he had felt himself shying away from those eyes. Just the feel of them upon his skin brought gooseflesh to the back of his neck and made his hairs stand on end.

He'd fought the urge to recoil from Baraghosa's gaze for years. For if he did ... if the sorcerer saw his fear, the way Jasen inched back from him ... then Jasen would surely be chosen.

Now, the instinct to recoil was gone. Baraghosa was a twisted man, but Jasen no longer feared the power he wielded.

He felt only hatred for him, and that hatred surged through him in waves with every beat of his heart.

With Scourgey's help, he approached the front of their entourage.

Baraghosa looked at him. He cocked his head slightly to one side.

He did not blink. That was another thing about those flat, terrible eyes. Jasen did not think he'd ever seen them close.

"You are here," Baraghosa said at last. There was the tiniest little hint of surprise in his voice. Yet, like always, he sounded barely interested at all.

"I've come to kill you," said Jasen.

That quirked Baraghosa's lips up.

Behind him, Trattorias boomed a laugh. "You? You can hardly stand. Is this one of your warriors, come to defeat me, cousin? A cripple gripping his malformed dog?"

Now Alixa moved forward. "Do *not* speak that way of him," she threatened, her dagger in hand.

"No—you bring two children." Trattorias smirked. His eyes glinted. "Is this the full force of your resistance, cousin?"

"I have brought all of Tarratam with me," said Huanatha. "Your slithering puppeteer locked them out."

As if on cue, the door to the throne room boomed. Many shoulders must have been rammed against it.

The rabble outside grew in volume. Shouts could be heard. They were muted by the thickness of the doors, but there were too many out there to be silenced.

Trattorias's mouth drooped and he swallowed.

"These traitors will be punished," he said, gathering himself once again.

"You will not lay a finger upon them," Huanatha said. "You have driven this city to desertion. You have brutalized and killed these citizens—*my* citizens. And you killed my family—your *own* family." Her glare burned with white-hot fire. "You are a conniving, traitorous, thieving, murderous bastard." Her lip curled. "And now your end has come."

She stepped forward—

"*Baraghosa!*" Trattorias cried, reeling backward.

But Huanatha stopped. She had not yet drawn Tanukke. Her hand rested upon it, though, and Jasen knew it would not be long.

She watched the sorcerer with equal contempt to that she surveyed Trattorias with. "And you—the serpent who pulled all these strings in the first place. You, who creeps in shadows, who whispers and sows dissent among a people."

He only watched her with distant curiosity.

"Your end approaches too, snake," Huanatha spat.

Baraghosa's mouth drew up at the corners. He looked at her, with his flat eyes, then at Longwell and Kuura and Burund, then Alixa, and finally Jasen and Scourgey.

And then—

He laughed.

It was an unnatural sound, pitched as high as a child's laugh and oddly mechanical.

It raised the hairs on the back of Jasen's neck.

"You will laugh no longer," said Longwell, "once we are through with you."

Baraghosa's chuckle did not stop so much as wind down. He caressed the corner of his right eye with a fingertip, his pinky finger extended, an almost dainty touch as he wiped away a tear.

"Of course, of course," he said. "You warmongers have sought me out once again."

"Warmongers?" repeated Longwell.

"You hear correctly. What else would I call you, when you sail across the seas to do battle with me?"

"We are purveyors of justice," Longwell said. "And you must now face it."

"Purveyors of justice ..." Baraghosa echoed. He almost tasted the words, letting them roll over his tongue, trying out their sound, their flavor. "We have discussed this before, Samwen Longwell. I will not be held to account for my father's crimes."

"We have discussed it," Longwell said, "and you will recall what I said to you then. Yartraak received his own justice at the hands of Vara Davidon. The crimes you are being held to account for are your own."

Baraghosa weighed this.

He looked to Burund, then Kuura. "And why do you stand against me?"

"You spread destruction in every land you touch," said Burund. "I have seen the fallout myself here in Tarratam, and in Nonthen."

"Ahh … Nonthen." Baraghosa nodded. "And you?" he asked Kuura.

"There are few people in the world I will allow to call me old," he answered. "My children and my wife. You are not among them."

A shallow smile lifted Baraghosa's lips again at that. "Fair enough." He steepled his fingers, tapping his forefinger and middle finger to his chin. Slowly, he paced away, turning his back to them—

Wrong move.

Longwell leapt, his lance raised high. So too did Huanatha—

Baraghosa spun.

Trattorias loosed his sword with an alarming *shick!*

"BEGONE!" he bellowed—

And they all surged as one—Huanatha for Achacthua and the rest of them for Baraghosa to end this—right here—and right now.

26

Longwell flew through the air in a blur, his lance speared out in front of him—

Baraghosa pivoted on his heel. He drew his folded cane from his jacket and extended it with a sharp flick.

The lights hovering over him spun down, so they rested just above his shoulders. Pulsing with white light, they shone brighter than Jasen had ever seen them, as if somehow the sorcerer had distilled the sun itself into the glowing orbs.

He jabbed at Longwell.

The tip of the cane exploded with energy. Jasen did not see it—but he felt it. It impacted Longwell with the force of a full mountain coming down on him. Longwell grunted as he was flung backward, over their heads, limbs spinning madly—

He crashed into the wall, rebounding with a clatter.

Kuura and Burund came as one, on either side of him. Burund stepped carefully, his sword drawn, but still low to his hip. He watched Baraghosa's movements with eagle eyes.

Kuura had an axe. Not quite as devastating as the one Huanatha had first lent to him, with its barbed prongs, it was still an impressive weapon. Its blade was polished steel, curving up to a pointed tip, so it more closely resembled a billhook.

He circled around Baraghosa,

Burund moving at ninety degrees to him.

They were not close enough to strike, but they were closing in—

Baraghosa sighed. "This is tiresome already." And he jabbed out with his cane again, the blast hitting Burund in the shoulder. He was punched backward, flipping end over end.

Kuura ran at Baraghosa.

The sorcerer flicked out with the cane, swiping it from floor to ceiling.

A laceration split open on Kuura's chest, up his neck, his face.

He stumbled, blood suddenly gouting—

"You *are* old," Baraghosa hissed. He thrust out with the cane. Shouting wordlessly, Kuura tumbled past Huanatha and Trattorias—

"*Your blade is pathetic, cousin!*" bellowed Trattorias. He swept his jewel-encrusted sword in a quick and powerful swing that suggested he had been trained by the same sword masters as Huanatha had. She had to duck into a roll to avoid being lopped in half by it. "*Lay it down, and I will make your death swift!*"

Huanatha bared her teeth. "*Serpent!*" And she threw herself at him again, the tiny stub of Tanukke flashing—

Longwell hurtled past, lance drawn.

"You will pay for—"

Baraghosa flicked out with the cane, and Longwell's words turned to a grunt as a blast of power bowled him over and backward again.

Baraghosa turned to Alixa, who approached with her dagger clutched very tight in white fists.

He appraised her as though he were looking curiously upon a toddler with a toy.

"You come at me again?" he asked. "After I showed you what I am capable of?"

"I know what you are capable of," said Alixa.

"And do you not fear it?"

"I do." She clenched her teeth. "But I wish to save others from that fear."

"Hmph," Baraghosa regarded her with curiosity. "Very well."

She stepped in—

Burund and Kuura hurtled back again, both their blades drawn, poised, and

Baraghosa ducked.

They yelped, narrowly dodging to avoid spearing the other, then Baraghosa thrust out his hands at each of their backs, and they were tossed across the room. Burund smashed hard into the throne, so hard it exploded in a shower.

"*Defiler!*" Huanatha roared at Baraghosa, her focus upon Trattorias momentarily forgotten.

Trattorias pressed. Swooping in with his blade, he swung high—

"Huanatha!" Jasen shouted.

She'd dodged already, but the blade winged her armor, sending a high-pitched whine into the air, like a bell struck with a hammer.

Longwell came in again. He was bloody, a dribble of red oozing from his lip. Teeth gritted, he moved in a blur past Alixa and thrust out with the lance.

Baraghosa flicked his cane—

—and Longwell froze.

He stared, eyes wide, his lance stuck out in front of him. And though he pulled at it, it did not yield. It was as if its tip had been buried in the cleft in a rock.

"What is this?" he breathed.

"My powers were already great," said Baraghosa, meandering forward easily, his expression calm. "But now they are greater still." And he flicked his fingers again, forefinger and middle finger together, in a spiral like he was imitating the twist of a funnel of air—

Longwell was whipped up and around on the end of the lance. He cried out, whirling overhead, a tangle of limbs. His grip faltered, and he came shooting off of it, across the room in an arc.

He crashed headlong into the sealed doors, then fell, dazed.

The lance hung in the air.

Baraghosa appraised it. "A godly weapon ... I suspected as much ... one does recognize these things. I could do great things with this. But then ... I can do great things already." His gaze flicked to Longwell's prone form. "You may have it back."

The lance turned in the air, so it pointed directly at Longwell.

It shot out, like an arrow fired from a bow—

Jasen gasped—

Kuura swept in. He deflected the blow with the axe, sending the lance spinning away, so it clattered upon the floor like a dropped broom.

"I must say," Baraghosa said, "I am impressed by all of you. To escape my island—no, none of that, little girl."

Alixa had crept in behind him. Now Baraghosa hit the ground at her feet with his cane. A rush of energy spilled her over, a head-over-heels roll that knocked the dagger out of her hand. She groped for it—

Baraghosa sent it spinning aside with a flick of his fingers. "But I find myself most impressed ... by you."

His gaze settled upon Jasen.

Scourgey growled.

They'd kept back so far. What little strength Jasen had managed to hoard during their journey from Nontham had been squandered on the climb up the hill to this fortress.

So he needed to pick his moment—even if it meant watching his friends get tossed about like they were a child's playthings.

"You are so close to the end," Baraghosa mused, looking down at him. "You know it now, don't you? Perhaps you did not believe it before. But now … you feel it. Yes, you know death lies within you. Every second is a second closer you are to its door."

"Leave him *alone!*" Alixa screamed, swooping in with her reclaimed dagger—

Baraghosa didn't even look back, didn't even move. The lights floating at his shoulders pulsed, and a blast of energy sent Alixa sailing through the air with a shriek, over the broken throne, over Huanatha and Trattorias as she dodged his wicked flurry of strikes.

"You're a murderer," Jasen said.

"So are you," Baraghosa returned. "I can see it—see what you've done. There is blood on your hands. You are no longer the innocent boy from Terreas, are you? You've become … something more."

Kuura swept in again. Blood soaked his tunic, and there was a wild look in his eyes. He spun the axe overhead—

At the same moment, Burund jagged inward. He brought the blade down low—

"*BARAGHOSA!*"

Longwell thundered forward, his lance pointed directly at the sorcerer's head.

All three of them hurtled in, coming almost a perfect one hundred and twenty degrees away from each other. They came high, they came low, they came at his midsection—

And yet Baraghosa barely flinched. He just twisted on his heel, sidestepping—yet it was as though his body flattened, somehow; he did not just dodge but thinned, so his entire body was a single plane, like a leaf of parchment—

And all three attackers missed.

Baraghosa clicked his fingers.

The blast of energy rolled out of him like an explosion. Kuura, Burund and Longwell all were thrown. Alixa, who was just tottering back onto her feet, was tossed backward.

It hit Jasen too.

He and Scourgey were thrown by it. Like a wave had rolled over them, it lifted the both of them off their feet, sending them backward—

For the first time in what seemed like days, his touch with the scourge was lost, and

he hit the hard floor.

It was stone, like the walls and ceilings of the fortress, a sunbaked brown that was decorated only by royal blue carpets. Yet even if it had been a distilled cloud he landed upon, Jasen's body was too far gone. It would have hurt under any circumstances.

The pain jolted through him, a white heat that twisted his stomach. He felt sick—and the *crack* that came with it! His spine had broken, it must have—

"Of course, I do not blame you," said Baraghosa, lazily strolling over, ignoring Huanatha and Trattorias's battle raging about the shattered throne. "The Prenasians deserve death—them and their trolls. You see, it's they who I've been working all this time to raise an army against."

The pact Huanatha said he had pushed for, the same he'd wanted from Nonthen.

"The threat they pose—it is like nothing your Luukessians, or the Arkarians, or these Coricuanthians have ever known."

"There are none worse than you," Jasen spat from where he lay. Fingers formed into claws, he raked them along the ground for a hold to pull himself up.

Baraghosa smiled. "Oh, but there are. The Prenasians. They will roll across these lands with a fury like no other, an unstoppable force whose only intent is to conquer and subjugate."

Jasen looked up at him, the dark ceiling above contrasting with the sorcerer's pale face. "What makes them any different than you?"

"What do you mean?" the sorcerer asked, a bemused look upon his face.

"You conquer the lands you touch too," said Jasen, and he rose, slowly, on legs that threatened to give out from under him. Scourgey looped around, limping—but she sidled under Jasen's arms, let him throw them about her neck, the pair of them upright and defiant.

She growled.

Baraghosa ignored her. "I have conquered no lands."

"You lie," said Longwell, pulling himself up from where he'd been thrown onto the floor. "You do not take the thrones yourself, but you usurp the leaders upon them. You bring about revolts of your own making in order to fell them, so that you may install puppets who do your bidding. You have done it here in Muratam, you tried it in Reikonos, and I have little doubt that you have done it in a thousand other places."

"A thousand!" Baraghosa echoed. "What a compliment you pay me. But alas, Lord Longwell of Reikonos ... or rather, *former* Lord Longwell of Reikonos ... I have barely scratched the surface yet."

Longwell's jaw clenched, a hard line. Teeth gritted, blood dribbling down his face from his split lip, he gripped his spear tight and leapt.

Baraghosa was too quick. Longwell moved in a blur, but the sorcerer's powers had grown in the weeks since their last battle. Longwell moved, but Baraghosa moved a fraction of a second before him, pre-empting the warrior's strike. So when the tri-point spear sailed through the air, where Baraghosa's neck had just been, the sorcerer had already moved.

He swung his cane out and around, like a conductor to an orchestra—

It tapped the back plate of Longwell's armor.

A flash of purple light, a *BOOM!*

The far wall exploded, dust raining out of it.

Longwell collapsed at its foot, a crater dug in it.

Burund and Kuura paused, Alixa with them.

"Thus far," said Baraghosa, turning casually, "I have been civil."

"You possess no civility," growled Huanatha over her shoulder, ducking the swing of Trattorias's blade. He was fast, dangerously so, and he drew her back in with a ferocious thrust across her knees. She leapt, dodging it, then rolled—

Trattorias brought the sword down overhead—

She jerked aside, so the blade clanged on the floor—then Tanukke flashed, hitting it, a resounding clang cutting through the chamber—

"I have not killed you," said Baraghosa, "when I could end any of you at any moment. Even when you come for my throat, again and again, I have spared all your lives. Likewise, you have shown me some civility. You have explained, all of you, the reasoning for wanting to do battle with me—a rare thing indeed." The sorcerer's face darkened. "But my civility has bounds. I will not stand for this."

"Nor will we."

This was Longwell. He had risen, behind Baraghosa, crept up with his lance in hand. Now he thrust out, the spear's jagged tip glinting—

Baraghosa caught it in his hand and

held it fast.

Longwell stared, terror dawning on his face.

Again, it was as though the lance had been buried deep within a rocky cleft, so tight it could not budge even an inch. Yet it was only Baraghosa's hand gripping it—gripping it right around the blade. It should have cut him, should have sliced him open, yet he held it as if it were nothing more than a stick.

"How—?" Longwell stammered.

Baraghosa's eyes glowed, with a light that was a color Jasen could not name, a queasy, nauseating color that had come from a world entirely separate to this one. The chill that ran up his spine threatened to turn him to ice and then shatter him into a thousand pieces.

The air electrified.

"My power has evolved," said Baraghosa in a low monotone. "And you are powerless against me."

And he pushed back with the lance, a sudden, sharp thrust—

The pole slammed into Longwell's chestplate, which shattered.

Crumpling inward, a spiderweb of fractures exploded across it. Shards of metal pinged out in all directions, like the vase Huanatha had thrown at the doors to the throne room.

Jasen saw this for the tiniest fraction of a second.

Then the blast of energy connected with Longwell's chest.

One moment he stood before the sorcerer, utterly dwarfing him.

The next he was gone, disappeared in a cloud of dust where he collided with the wall.

"Longwell!" cried Alixa—

Huanatha, too, shouted his name. Her focus on Trattorias lost for a moment, she thrust out a hand, as if she could catch Longwell with it—

The king swung the sword—

The blade crashed against her chest.

Her own armor protected her. But Trattorias was strong too—not in the way that Baraghosa was, but in a physical, brutish way. Huanatha grunted, careening backward.

"*HAH!*" Trattorias bellowed. He brandished his sword. "Foolish traitor."

Huanatha staggered to her knees. Her head spun; Jasen could see her eyes flicking back and back to Trattorias before drifting off each time, following a dizzy world while her brain fought to reorient itself.

Tanukke hung almost limp in her hand.

Trattorias stepped before her.

He leered down at her, lips curled in a familiar way that must also have come from some distant ancestor, passed down through the family. This was not just a sneer though, but a victorious smirk.

He lifted the sword.

Its jewels glinted, blue and red and purple.

"Bow before your true king," he breathed, "and I will make this quick."

Huanatha looked up at him. Still spinning, she seemed not to be able to focus. Her own energy had wavered too; she almost sagged there, upon her knees before him.

But she met his eyes … and she growled, "No."

And she swung out with Tanukke at the same time as she rolled—

Trattorias screamed.

Blood erupted from behind his knee, where the stubby blade had pierced the gap between the two metal plates that gripped him about thigh and shin and torn him open.

"I will *never* bow to you," Huanatha roared,

and she flew at him again.

So did Kuura, hurtling at Baraghosa in the moment's distraction like a cannonball.

The billhook-like axe rose—

Baraghosa spun, swiping his cane through the air.

One second Kuura surged toward the sorcerer; the next he flipped through the air like a fly slapped with a piece of leather.

Burund—

He'd no more than stepped forward before Baraghosa sent him bowling over with a thrust of his cane.

"Meddling busybody," Baraghosa said. "Following me from Luukessia to Chaarland to Necromancer Isle ... I wrecked your ship upon the rocks, just as I wrecked this Longwell's to get you off my arse ... and still you took it upon yourself to find me."

Burund staggered up—

Baraghosa thrust out again.

Another burst of power, like a wave, shot out from his hand.

Blood sprayed from Burund's nose as he careened backward.

"Stop," Jasen wheezed.

Baraghosa glanced at him.

"No."

And he flicked out his fingers—

Alixa, who crouched beside the prone form of Longwell, his eyes closed and unmoving, shrieked as she was lifted into the air on invisible strings and drawn toward him.

Jasen recalled the battle in Baraghosa's tower. The way he had bound Alixa in invisible ropes, the way he had lifted her own dagger, pressed it against her stomach—

"No," he breathed.

He drew forward on legs that were unwilling to carry him.

"Desist, child," sighed Baraghosa, and Jasen, too, was thrown across the room, Scourgey with him. He sailed, the breath forced from his lungs—

CRACK!

This one was worse. If the burst of pain that had ripped through Jasen before was a ten on the scale, this blew past it and rendered obsolete every former measure of pain he had known. It *must* have broken his spine, not just snapped it but ground every vertebrae into dust. Oh, it was so searing and hot, overspilling his senses—he screamed, or coughed, or only wheezed—whatever sound he was capable of making now, it was not enough to convey the sheer, utter *agony* …

"I tire of your cousin," Baraghosa muttered. "But you, little girl … I see *very* interesting things for you. A shame—you could have achieved much indeed … been a great ally … but you aligned yourself with these simpleminded fools. All those opportunities to leave them wasted …" He tutted. "How stupid of you. Never mind, though … you will be reunited with your mother and father soon."

"Don't you speak of them," Alixa growled, and she spat, a fat glob of saliva that struck Baraghosa in the eye.

He winced.

For a moment, there was a deathly silence. Even Huanatha's battle with Trattorias seemed to have stopped.

Then,

for the first time, Baraghosa's voice rose with anger. "You disgusting little—"

"*UNHAND HER!*" Huanatha roared.

Jasen lifted his head—no, that was Scourgey lifting him, snaking under him again, whining, questioning in her own way if he were okay—just in time to see Huanatha sail through the air between Baraghosa and the suspended Alixa, Tanukke's stub flashing. She swept with it at the sorcerer's face, Alixa's spit still glistening upon it.

Baraghosa let Alixa drop with a clatter—

He caught Tanukke in the same way as he had Longwell's spear.

Then he thrust up, sending Huanatha and her blade spinning backward in an airborne cartwheel.

"You have your own battle to fight, *queen*," he sneered.

He rounded on Alixa, looming over her. "As for you—"

"*LEAVE HER ALONE!*"

Jasen's voice ripped through the throne room.

On Scourgey's back, he bounded across the stone floor, teeth gritted, pain roaring through him, his steely gaze set upon Baraghosa, fixed on the sorcerer who he would kill, would use the very last of his energy to destroy—

Baraghosa's expression flashed with surprise, then he swiped with his cane.

Jasen hit the wall, rebounded, and lay face down in the dust and cracked stone that had skittered over the floor, Scourgey sprawled somewhere beside him.

The world seemed to fall away from him. A fog crept in. It had been clouding his mind for days now—not just his mind, but all of him, lurking in the shadows. It came with the blackness that was eating its way through him. He'd staved it off, waiting for this moment ...

But they were losing. For all their trying, Baraghosa was stronger than he ever had been.

How could he be beaten?

How could Jasen beat him, when he lay here like this, broken and crumpled?

He might as well stop now ... might as well give in to the fog ...

He was so tired ...

He could rest ...

He breathed ... and the pendant dug into his chest as his lungs filled with dusty air.

His mother's pendant.

We are so proud of you.

But you aren't done yet, son.

He had promised to stop Baraghosa. If it took the last of his strength—he had promised them, his ancestors— that he would see it done.

He could not stop now.

He had to rise.

Across the distant clanging of Huanatha's and Trattorias's swords came footsteps. They should've been muted by the battle going on between former queen and false king. Yet Baraghosa had a strange way of overpowering sound. In the storms over Aiger Cliffs, Jasen had been able to hear him easily, even when thunder ripped open the skies and boomed every few seconds and rain poured down like a thousand drums all beaten at once.

"You would have been useful, you know," Baraghosa mused quietly. "The children I took from Terreas ... they were all useful, of course ... life is power, you know—yes, of course you know, for you feel it deserting you. It is why you lie powerless before me.

"But in life, you would have been useful, yes, very useful. You have a certain ... determination to you. Oh, I could have put that to great purpose ... but of course, I have gained a different sort of power now."

An echo of the clifftop battle came back to Jasen—the lightning, flashing white, its energy harvested. The people of Aiger Cliffs had been against it ... but even there, Baraghosa had been able to worm his way into achieving his ends, as he always did.

"I had to expend some of it putting down that useless wretch," Baraghosa went on—Longwell flashed in Jasen's mind now, lying upon a piece of wreckage of the boat he had commanded out of Reikonos—"and still more to dispense with you and your captain. And what to say of Nonthen?" He sighed, a heavy, weary breath. "I wished not to, I truly did … but I offered them an alliance, many times. Yet when they refused to listen—when they attempted to banish me from their city … well, I had to act. A shame; they would have been helpful against the Prenasians, when they come … But there are others. And their end will serve as a warning to others.

"You know, Jasen," said Baraghosa. "We are not so different."

He stooped down—and his hand reached under Jasen's face, taking his chin in a grip that was deathly cold and somehow unnaturally smooth, as though his hands possessed no lines, his fingertips no prints—

He lifted Jasen's head.

Jasen looked at him through a whirl of dancing white spots.

"You wished to protect your homeland," said Baraghosa, gazing at Jasen with his awful flat eyes, the pulsing lights perched upon his shoulders. "And I wish to do the same. It is why I work to bring about this alliance, so that when they spread from the east—which they will—I can protect it."

"You will fail," Jasen wheezed.

Baraghosa's mouth rose in a faintly amused smile. "No, Jasen Rabinn. I will not fail. For unlike you … I am not powerless."

He smiled now, a ruthless grin, his teeth showing—

He meant to kill him.

Jasen braced for it, the white dots clouding his vision, swirling, swirling—

And then he saw—

There were souls here. Dozens and dozens of them, all surrounding Baraghosa.

And among them, at the forefront, right over the sorcerer's shoulder, a face Jasen recognized.

Pityr.

27

Pityr smiled at Jasen, a boyish grin. Warm, comforting, it was a grin that Jasen recalled as if he had last seen his friend only yesterday. It had etched itself into his mind, the same way his mother and father's voices had, their faces.

His mouth fell open. His eyebrows knitted.

His friend? Here?

But of course. It had been Baraghosa who Pityr died with.

Baraghosa ... who killed him.

And as Jasen looked upon him, he thought—he could find out how it happened. In the same way as he'd been able to pick through the souls out at the gates, souls who, he realized now, were also tethered to Baraghosa, tied to the sorcerer because it had been his destruction and discord that had wrested them from their bodies—Jasen could sift through the last parts of Pityr's life.

He could know, finally, how he died.

He could know if it hurt.

But as he reached out to do it, with invisible hands, Pityr held them, stopped him from going any farther.

He only smiled down at Jasen, yet Jasen felt his response, even without Pityr saying it.

The circumstances do not matter.

But— Jasen began to protest. He needed to know—needed to know how his friend had been loosed from the earth ...

And he needed to know if it would hurt him, when death finally came to take him.

It may, Pityr thought, as kindly as he could. *But only for a moment.*

Jasen blinked. *I'm scared.*

Pityr nodded. *It's not so bad.*

Seemingly out of nowhere, Longwell flung himself at Baraghosa once more, his lance whirling. It swept through the air in a mad blur, impossible to dodge—

And still the sorcerer avoided it. He sidestepped as though he moved out of the way of a pair of dancing butterflies rather than an armored warrior who thrust a spear at his neck. Then he put out his palm—the lights above his shoulders, down very low to him now, pulsed with a flash—and Longwell careened across the throne room, smashing into the far wall. The impact was vicious: cracks spread out from where he slammed into it.

He dropped hard, lance fallen—and he did not rise.

Only Huanatha stood now, swinging with Tanukke, its broken blade almost comical against the curving blade Trattorias wielded. Yet still she battled, still she ducked and wove and pivoted and parried, pushing her advantage where she could, dropping back when she could not.

Baraghosa turned back to Jasen, favoring him with a flat smile.

Scourgey growled, teeth bared.

"You know it's hopeless," said the sorcerer. "You can feel it, can't you? The end?" He stepped closer, peering down at him with eyes that were almost flat—peering into him. "There's almost nothing left in you."

Pityr loomed beside Baraghosa. He looked at Jasen, his smile fading … and then he glanced at the glowing orbs positioned just above Baraghosa's shoulders.

He nodded.

And suddenly, Shilara's voice filled his head, even at the moment he realized.

How is he different?

You already know. You just don't know that you know.

The lights.

They were not beacons at all, dancing in the air to herald Baraghosa's arrival to the many lands he sowed division within.

They held his power.

Upon wobbly feet, Jasen rose. He had to brace himself again the wall behind him with both hands, pushing himself upward with all the energy he had in him. Baraghosa was right: the end was almost upon him. Those black tendrils had penetrated almost to his very core, at long last. He could feel them, winding around and around it, the last light place in him. But he'd held them off—for this.

He reached out—

Baraghosa's smile faltered. His eyebrows flickered in toward each other, the only time Jasen had ever seen confusion upon him.

He reeled backward, asked, "What are you doing—?"

Jasen's fingers touched the orb.

Light flashed. It was like the flaring of a fire—wait, no, that was wrong. It was like the flaring of every fire across the whole world, all of them burning in one huge, continent-sized pyre. A blinding white, whiter than anything Jasen had ever experienced, it enveloped every single one of his senses, as if somehow his eyes could not take it all in, so it flowed into his ears, through his nose, into his skin—

Then he was in Terreas.

And it was peaceful. So, so peaceful.

The village spread before him under a clear blue sky. The mountains were picturesque and quaint. The grasses were just coming midway to knee-height—early summer, a comfortable warmth beamed down from the sun, not yet so hot that seeking shade became Jasen's most common pastime. Smells came to him, breads and pastries wafting from the bakery. Meat was cooking, and though it had none of the exotic, interesting spices that he had discovered out in the world beyond Luukessia, it was the most delicious smell he had ever known.

But of course it was. It was the smell of home.

The village was quiet ... and yet it was bustling too. People passed by, faces he recognized—there was Griega Marks from the assembly, talking amiably with Euonice and a rather moderate-looking Hanrey. And farther down the street, Stewert Wells, walking his faithful old dog, its white fur stained by mud where it had dived into the stream on its morning walk.

But there were so many others, people that Jasen did not recognize. Had he forgotten all of Terreas's people already?

No—he realized, with widening eyes. He hadn't forgotten.

These were people he had not met.

These were his ancestors.

He stared at them, and they smiled as they went past, like he were a gawping child—which he supposed he was.

He turned on his heel, around the village square, to take in the full shape of it ...

And his heart skipped—not just one beat, but a dozen, surely.

A space within the moving crowd had formed, quite naturally. And within it, hand in hand—were his mother and father.

Jasen stared. His breath caught in his chest—if indeed there was breath to fill it.

His mother laughed ... and oh, how he'd missed that sound. His stomach squeezed as it came to his ears, soft and gentle and so much like home.

He staggered for them, tears in his eyes.

"Easy, son," said Adem, reaching forward to take him by the shoulders.

Jasen gripped him.

His mother came around his side—and he reached out for her too, winding an arm around her waist. He was as tall as her now, but in her embrace it was like he was a child again—and he held fast, firm, crying in the square.

She was warm.

This was home.

And he'd been gone from it for so long.

"We are so proud of you," his mother said. There were tears of her own in her voice, he could hear them. He could feel the ache in her chest too, as if their touch made a bridge between them, and he could cross it, could physically feel her emotions.

"I love you," he sobbed.

"We love you too," said his mother.

He pulled away from them, at least far enough that he could look them both in the eyes, ascertain that they were real, not some—some figment of his imagination that Baraghosa had conjured to ensnare him with. But no, those were his real parents. His father had the same hair, all the right lines upon his face, where the stress of running the assembly had weathered him a little more than time alone would have. And this was his mother, her face soft, her eyes the same brown Jasen remembered, with its dark little flecks like the jewels inlaid on Trattorias's stolen crown. This was their scent, this heat he felt from them was theirs.

He was home. At long, long last—he was home.

"Am I dead?" he asked.

Adem shook his head. "You're not done yet."

"But … how …?"

"Feel death," said his mother, leaning in. Her gaze was so loving—oh, he'd missed it so—but she implored him with it too. "It's here, in your hands." She touched him, then, a palm stroking across the back of his hand, and he *did* feel it—

Terreas vanished.

He was back in the throne room.

Baraghosa's orb glowed in his hands.

Pityr nodded at him over Baraghosa's shoulder. He had a faint smile upon his lips still—but he stared at Jasen, very intensely, meeting his gaze hard.

He was not alone.

The veil had fallen again—not a slip, like the short bursts he'd had before today, but like an entire curtain had been ripped from its rail. There were so many dead here, all those souls who he'd touched in Tarratam, he'd been brushed by. Every last one of them was like Pityr, anchored to Baraghosa, carried across the land and the sea to places far beyond where they ought to have gone to rest—

They whirled around him, constantly, out of sight of all but never gone, because the sorcerer held them close, always.

And they hated him.

Baraghosa was oblivious. He saw only one thing: Jasen, grasping the glowing orb that had danced so lazily, like a firefly, innocuous and yet the source of all of his vast power. And no matter how he pulled back—the orb remained in Jasen's hand. It had no surface, nothing solid about it—but he held it there, held it firm.

Panic rose on Baraghosa's face. He stared at the orb, at Jasen.

"What are you doing?" he asked, voice rising in alarm.

"You make people feel alone," Jasen whispered. "You spread fear, and you divide, so those you have most strongly wronged feel alone, alone in hating you, and in being able to take their revenge upon you. But I am not."

The voices of the dead rose around him, baying for Baraghosa's blood. Yes, there were so many lonely souls here, people who had been cut off or forced out. And sorry as Jasen had felt, consumed by self-pity in equal measure to his determination at times, he realized he had felt only a fraction of what these people had. Exiled from villages or cities, or simply cut off from their friends and families, loved ones all pulled away by an invisible chasm that Baraghosa grew, they'd thought themselves against an entire world. They had not found friends like Jasen had, warriors willing to stand with him, or those, like Alixa and Kuura and Burund, who simply took up the mantle because it was right.

They'd been so alone, in life.

But in death—they were many.

"You do not know power," Jasen said, and he rose, straightening for the first time in days, as if the souls of the dead fed him, brought new energy to his failing body. "*Life* has power. Death is powerless."

Baraghosa stared. His face was haggard. "What are you doing?"

"You did not kill my family," Jasen said. "But you did kill Pityr. And you have killed many more. They're here now. Do you feel them?"

Now the sorcerer's face twisted in panic.

His mouth opened and closed, the way a fish's did. But no words came out. He could only stare.

And then, gritting his teeth, he lunged forward, but Jasen snatched the ball of light out of his reach.

Baraghosa staggered backward. His alarm ratcheted higher. His face, always pale, was now ghostly white.

"You do feel them, don't you?" Jasen asked, still cradling the orb of light, now separated from its master. "You see them all around you—the people you have murdered. They follow you, night and day." His lip curled. "They hate you, Baraghosa."

A terror like no other filled Baraghosa's face. His neck jerked around, following the dead—they spiraled around him, a tornado of the dead, their faces twisted and angry and all of them screaming at him—he took them in, perhaps acknowledging them for the very first time, understanding the full might of their united hatred—

And then a dagger ripped through his chest from behind.

He stared, horrified, at its bloody tip pointing out from his ribs.

Behind him, Alixa gritted her teeth, clutching the blade's handle tight.

"You are a bastard," she said—and she twisted the knife.

Baraghosa howled.

The lights faded, like candles going out.

The power within them ebbed. Jasen could feel it, like water flowing past his hands and out, an ocean's worth of it pouring away.

Baraghosa hung for a moment, then Alixa yanked back the dagger and blood gushed from him, pooling at his feet. The corners of his lips down as far as they would go, his eyes flat, he looked almost like a child's drawing, a rendering of what stalked through nightmares, then he slid slowly to his knees.

He lifted a weak hand, touched the hole the knife had left as if he was checking it had really happened—that he had really been mortally wounded.

At the far end of the room, Longwell rose up from the heap of broken masonry and staggered over to them.

"Your reign of terror has reached its end," he said.

"Reign of t-terror?" Baraghosa wheezed. His flat eyes landed upon Longwell—but they were fading now too, the light in them vanishing the way his glowing orbs were rapidly diminishing to nothing. "I was trying to protect ... all of them."

"You protected only yourself," said Longwell. "And you failed at it."

Baraghosa's dimming gaze turned to Jasen. He looked at him almost blankly.

Death came for him—came far faster than it came for Jasen.

"I see them," the sorcerer wheezed. His spittle was bloody. Crimson liquid spilled from his mouth. "But you … do you see wh-what comes?" He coughed, spraying red, and his eyes met Jasen's. "What will you do … to protect them? You won't even … be here …"

Jasen looked back with all the defiance in his soul. "Neither will you."

"Before the end …" Baraghosa choked. "They'll be sorry I'm not."

He coughed again—

The light in Jasen's hand vanished.

And there, in the throne room, as Huanatha finally took the upper hand over Trattorias and knocked the blade from his hand, then stood over him where he cowered, hands above his head—it was done.

Baraghosa stilled.

And at long, long last, the sorcerer was no more.

28

All of Tarratam came to witness the coronation of the queen—or rather, the re-coronation. Jasen waited for it from a pillow in the corner of the throne room, weariness settled on him as it played out before his eyes. There were still not a great many of them, but already, in the short twenty-four hours since Trattorias had been defeated and thrown into the dungeons and Baraghosa had finally been felled, the citizens of this land were coming back.

They would never number as many as they once had. Trattorias had killed too many for that. And though Huanatha once more took the throne, Trattorias's actions had sullied the name of Muratam. It would be sullied for decades. Tough work ahead for the queen, to repair its reputation, but she would achieve it. Of that, Jasen had no doubt.

It was just a shame that he would not be here to see it.

He could not see much of anything now. The battle with Baraghosa had pushed him very close to the edge. His life now neared a cliff, one which he would inevitably tumble down before much longer. Hours? Days? No more than a week—he was much too tired for that.

However long he had left, it did not matter. He had defeated Baraghosa—all of them had. The sorcerer had faced justice for his crimes.

Baraghosa could sow discord no longer.

Jasen could die peacefully.

Except there was one other thing. He had seen Baraghosa's demise ...

Now, in the hours following his death, he wondered if perhaps he might see one last thing before he left this world behind and rejoined his ancestors.

The coronation took place at the castle. The courtyards were opened to all of Tarratam, the gates open wide for what was likely the first time since Trattorias had ascended to the throne, the celebration spilling out beyond the gates and around the walls.

Music played. People laughed. Families clutched each other tight.

The fear that had besieged this place only a day before had evaporated, gone like a puff of cloud pulled into strands by the wind and then vanished into nothing.

And when Huanatha came out—the cheers! Jasen had never heard such a glorious, happy, wondrous sound. It lifted his face in a grin, from where he watched upon the parapets with Alixa, Kuura, Burund, and Longwell. It was a tired grin; he could hardly hold it up, let alone himself—he lay slumped next to Scourgey more often than not—but it was a grin nonetheless.

Jasen listened to it. Kuura translated.

But he was so tired.

He did rouse enough to see the crown placed atop Huanatha's head. The thunder of applause that came after that was likely the cause of his waking, for it was so loud it vibrated even the walls around the castle.

He smiled again.

Alixa squeezed his wrist.

Then Huanatha took to the center of her podium to give a speech. It was in her native tongue, and again Kuura took to translating it.

"People of Tarratam: I stand before you today after long years in exile. Through that exile, there were times I believed I would not see this land again. Likewise, I am certain that there were times when all of you believed you would not see it prosper, or would not wake without fearing for your lives.

"Those days are over."

Applause thundered again.

Huanatha let it run its course. Then, when it began to diminish, she started again.

"Our wounds will take a long time to heal. In so doing, I feel it is important that we understand their context—this, I believe, is the only way to truly move on from them.

"Many years ago, a man came to this place. This man ..."

Jasen drifted.

*

The celebration lasted long into the night.

Tarratam was alive—with music, with the smells of wonderful food and heady, fruity wines—but most of all, it was alive with people.

Where the roads throughout the city had barely been walked these past months, they now bustled again. Friends and neighbors came together as if they had been parted for years, and this was a long-awaited reunion.

Jasen supposed it was.

The courtyards remained open. And Huanatha partook in her own celebrations too, with the skeleton of staff that she had already put together, most of whom were her former guards and maids and butlers. But there was much work to do, and she had little time for drinks.

She found some, though, late that evening.

They were arrayed in a library of sorts, Jasen, Alixa, Burund, Kuura and Longwell—and of course, Scourgey; Jasen could not get anywhere without the faithful creature—no, woman ... ex-woman ...Niamh. Huanatha joined them, a flask of wine in hand. A butler came in with a tray of beautifully blown glasses.

"Queen Huanatha," Longwell greeted, stooping into a low bow.

Huanatha stilled him with a cutting motion. "Rise. You do not bow here, Samwen Longwell, for many reasons —you have ruled two lands, we have been through too much, and you are not one of my subjects."

"All fair," Longwell said, and nodded as the lightest version of deference. "But still, respect must be shown. This is, as you say, your land."

"I would like to propose a toast," said Huanatha, uncorking the wine bottle.

Her butler stepped forward to hand out glasses. Then he took the bottle from the queen and decanted a portion into each, no more than a swig.

"Shilara would be so envious," murmured Alixa.

Jasen breathed a weak laugh. "Shilara would be terribly disappointed."

"Ooh, yes, very true. A single mouthful of drink—how unsatisfying."

They chortled. Then Jasen said, "We're being cruel to her."

"We are," said Alixa. "She does not deserve that."

He nodded, looking into the liquid in his glass. It was crimson, the color of ripe cherries, but it did not smell of them. Probably it was brewed from some other fruit native to Muratam.

When all their glasses were filled, and the butler was dismissed, Huanatha raised her glass.

"First, to Shipmaster Burund."

His eyebrows rose.

"I alternately thought you a buffoon and a good man who was willing to do what was right and true."

His eyebrows climbed higher. "And now?"

"You may still be part buffoon," said Huanatha, to laughs from the room—"but you came through, and you battled when it mattered most. For that, I thank you.

"Next, to Kuura of Nunahk. I could say the very same about you."

"How touching," same Kuura, grinning widely, clutching his heart. "You are so kind, Queen Huanatha." He was bandaged thickly where Baraghosa's laceration had split him open, the bindings wrapped around his neck and taped to the side of his chin. The look would have been almost funny, if not for the damage that had caused it to be necessary.

"You have shown yourself to be a man of great honor," said Huanatha. "Among the very first willing to stand before Baraghosa, even before understanding the full threat he posed, you put your neck on the line time and again. For that, I thank you."

Kuura tipped his glass. "My pleasure, Queen Huanatha."

"And you are not so old—yet," Huanatha said, causing a chorus of laughter. Kuura's eyes sparkled as he appeared to try and hold in the liquid he'd just drunk.

"Samwen Longwell." Huanatha turned to him. Her eyes sparkled as she appraised him for a long moment. "Your armor is broken." She nodded to the chestplate he still wore, crumpled in and fragmented. "But your spirit never once wavered. I pray you find a Reikonos willing to have you once you return to it."

"Thank you," Longwell said, but there was a distance in how he said it, as though he were contemplating that question himself and finding the answer … unsatisfying.

"To Alixa Weltan." The Queen licked her lips. "You, too, joined in a battle, one you have said many times was not your own. I may have disagreed with you, but your resolution is admirable. You are steadfast and sure, and I know that you have great things before you; you need only dare to dream them. Thank you for fighting at my side. You will always find yourself welcome in Muratam."

Alixa swallowed. Her eyes were suddenly pink. She nodded, unable to state her thanks.

"To your scourge." Huanatha nodded at Scourgey. She bowed now, below Jasen, and took Scourgey's head in her hand, resting the tips of her fingers against it. "Thank you, Niamh," she breathed.

Scourgey pressed her nose to Huanatha's forehead.

"And lastly … to you, Jasen." Huanatha looked up at him, from where she knelt. She did not move—just looked into his face, his eyes, with a steely, unwavering gaze. "You, who have been surest of all, who has fought with everything you possess and more, even when you knew you might die, and even harder, when you knew that you would. Few are hewn from the same steel as you. Your ancestors are proud. As am I—and all of us here, I believe." She raised her glass. "We are here for but a short spell in this world, and during mine ... it is a great honor to have fought at your side, Jasen Rabinn."

The rest of them lifted theirs, eyes on him.

"Hear, hear," said Longwell.

They echoed him—and they drank.

Jasen swallowed too, gulping it down so quickly he almost spluttered it out of his nose. It went down surprisingly smoothly given his difficulty with eating or drinking of late. His face was rosy, he could feel its heat, and all those eyes on him only seemed to stoke the fires that burned it.

"I believe there is one final toast in order," said Longwell, standing. "To Queen Huanatha: a fury made flesh. I hope never to cross her for as long as I live."

Kuura chortled. "I will drink to that."

They upended their glasses again, draining them.

When they were emptied, Huanatha said, "I say to each of you what I offered Alixa—all of you will find welcome here in Muratam for as long as you may live—as guests to the state ..." She glanced to Longwell. "Or, if you wish, on a more permanent basis."

"Thank you, Queen Huanatha," said Longwell. "I appreciate your extended welcome greatly. Although, as you may surmise, I cannot remain here. I have an adopted homeland of my own to return to. One that I have sorely missed—and which has, I hope, sorely missed me."

"Of course," said Huanatha. "I expected nothing less." Still, was that disappointment on her face? Only the smallest amount of it, of course—but no, it couldn't have been. If it was, she had wiped it off very, very quickly. "Well, you have my favor. When you have returned to your own rightful post, I would be very happy to extend trade deals to your nation of Reikonos. Our Muratam steel would be very beneficial to you. Perhaps we could even forge you a new suit of armor, after the damage Baraghosa did to yours."

"Ah ..." said Longwell, looking down at his ruined chestplate. "That would be very kind of you ... but I must admit that, over the years, I have grown quite fond of this armor. It was a gift from my late father. And near-impervious as I am sure your Muratam steel is, I believe I know a smith who could repair this one for me."

Huanatha scowled—but it was not a truly angry scowl. "Your head has been muddled."

"It may well have been. Or I grow sentimental in my years. Nevertheless, I will accept your trade deals."

Huanatha nodded. Then, turning, she said, "You, Shipmaster Burund and Kuura of Nunahk, I cannot offer a trade deal. However, I can employ the both of you—and I can likewise reward you."

Kuura's eyebrows rose. "With some of that Muratam steel you mentioned?"

Huanatha tamped down a smile. "That may be possible. As well as, perhaps a ship of your own. To aid in rebuilding Muratam's trade."

Kuura's eyes lit. He threw his head back and hooted, all of his teeth on proud display. Suddenly on his feet, he leapt and danced around, chanting words Jasen did not understand.

Alixa looked baffled. "What's he saying?"

"He is singing," said Burund. "I believe an appropriate translation would be, 'I am rich.'"

Alixa raised an eyebrow. "Appropriate?"

"He is quite profane about it," said Huanatha, watching him with a smirk.

When Kuura finally settled, he cleared his throat. "Ahem. So sorry. That is … very kind of you, Queen Huanatha. Very kind indeed." He looked sideways at Burund. "I don't mean to dishonor you—"

"You do me no dishonor," Burund said. "You will make a fine shipmaster, Kuura." His eyes glittered. "And you have earned it."

"Indeed he has," Huanatha said. "Alixa? I am sure I know your answer already, with regard to remaining in Muratam."

Alixa nodded. "Thank you, Queen Huanatha. But I must go to be with my brethren, at Emerald Fields." She glanced nervously to Longwell. "That is, assuming your offer to take me still stands?"

"It does," Longwell said. "Of course, there is the little matter of a boat."

"I will take you there," said Burund. "May our last journey together across the seas be more peaceful than those we have had before."

"Hear, hear," said Kuura, raising his empty glass. "I will accompany you as well." He looked a little sheepishly at Huanatha. "If this would be all right with you?"

"It is very fine with me," said Huanatha. "Return, and we will have a ship for you."

Kuura kissed his hands and extended them in front of his face. "Thank you, your majesty."

She nodded, and turned her attention to Jasen. "And what about you? Your days grow short. Travel will be difficult on you. Will you stay, here in Muratam ...? We would take greatest care of you, I would see to it."

He hesitated. "I ..."

"You are very welcome to stay out the rest of your days here," she said, as kindly as she could, "however few or many there are. Muratam is a beautiful land. Tarratam is perhaps somewhat dry, a little dusty ... but there is great beauty in this place."

Jasen felt a slight crawl over his flesh, chill and clammy despite the warm air. No answer came, though he felt one tugging at his heart.

"You needn't stay here, of course," she went on quickly. "Where the river flows—there are many lush villages, canopied in green, with towering trees and plants, and animals like you can hardly have imagined. I can arrange your travel there. Any part of my land, you need only say the word—and I will take you there."

Jasen bit his lip. "I ... thank you for your offer," he said carefully. It hurt him to say. How did his throat feel as though shards of glass had been raked along it? "However ... Shipmaster Burund, I wondered if ... perhaps ..."

He struggled with it, for a moment, not sure whether to ask it outright or not. It had been nagging at him increasingly today. And if there was any time for it, then surely it was now.

Finally, he said, "Is Terreas on the way to Emerald Fields?"

Alixa let out a small, "Oh." She touched her hand to her mouth.

Her eyes, again, were suddenly pink, and wet. She blinked against it.

"Terreas," said Burund, "is that the village you came from? On Luukessia?"

"Yes," said Jasen. "I would like to see it ... one last time ... if I may." He felt a lump in his throat, hard to swallow around. "I would like to go ... home."

Burund licked his bottom lip—and now he, too, looked as if he might break with tears.

He did not. But he stepped forward, and laid a gentle hand upon Jasen's shoulder, the lightest of touches—any weight to it and it would crumple Jasen to the floor.

"It is on our way," Burund said. "And I will take you there."

29

A wind picked up like no other the sailors had ever known. Blowing across the sea, it gusted endlessly, a bluster that filled every sail of the *Lady Vizola* II and pointed them on a straight-line course to Luukessia.

"I have never known anything like it," Burund mused.

"No," said Longwell. "Nor I."

They wondered about it in quiet, as the *Lady Vizola* II practically raced across the ocean. Perhaps inclement weather from the tropics had condensed into a front of wind that blew out from Coricuanthi and over the ocean. Maybe a seasonal storm had been too long-lived somewhere farther around the coast, hundreds of miles away, and had carried on long past the place where it should have died away.

They had no answers for it.

But Jasen knew.

The souls that he had freed from Baraghosa—they did this.

It was as Huanatha had said: the ancestors could guide the living. Alone, they could give only the smallest of nudges … but when thousands of slight touches were combined, they grew into a great, unstoppable force—a force that now carried Jasen across the sea, in the last days he had left to the place where he could rest.

How many days it took, he could not say. Certainly the trip was much swifter than it had any right to be. The days and nights vanished in a blur.

The last fight with Baraghosa had taken almost the last of Jasen's energy from him. The black tendrils snaking through his innards had found the deepest part of him now. They grew into it, the soft, vulnerable pinkness left there, and they sucked at it like dozens of leeches, slowly draining what life was left.

He was not vomiting now. Yet he did not eat either. He drank little.

His consciousness faded in and out, in and out.

But he lay upon the deck, propped up, with Scourgey always by his side. Alixa was there with him too, every time he awoke. She held his hand constantly. And when he stirred, when he opened eyes to a blearier and blearier world, full of white spots that he could not vanquish—she smiled at him.

Her eyes were pink. Always pink. But she smiled.

Longwell was there too. He spoke to Jasen kindly, things that … he did not remember, honestly. But they were kind things, he thought. Stories of his people. Tales of Reikonos, of a place with warm hearths and noble hearts called Sanctuary. He reminded him, at every stage, that Jasen was strong, a warrior, that he was noble and good and had done him and his ancestors and his brethren in the Emerald Fields, and a whole world who did not know it yet, proud.

And one other thing, one thing that Jasen did remember properly, not in the ghostly, vague way that the world seemed to hang now, swimming rather than solid.

"You will be home soon."

Home. He held on to that. He gripped it when he was awake, and the days passed him by, the sea unbroken, the sails full of the wind blown by the dead. And he held onto it while he slept, fallen into dark places that were more like voids than dreamscapes.

Home. He was going home.

He just needed to hold on a little longer.

"We will be there soon." This was Alixa. She came from far away.

The air was so salty.

Scourgey smelled … bad. Awful. She was so rotten—or was that him? Was that the scent coming from his own innards, leaking out of him as the small bit of life left in him was blotted out?

Skies were blue. Then twilit. He was carried, into the ship, into his quarters.

Comfortable here, yet it was not right.

A long gap.

He was dead?

But no—it was morning again, midday, afternoon, early evening—hard to tell. Blue though. Very blue.

Salty.

Scourgey reeked.

Luckily, he had nothing more to vomit. There was no bile left, except maybe a dribble. And he didn't possess the strength to cough it up.

Someone crouched before him. A hand on his shoulder, big, but holding him gently.

Someone else fussed.

Medleigh.

And Burund—it was the shipmaster who gripped Jasen's shoulder. He looked into his eyes.

"Jasen."

Jasen lifted his head.

So many white spots.

He could see the dead again. They were on the deck—but he could not focus on them, could not pick out who they might be.

Burund smiled a kindly smile.

"Hold on," he said, from a long way away. "We are close."

How close?

"Tomorrow," said the shipmaster—had Jasen asked? He didn't remember it … but he must have.

Tomorrow. Home. Tomorrow.

Hold on.

The blackness was so deep, though—so deep down. He could feel it, in the very core of him, like a wolf eating the soft parts of a mountain goat. It hurt—but the pain was not all-encompassing. He did not feel bruised throughout his whole body, the way he had in the days after leaving Nonthen behind. As his body failed, he felt less and less.

Tomorrow—he would be home tomorrow.

He held onto that … and he slept.

*

There was a knocking at his door.

He left the dark place that had been his dreamless sleep.

The dark, though … it did not leave him. Not entirely.

The fog was close now. Very, very close.

"Yes?" he called out, his voice almost inaudible.

The door opened.

Alixa stood there, with Longwell.

"We are here," she said.

Jasen's heart, weak that it was, skipped. "Luukessia?" he breathed.

"Yes," said Longwell.

"Help me—please," said Jasen.

The two of them came in, to his bed. They let him drape an arm over either of their shoulders. It would be a particularly lopsided sort of walk—their heights were so far apart.

Scourgey loosed a low, cooing sort of a noise.

They lifted Jasen out of bed.

He was weak now, very frail. The muscles that had once carried him seemed to have vanished away. Without the stomach for food, and less and less capacity for water, he had withered. He could feel it, and if he looked down, he could see it: his trousers, which he slept in—far too difficult pulling the things on and off now—hung down from his hips in straight lines, like they were clipped to a drying line, nothing at all filling them.

Alixa and Longwell placed Jasen gingerly onto feet no longer capable of holding him.

Scourgey ducked under his legs.

Carefully, they lowered him forward, so he could wrap his arms about her neck.

"Good girl," said Alixa softly.

Her eyes were pink. Yet when they met with Jasen's, she smiled—a radiant smile that one day, and one day very soon, men would find beautiful—that would inspire hearts and minds.

"I'm sorry," he said—

She frowned. "For what?"

How could he put it into words? There was much. His regrets were many. The way he had bullied Alixa into coming down to the wall on that first fateful crossing of it, goading her into something he knew she was deeply uncomfortable with. Their falling-out in the long days upon this war galley.

Not telling her that he was dying.

And he was sorry, too, for all the things he would miss out on. He would not have a life of his own, but now, lying upon Scourgey as he and Longwell and Alixa made their way through the labyrinthine corridors of the war galley for the last time together, he was sorrier that he would not see how Alixa's would turn out.

She had grown so much, changed so drastically, in such a little time. It was not a complete change—she had not ceased to be the girl she once had been in Terreas—but this Alixa was one Jasen could never have imagined she would grow to be. Very likely it was an Alixa she would not have been, period. Terreas, for all that it meant to Jasen, had shaped her to be meek; now he saw the woman she would become.

So much he could apologize for. But he hadn't the energy, so he said only, "Tugging on your braids ... on the mossy rock."

Alixa burst out with a laugh, a cathartic sound that was jubilant and light and tinged with so much sadness all at once.

"I forgive you, Jasen," she said when she'd laughed herself out. "For that, and for everything else you're not saying."

He nodded. "Thank you."

They walked slowly through the ship, through halls, round corners that Jasen was still not sure he had ever really wrapped his head around ... and then up the steps, through the door to the deck ...

The sun was bright. It must be close to midday now, perhaps even a little past it, because it hung almost at its apex. The skies were a perfect, clear blue.

The winds that had brought them here had ceased. So now the *Lady Vizola* II lay lazily upon the water—at the shores of Luukessia.

"There it is," said Alixa softly, fondly. "Home."

Jasen tried to focus on it. His sight was so full of those blind spots now. Had cataracts grown upon his eyes in these last days? He could not rid himself of them, no matter how he blinked. They blurred the world, turning it into a smear.

But he would recognize Luukessia anywhere. He had seen it from the waters only once, and yet the sight of the shoreline had been burned into his mind, this land that was all he had ever known until just two short months ago, a network of rising hills and green, overgrown meadows, nature untamed and thriving where the scourge did not bring their death ... and at the very peak of it all, the cluster of mountains in which Terreas was nestled.

No smoke poured from any of them, no puffs of white cotton breathed into the sky.

The cratered mountain had stilled once more.

There were men upon the deck, the crew of the *Lady Vizola*. Which, Jasen didn't know—at least, until Burund and Kuura swam out of the smearscape.

"Good morning, Jasen," said Burund. "We have arrived."

"Thank you."

There was a tense, disquieted moment, where no one appeared sure of exactly what to do or say.

Longwell broke it. "Well then ... shall we take a rowboat?"

"One is already prepared," said Kuura.

They started out.

"We're all going?" said Alixa, surprised.

"Of course we are," said Kuura, grinning widely. "You did not think we would send him out there alone, did you?"

"You are sending me out alone," Jasen wheezed.

Kuura smiled. "Ah, yes, but not to the shore. That much, we can manage."

Scourgey could not guide him down the ropes to the boat that lay waiting. So Longwell gently lifted him into his arms. Clutching him with one—he seemed so small at the dragoon's hip—he descended.

Scourgey whined softly.

"I will be back for you in just a moment," said Longwell. "I promise."

He lowered Jasen into the boat. Then he climbed back up.

Alixa clambered down beside him.

"Are you comfortable?" she asked.

"Yes," he said. At least, he was as far as he could be. Here, lying against the rowboat's frontmost seat, death gripping him, comfort was relative. The sun beat down upon him, burning his tender flesh. He didn't much care—it wouldn't matter for much longer.

Longwell returned a few moments later, with Scourgey upon his shoulders. She leapt down, her claws clacking upon the rowboat's bottom. Easing her head under Jasen's hand, she slumped down against the side of the boat so that she was touching his leg but putting no weight on him.

"She will stay with you," said Longwell. "To the very end."

Jasen knew. And though he hadn't the energy to do so aloud, he thanked her.

She lifted her head to look at him. Hearing it? Just knowing, in her strange way?

The boat began to move. Oars plunged into the water in a steady cadence.

The rowboat pulled out of the small shade thrown by the *Lady Vizola* II.

Jasen winced against the sun's brightness.

"Close your eyes," said Alixa softly. "We'll be there soon."

He did.

The boat moved …

The dark place came in again.

He was so tired.

"Jasen."

He opened his eyes.

Bleary.

The sun was bright.

Alixa bowed over him. Concern wrought upon her face, a smile flickered upon her lips as he roused. There was relief in it—he was not yet dead.

"We're here," she said.

He gripped the edge of the boat, floundering—

"Help," he breathed.

Alixa gently took his hands.

She was so warm.

Or was it him that was cold?

Of course it was. He was dying—today.

She straightened him, and it came into view again, this smeared, blurry rendition of Luukessia, with its green, rolling hills, the bar of sand streaked around its edge some twenty feet off ...

And a fleshy, greyish line of bustling scourge, right up to the water's edge, snarling and gnashing their teeth.

"Foul creatures," said Longwell. Then, with a sideways glance at Scourgey: "Uhh—no offense, Niamh."

Burund peered at the shore. Frowning, he murmured, "Are you sure you wish to do this, Jasen?"

"I'm sure," Jasen breathed.

"You are certain when you say they will not attack you?" Kuura muttered.

"I'm sure," said Jasen. "They have no interest ... in the dead."

"But you are not dead yet," Kuura's voice was strained.

"I will be safe," Jasen replied. "I know this."

Again, there was a long and tense silence, as if none of them knew what to do, or to say.

It was Longwell who broke the quiet.

Taking a great breath, as if the dragoon were steadying himself, he stepped forward in the rowboat. "Jasen Rabinn—I must echo Queen Huanatha of Muratam when I say that it has been an honor—one of the very highest—in fighting alongside you. Truly, you are the pride of Luukessia, a great tribute to your ancestors. And though you leave behind no blood lineage of your own, know this: the things you have done will carry forth a great legacy from here, one that is everlasting." He bowed his head. "You are barely a man, and yet a greater man I have rarely known. And I will not forget you."

"Nor will I," said Burund. "You may have helped save all of Coricuanthi by your deeds."

"And," said Kuura with a faint grin, "you have made me a very rich man indeed." He laughed ... and then it fell, and he looked at Jasen very earnestly, not with a smile that was so wide as to show off all of his teeth, but a sweet, small one. "Thank you, Jasen. I shall not forget you."

"And neither will I," said Alixa. Her voice warbled, shook. Her eyes were not just pink but red, and they shone with a sheen that did not leave her no matter how fast she blinked at it. Yet she held it in—and for the last time, he was glad of it.

"You will go on," Jasen wheezed. "To our brethren."

Alixa nodded, firmly. "And I will tell them tales of my cousin—who was brave, and adventurous; who challenged me; who made me better … and who saved my life."

Her voice trembled at this last part.

Now she would surely break.

But still she did not. The girl was made of steel, through and through.

"I will remember you," she whispered. "Always. And I will make sure, however I can, that none of this was in vain."

"I know," said Jasen. "You have a … great destiny before you. You will … carry on … for all of us." Ancestors, this hurt so much—his throat was so shredded. But he spoke, tapping into the last reservoir of his energy, once so full yet now close to empty. "For Terreas," he finished, voice fading.

Alixa nodded. "I promise," she said.

That long quiet again.

Then Longwell said: "Well. I suppose it is time to do this. Niamh?"

He clambered out into the water. Bowing low, he stooped so that Scourgey could clamber onto his back. Once she was comfortably positioned, he straightened, and took his lance in hand. "I'll be back in just a moment," he said, flashing a smile. Then he trudged out into the water, his legs cutting through it, sending waves sloshing out with every step he made closer to the shore.

The scourge arrayed there clamored for him.

Longwell shouted—something that Jasen could not make out.

He could hardly see what he was doing. But there were louder splashes all of a sudden, then whines—

And then Longwell was on his way back again.

"Poxy bastards," he grumbled when he reached the rowboat again, sans Scourgey. "Thought they'd have a bite of me, did they? Never mind—Amnis showed them what for." He dripped, water pooling beneath him in the boat. "This is it, Jasen. Last goodbyes."

Jasen looked at them—at Burund, and Kuura, and lastly Alixa, who had stayed by his side all this time and gripped his hand in hers, warm, so very warm, so alive …

"Thank you, all," he wheezed. "For everything."

Burund nodded. Kuura too.

Alixa bit her trembling lip. "No … thank you."

She hugged him. Kissed him upon the cheek.

It there was any place he could choose to die—any place that was not his former home—it would surely be here.

But his time was finite. So Alixa released him. She favored him one last look, her eyes glistening with tears … and then she let Longwell gently lift him from the boat, turn … and carry him on his back to the shores from which they had both come … but where only one of them would remain.

"She waits for you," Longwell murmured to Jasen. "The scourge detest water … and yet she waits for you, submerged to her haunches in it."

Jasen opened his eyes to see.

It was so hard to make out.

"She's a good girl," he said.

"Oh, yes, she is," Longwell agreed. "One of the finest I ever knew."

The shore's proximity announced itself by the clamoring of the scourge.

"We are here," said Longwell.

Jasen opened one eye. He could see better that way—something about both of them open at once only smeared the world more, like his eyes could no longer point in quite the same direction, and his brain was failing to stitch the images from each together.

There was Scourgey. She quaked in the water, but she waited, apart from the rest of them, looking up with her coal-lump eyes.

Longwell stooped, and gently lowered Jasen onto her back.

"You got her?" he asked.

"Yes," said Jasen. His arms were looped round Scourgey's neck. Of course, he did not have her, really; he had no grip at all; but Scourgey kept him balanced. She would not let him fall.

"Your faith has never once wavered, has it," Longwell demurred, looking fondly at Scourgey as he straightened. "Farewell, Niamh. And farewell, Jasen. Until we meet again."

"Thank you," said Jasen.

Scourgey turned, the water making waves about her.

She came to the shore.

The scourge thrashed, all in a line, pressed right up to the water's edge. Jasen could imagine the rest of them on the boat, Kuura most of all watching in fear that Jasen was wrong …

Yet it was not he who the scourge wanted. They desired Longwell, and the boat farther out. They did not so much as spare Jasen, already mostly dead, a look as Scourgey moved through their mass, undeterred, and then onward, inland.

"You know where we're going," Jasen whispered into her ear. It was all he had the strength for now. "Don't you?"

Scourgey whined softly.

She knew.

And she with uneven steps, bearing him upon her back, she bore him inland, toward the heart of Luukessia.

Home.

30

He slept through much of it.

Luukessia passed him by, the hills disappearing under Scourgey's feet, the overgrown meadows vanishing behind like they were squares in an enormous patchwork blanket.

She moved quickly. Even when he fell into the dark place, he had a sense of it, could feel the thrumming of her feet below. His time was short, shrinking away with every second—she had to run.

When Jasen woke, though, she slowed. How she knew he was awake, Jasen did not know, for he did not move, could not. Perhaps now the veil was so thin there was a bridge between them. Perhaps the same way she could detect death, she could feel Jasen in other ways too.

Those waking moments were like a fever dream. The world was washed out, over-bright, so very blurred ... he could smell wildflowers, but they were heady, their pungence overpowering.

And death. Always the smell of death.

What had Scourgey bathed in?

But no. This was not Scourgey.

This rot was his own. It came from within him, festering and foul.

Just a little farther though. Just a little more.

He drifted.

Scourgey sped.

And Luukessia fell away behind them.

*

He woke under the evening sun.

It was cooler now.

And the air ... it smelled different too. It had something ... *wrong* in it—there was no other way Jasen could think to describe it.

Scourgey whined, low in her throat.

Jasen raised his head.

At first he could not make head or tail of what he was seeing. Everything was grey-white. For a confusing moment he thought it was rock. Then, as his vision came slowly back to focus, he wondered—was this *snow*? But this was the height of summer. The mountains had no caps upon them this time of year. Luukessia could not get so cold as to be covered in ice.

He turned, puzzled …

And then he saw it—the outline of a village, layered under the stuff.

This was not snow at all.

It was ash.

He was back at Terreas.

Scourgey waited beside the wall. She whined again, rousing Jasen higher from the dark place he had fallen into.

As Huanatha had predicted, the destruction that the scourge detected had indeed not come past the wall at all. The grasses here at the very edge of the village, where the boundary lay, were barely touched by it, only a light dust settled on their blades. And beyond the wall, where Scourgey stood with Jasen lying upon her back—it was nearly pristine. As though no mountain had ever erupted here.

"You knew," Jasen wheezed.

Scourgey whined.

"Can you … cross it now?"

She seemed unsure. Still, she tested, raising a paw onto the wall, just the one at first—then she added another, and stepped in—

She flinched, at the feel of the grass carpeted in ash.

But she was across.

They both were.

He was home.

But then … was this home? It had been once. Now, though, coated in a layer of ash that grew closer to the village proper—and half of it buried under dark rock, magma that had spilled out in a great tide and solidified … this was not the Terreas he had known.

This was a Terreas as destroyed as him.

His stomach dropped at that.

But then—how stupid. What had he expected to see? Had he really thought Terreas would be as it once was, when he came here? He'd seen the mountain erupt with his own eyes. He'd seen the lava stream out of it, smothering Terreas in an instant.

Of course this was the village he was coming back to.

He sighed. "Well ... I guess let's just ... walk."

Scourgey began a slow clamber up the hill.

Jasen surveyed it sadly. The lava flow had come down over the very central portion of the village. It had frozen almost into waves where it rebounded, coursing up in another great flow like a stream, and eaten up even more of the village.

All the fields were gone, all the ones they'd used to grow food. So were the stables, where Shilara had borrowed Milo for their last fateful excursion.

The assembly hall was gone too.

Shilara's home sat upon the edge of the village. That remained, coated in a greyish-white layer of solidified ash, like plaque on a tooth. Only—it was not all there, Jasen saw, rounding it with Scourgey. A rock had plowed through the front, collapsing it. From the back, it could pass for whole. But it definitely was not inhabitable now.

Of course, there was no one to inhabit it. There was no one here but him.

What a stupid, pointless exercise this had been. He should have stayed upon the rowboat, and just drifted into the blackness in Alixa's arms.

He resting his head against Scourgey's uneven spine.

Damn this. Damn it all.

She whined—asking him, through the bridge, where she should go. "I don't know."

His home was not there anymore; it had been burned down before he left for Wayforth ... for Aiger Cliffs, for Necromancer Isle, and Nonthen, and Tarratam. Besides, his sweeping assessment, through a blear of white spots, told him that the place where he had once lived was now buried under a three-foot-thick layer of solidified magma.

Scourgey whined again.

"I ... don't know," he wheezed. Just that was enough to sap his strength further still.

She whined again. Then she plodded on.

He lay there against her, his eyes closed.

The dark pressed in, nearing ...

Breathing was hard. So hard. Shallow breaths were all he could manage.

His hand slipped from around Scourgey's neck.

He was going.

This was it.

His eyes drooped closed ...

The darkness closed in around him—

Scourgey whined.

She was far away—so far.

Just let me sleep, Jasen thought.

Scourgey whined again, more insistent this time. The noise cut through the blackness encroaching on all sides, banishing it—at least a little farther away.

But it was still close.

He opened one eye.

The ground before him was ashen.

Scourgey whined.

Jasen blinked.

Let me rest …

She whined—and now she bucked him.

It was a small jerk of her body. This far gone, it brought no pain to him—but it did jolt him, scaring the darkness away a little more again—and he opened his eyes, both of them, swimming with white dots, to see—

He stared.

This was the Weltan house. It was remarkably whole, all things considered—or rather, the back half of it was, where the mossy rock rested beside the vineyard. Most of it had been devoured by black magma.

Yet this place was not what gave Jasen pause.

It was the rock.

For there, under it, where the ash had not entirely been able to snow … there rose a single flower, its petals pointed like a child's drawing of a star, all bluish-white.

He stared at it. Squinted. Surely not?

Scourgey whined again. She eased him closer.

He looked down upon it, hanging over her side.

That was a flower.

"Put me down," he wheezed.

Scourgey lowered.

Jasen clambered off—fell, really. It did not matter though: he was off.

Resting against the mossy rock, he stared into those white-blue petals like they were the most beautiful thing he had ever seen. They swam, blotted out by the white spots that clouded his vision—so much of it was gone—but he did his very best to focus on it, on this flower—this little piece of life that flourished.

And it would. In the same way as Terreas had eked out survival even when the scourge overran the lands of Luukessia … in the same way as the people from Nonthen drew together, dug out the survivors and fought to keep them alive another day … in the same way Tarratam would return to its former glory, even if it were decades from now … life went on.

Alixa went on.

Longwell went on.

And the Emerald Fields, they went on too, with a new line of Luukessians.

And perhaps … it was thanks to him. Not entirely—but he had a small part in it. A *big* small part, maybe.

This was the legacy Longwell spoke of, the lineage that went on after Jasen passed. A chain that bound them all together, from the first of the Luukessians …

To him, here, now.

And to Alixa … on her way across the sea.

Safe.

He closed his eyes …

The veil slipped. And here, here, at last—was the Terreas he had known. A Terreas filled with smiling faces, bustling, not a hint of the ash or magma spilled over it. It was a whole place, alive, and he was whole again too. He did not lay prone, with a scourge at his side, in the ash and dust spewed out from a mountain, but stood tall, among a field of people, all moving, all smiling at him, all reaching out for his hands and welcoming him, saying they were so proud of him, so grateful for what he had done …

And then—them. The throng parted, its mad swirl about Jasen paused … and there was Pityr, smiling. There was Shilara, a flask of whiskey in her hand, a sparkle in her eye. There was his aunt and his uncle and his cousins, and his grandparents, and their parents and grandparents too … all a part of the same great chain as he was, links in their own way …

And at the very forefront were his mother and his father.

Jasen stepped forward to meet them.

His mother smiled, a beautiful smile. "Oh, Jasen. You don't know how proud I am of you."

Adem squeezed his shoulder. "You did wonderfully, son."

And they wrapped him into an embrace that was so warm, so gloriously, beautifully warm …

"I've missed you," he said, breathing in their scent—a flowery perfume from his mother that he had somehow forgotten, but it came back to him now in a rush—a bookish sort of smell from his father, the slightly musty smell of the assembly hall, its odor impossible to purge even with those pungent candles in their sconces ...

He was home.

At long, long last ... he was home.

And he realized, then, as he was swept up among the flow of his ancestors, these souls who had watched over him as they watched over his parents before him, and theirs, one final truth:

Luukessia would return someday.

The knowledge filled him like the summer sun, white light shining from above as he lay beside the mossy rock where all of this had begun, Niamh the scourge at his side, company to the very last.

And as he finally faded into the white ... he smiled.

Alixa Will Return in

ASHES OF LUUKESSIA

Volume Four

Coming in 2018/2019!

Author's Note

Thanks for reading! If you want to know immediately when future books become available, take sixty seconds and sign up for my NEW RELEASE EMAIL ALERTS by visiting my website. I don't sell your information and I only send out emails when I have a new book out. The reason you should sign up for this is because I don't always set release dates, and even if you're following me on Facebook (robertJcrane (Author)) or Twitter (@robertJcrane), it's easy to miss my book announcements because...well, because social media is an imprecise thing.

Come join the discussion on my website:
http://www.robertjcrane.com!

Cheers,
Robert J. Crane

ACKNOWLEDGMENTS

Editorial/Literary Janitorial duties performed by Sarah Barbour and Nick Bowman. Final proofing was handled by the Jeff Bryan. Any errors you see in the text, however, are the result of me rejecting changes.

The cover was once more designed with exceeding skill by Karri Klawiter of artbykarri.com.

Thanks again to my co-author, an amazing life-saver who makes my life easier in pretty much every way in which his life intersects mine.

The formatting was provided by nickbowman-editing.com.

Once more, thanks to my parents, my in-laws, my kids and my wife, for helping me keep things together.

Other Works by Robert J. Crane

The Girl in the Box
and
Out of the Box
Contemporary Urban Fantasy

Alone: The Girl in the Box, Book 1
Untouched: The Girl in the Box, Book 2
Soulless: The Girl in the Box, Book 3
Family: The Girl in the Box, Book 4
Omega: The Girl in the Box, Book 5
Broken: The Girl in the Box, Book 6
Enemies: The Girl in the Box, Book 7
Legacy: The Girl in the Box, Book 8
Destiny: The Girl in the Box, Book 9
Power: The Girl in the Box, Book 10

Limitless: Out of the Box, Book 1
In the Wind: Out of the Box, Book 2
Ruthless: Out of the Box, Book 3
Grounded: Out of the Box, Book 4
Tormented: Out of the Box, Book 5
Vengeful: Out of the Box, Book 6
Sea Change: Out of the Box, Book 7
Painkiller: Out of the Box, Book 8
Masks: Out of the Box, Book 9
Prisoners: Out of the Box, Book 10
Unyielding: Out of the Box, Book 11
Hollow: Out of the Box, Book 12
Toxicity: Out of the Box, Book 13
Small Things: Out of the Box, Book 14
Hunters: Out of the Box, Book 15
Badder: Out of the Box, Book 16
Apex: Out of the Box, Book 18
Time: Out of the Box, Book 19
Driven: Out of the Box, Book 20
Remember: Out of the Box, Book 21
Hero: Out of the Box, Book 22* *(Coming October 2018!)*
Flashback: Out of the Box, Book 23* *(Coming December 2018!)*
Walk Through Fire: Out of the Box, Book 24* *(Coming in 2019!)*

World of Sanctuary
Epic Fantasy

Defender: The Sanctuary Series, Volume One
Avenger: The Sanctuary Series, Volume Two
Champion: The Sanctuary Series, Volume Three
Crusader: The Sanctuary Series, Volume Four
Sanctuary Tales, Volume One - A Short Story Collection
Thy Father's Shadow: The Sanctuary Series, Volume 4.5
Master: The Sanctuary Series, Volume Five
Fated in Darkness: The Sanctuary Series, Volume 5.5
Warlord: The Sanctuary Series, Volume Six
Heretic: The Sanctuary Series, Volume Seven
Legend: The Sanctuary Series, Volume Eight
Ghosts of Sanctuary: The Sanctuary Series, Volume Nine
Call of the Hero: The Sanctuary Series, Volume Ten* *(Coming Late 2018!)*

A Haven in Ash: Ashes of Luukessia, Volume One *(with Michael Winstone)*
A Respite From Storms: Ashes of Luukessia, Volume Two
A Home in the Hills: Ashes of Luukessia, Volume Three *(with Michael Winstone)*

Southern Watch
Contemporary Urban Fantasy

Called: Southern Watch, Book 1
Depths: Southern Watch, Book 2
Corrupted: Southern Watch, Book 3
Unearthed: Southern Watch, Book 4
Legion: Southern Watch, Book 5
Starling: Southern Watch, Book 6
Forsaken: Southern Watch, Book 7
Hallowed: Southern Watch, Book 8* *(Coming Late 2018/Early 2019!)*

The Shattered Dome Series
(with Nicholas J. Ambrose)
Sci-Fi

Voiceless: The Shattered Dome, Book 1
Unspeakable: The Shattered Dome, Book 2* *(Coming 2018!)*

The Mira Brand Adventures
Contemporary Urban Fantasy

The World Beneath: The Mira Brand Adventures, Book 1
The Tide of Ages: The Mira Brand Adventures, Book 2
The City of Lies: The Mira Brand Adventures, Book 3
The King of the Skies: The Mira Brand Adventures, Book 4
The Best of Us: The Mira Brand Adventures, Book 5
We Aimless Few: The Mira Brand Adventures, Book 6* *(Coming 2018!)*

Liars and Vampires
(with Lauren Harper)
Contemporary Urban Fantasy

No One Will Believe You: Liars and Vampires, Book 1
Someone Should Save Her: Liars and Vampires, Book 2
You Can't Go Home Again: Liars and Vampires, Book 3
In The Dark: Liars and Vampires, Book 4
Her Lying Days Are Done: Liars and Vampires, Book 5* *(Coming August 2018!)*
Heir of the Dog: Liars and Vampires, Book 6* *(Coming September 2018!)*
Hit You Where You Live: Liars and Vampires, Book 7* *(Coming October 2018!)*

* Forthcoming, Subject to Change

Printed in Great Britain
by Amazon

84000394R00129